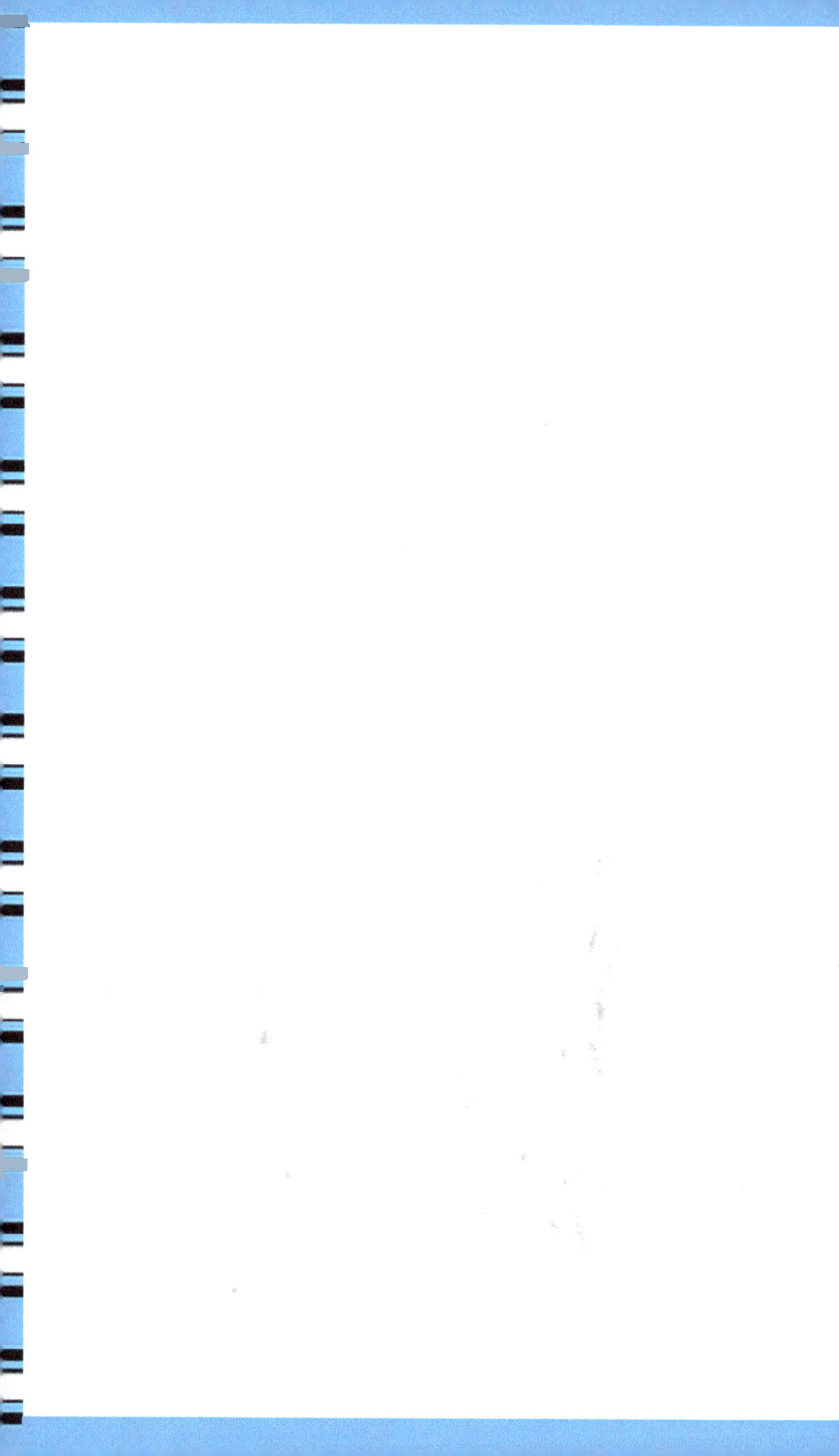

A BOOKISH STORY

HEATHERLY BELL

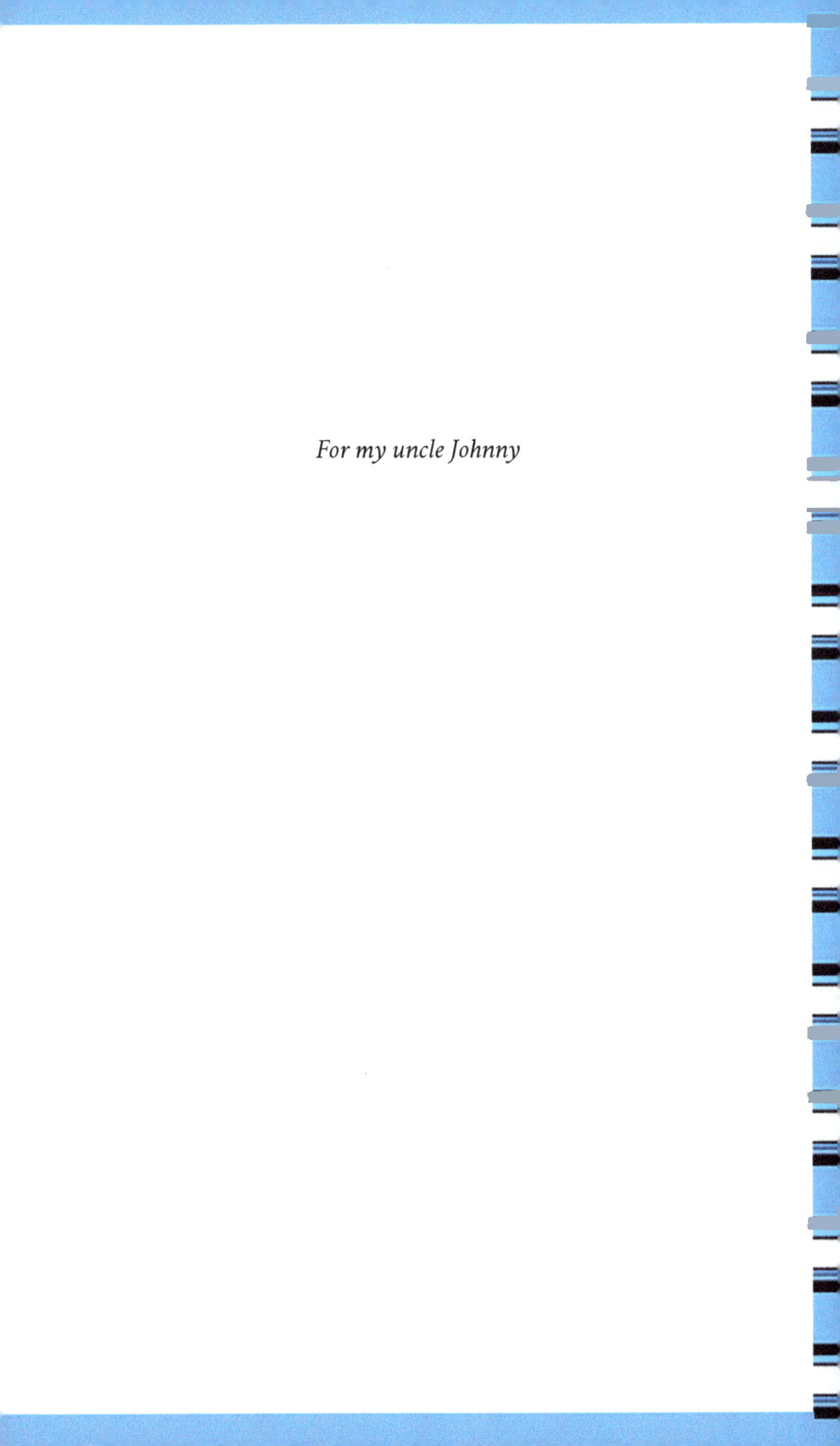

For my uncle Johnny

CHAPTER 1

Nobody plans to live in a converted garden shed when they're on the cusp of turning thirty. But that's exactly where I live, in the backyard of my abuelita's home, since rent in my small town in the Bay Area is such that most people my age can't afford to live alone. The threat of months in my she-shed has brought me to this moment. Something has to change.

And behind the door of the charming bungalow residential house standing before me, there is possibility. This leafy tree-lined area is commonly referred to as Professorville, one of the oldest neighborhoods in Seven Trees, closest to the university.

I need this second job as a research assistant to a visiting history professor. It pays well, and once your fiancé dumps you weeks before the wedding, a girl needs a second job. This position would be perfect, with the flexible hours I can use to work around my main job as a ghostwriter.

I walk up the short flight of steps to the porch of the home with a pitch-style roof, a stone chimney, and a large picture window facing the front. The door is painted a forest green, giving the cottage a secret-garden quality.

Fist raised to the door, I'm ready to state my case as to why *I* should be hired.

But before I knock, the door swings open, and a middle-aged man who looks like the professor of my former MFA program in creative writing greets me. My shoulders unstiffen and I relax. This is perfect. He resembles every other professor I've ever met, and I've met a lot of them. Portly, barrel-chested, wearing tweed, beard. Check, check, check, check.

"Well, hello! You must be here for the research position," he says and waves me inside. "Please do come in."

"Thank you! I'm so glad to meet you. My name is Lucia Milagros Santana but please call me Luci. Let me just say first off, I'm anxious to start working, and I can start today. The salary posted is more than adequate."

"Um…" he says, probably not accustomed to someone as energetic.

If there's anything I hear quite often, it's "care to tone it down a bit?" It's as if I have two dials: high and off. But certainly, this is not the time to find that middle ground.

"A little about me! I have my MFA in creative writing and I'm also a writer. I ghostwrite mostly but I also have my own novel, which I'm querying. Also, I'm a *huge* fan of history so this is perfect. I understand you're a history professor and an author. This is a good fit, believe me. I love historical fiction, the older the better!"

Older the better? I internally roll my eyes. I'm constantly self-editing but life is not a book.

I must keep going.

He smiles. "Well, my dear, you are quite enthusiastic, aren't you?"

"Yes! And I will work hard, I promise you. I've lived in

Seven Trees for most of my life," I say, because he should know everything about me, or everything that's legally required. "My family lives here, my grandmother and uncle. My grandfather actually built the house they lived in, back in the nineteen sixties."

He quirks a brow. "My, how grand. So, your family was here before the tech revolution."

I'm excited because I think he likes me, and I've succeeded in making the good first impression one must make within the first few minutes of an introduction. It's only then I notice the large suitcase sitting beside the professor. This is confusing for a moment, as the agency said the professor would be renting this house for at least a month and I'm told he's been here only a week. The professor glances behind him, where a younger man entered the room at some point in my monologue. I look from the professor to the other man, waiting for someone to speak. I've been commanding the floor, which may have been a mistake, but did I mention how much I need this job?

"Ryan," the professor says, turning to the younger man. "I believe your candidate has arrived."

"I believe you're right, Henry."

My heart flutters in my chest. I've been selling myself to the *wrong person*. While they speak as if we're all in a Jane Austen novel, my brain catches up with my mouth. The younger man is the antithesis of the older one. He's wearing slacks and a Dodgers T-shirt, which might get him killed in these parts, and he looks more like a TA than an actual professor.

"Oh," I say, and add an impromptu curtsy as I recover. "Mayhap I have made an error."

The older professor bursts into laughter while the younger one continues to stare like he can't believe they let people like me wander around town unattended. His head is cocked to the side, his black-rimmed Superman-style glasses sit slightly askew on his face. The urge to reach out and straighten them is distracting me.

"Yes, you have erred, my dear," he says and chuckles, waving to Ryan. "But that's completely understandable. This is Professor Brady, who will be staying in my home while I'm off for my six-month sabbatical in Egypt! I leave you in good hands."

A wave of discomfort hits me, because this other man is not at all what I expected. For one thing, he's *young*. For another, he's got that Clark Kent, geeky, studious appearance only handsome men like him can pull off and still be cool. His hair is so dark it's almost black, eyes a deep indigo blue. They droop slightly at the corners, giving him a sad puppy dog look.

"Let me help you out," Ryan says, and bends to pick up another one of Professor Henry's suitcases.

"Goodbye, my dear, and good luck! I'm off to see the pyramids!" Henry says.

"Bye, sir."

Safe to say I will think of him often, every time I blow a job interview.

I walk a bit further into the home. Since I'm a writer, by nature I'm a snoop, but I dial it down with strangers. I've never been in one of these craftsman-style bungalows and I'm curious. There's a fireplace to the left in the family room, dark gold paisley drapes, bookcases, and plants, with the kitchen straight ahead. Down the hallway must be the bedrooms. To the right is presumably the dining room and taking a few steps in, I find a farmhouse table filled with papers and books. Here, through the wide picture window, I have a clear view to the sidewalk where the two professors are engaged in an animated conversation.

Mr. Brady assembles luggage in the trunk of the sedan

while Henry waves his hands in the air, then gestures to the house. Probably giving him instructions on how to water and care for the assemblage of cactuses and ferns. But Mr. Brady shakes his head, as if no way, can't do it.

Oh my god, are they discussing whether or not he should *hire* me? That must mean I still have a chance! I take a step closer to see if I might be able to read their lips, and that's when Ryan turns and sees me in the window. I know he does, because I see him, and for a second in time we just simply gawk at each other like time has stopped. Then I snap out of it and move away.

When Mr. Brady returns after seeing his friend off, I wonder if I still have a chance to get this job, and if I should still want it. He caught me in the window snooping. Also, it's possible the cleft in the professor's chin might make it difficult to concentrate on my work. He's handsome and young, and I'm on the rebound. Not a great combination.

Then I remember my she-shed and how much I'd like to live in a place where I don't have to leave my home to take a shower or have a homecooked meal. Where I'll have some privacy from my loud and intrusive but well-meaning family who is still worried about me over the breakup that caused me to be here today in the first place.

But I need this job far more than I'm worried about crushing on the professor, so I will put a block on him. It's the same thing I do when my cousin Sofia introduces me to her latest boyfriend. They're always hot and the block allows me to appreciate them in the same way I do a beautiful sunset from a safe and healthy distance.

"Well, this is embarrassing," I say, when Mr. Brady returns and closes the front door.

Something resembling the start of a smile seems to be fighting his mouth, and he's winning. He doesn't want to smile. Still, the hint of laughter is shimmering in his eyes and I can see it. It gives me hope.

"So, I feel like I know everything about you already other than possibly your blood type," he says, hands tucked in the pockets of his dockers. "And…no notes."

"He opened the door, so I thought—"

"Don't apologize, it makes perfect sense."

"Okay. Thank you."

"You mentioned the salary is more than adequate," he says.

"Yes, and please excuse me for being so enthusiastic. It's just I really need this job. Have you seen the rent for a studio apartment in Seven Trees? I'd have to sell a kidney on my salary."

"No need for that."

He walks into the dining room, and I follow him. The home of the older professor smells like paper and moths and is filled with shelves upon shelves of thick books. The books are interspersed occasionally with interesting…um, art? Some of the pieces are embarrassingly erotic, like maybe I should turn my head and give them privacy.

Ryan catches me looking. "The professor travels a lot and collects…art. Last year he went to India."

"Uh-huh. Nice man. Have you known him long?"

"He's my mentor," Ryan says. "He used to teach at UCLA, which was where we met. Now he's Professor Emeritus at the university here."

"You're from Los Angeles?"

"Originally from Ohio but live in Pasadena," he says, sitting at the dining table, which he's clearly using as a desk and gestures for me to sit. "In your soliloquy, you mentioned you're from here."

"I'm one of those rarities, someone whose middle-class family has lived in the Bay Area for decades."

We were here first, before the tech companies settled and changed the price of everything from housing to gas.

I pick up a paper with handwritten scribbles all over it. If this is his penmanship its atrocious. And were this truly a Jane Austen novel, I'd tell faux Mr. Darcy, "Pray tell, is this handwriting or hieroglyphics? Mayhap you can do better or risk offending a possible suitor with your careless efforts at penmanship."

"I need help organizing this"—he waves his hand in the direction of papers, books, pens, pencils, laptop, and other detritus of a working writer—"into something cohesive I can use."

I almost say, "Fear not, I will handily execute this," but decide it's time to abandon Jane Austen impressions.

"No problem," I say. "I've got you."

"What about hours?" Ryan says. "They're flexible, but I want to know when to expect you."

"Mornings around eight? I'll bring the coffee!"

"The only exception is if I've had a rough night and stayed up all night writing. That happens. You don't want to be around me then."

"Um, okay. Does that happen…often?"

"More than I'd like." He shakes his head, like angsty Mr. Darcy, regretting his life choices. He has floppy and wavy hair, a little longer in the front, and a lock of it falls over one side before he brushes it away.

"When do you start writing your book?"

"Soon," he says. "My method is research first, then write the book. It takes me about nine months altogether, and yes, I realize that's how long it takes to grow a baby."

I smother a laugh in my effort to remain serious while privately thinking of more Jane Austen references.

"What do you write? The post said literary fiction."

"World War II spy novels," he says, not meeting my eyes.

"I heard you say you love history. What's your favorite period?"

I don't know if this is a trick question but there's really no other way I can answer honestly. "Regency."

"Of course," he says, and I'm not going to take this personally even if he sounds disappointed.

In his spare time, I imagine he makes fun of genre fiction as do most highbrow types. Well, to each his own.

There's a knock on the door and the professor's brow furrows.

"Should I…should I get it?" I ask.

"No," he says.

Head down, he marches toward the door and a few seconds later I hear him say, "The position is filled."

I look out the window and see a guy, probably a university student, getting back on his bicycle.

My day is made!

When he joins me again, my hands are clasped together. "Really? I got the job?"

"Well, as Henry said, I'd be an idiot not to hire you." He shrugs. "And you got here first."

"High praise indeed," I say, holding out my hand. "I accept!"

THAT AFTERNOON, I return to my shed with a second job.

My she-shed might not be much of a living space but for now it's all I have. There's barely enough room for my twin bed, a mini fridge, a hot plate, one big chair, which doubles as a love seat, and a bookshelf. When I had to give up the condo I shared with my ex, I moved most of my things into storage, another monthly bill.

Here I have electrical outlets, but I can't use the blender and the light at the same time. Ask me how I know. There's only one small mirror, which is more than enough to check to see if my blonde curly hair has decided to behave today. I shower in the main house, use the bathroom facilities, and eat dinner with the family every night.

Not going to lie. Living in my abuelita's backyard took some getting used to. This used to be a garden and tool shed, but it's always had windows. Two of them, now decorated with yellow and white frilly curtains that cheer me up. My Tio Eddie emptied the tools, lawn mower, and potting soil, painted and cleaned, and suggested I live there until I got back on my feet after Chris abandoned me. He left me six months ago, get this, *to join the Peace Corps*. No explanation but the desire to "give back." Barely enough notice to let our guests know the wedding would be canceled. Jerk.

Later that day, I check in with Abuelita. Eddie is at work in San Francisco at his dentistry office, so it's just the two of us. I sort through the mail that comes to the main house because asking them to deliver it to a shed would be too confusing. Packages are another story but you should have seen the look on the UPS guy when he delivered a box of books to the shed.

It was nice of Eddie to convert the garden shed to a living space for me, but I have to confess that moving here feels like the physical representation of how badly my life is progressing so far. Not how I expected.

By now, I thought I'd be published, but so far, no one wants my romance novel so I continue to pay the bills by ghostwriting vampire romance for the estate of the late Desdemona Hill.

Abuelita pats the couch after she says hello. "Come sit and watch the telenovela with me."

I'm not a fan and she usually watches these with Eddie, but I plop down on the couch beside her. "Good news. I got a second job."

"Bueno," she says, eyes riveted to the screen.

She's lying. If left to her own devices, my grandmother would keep me here with her forever. She wanted me to take the only spare bedroom available since Eddie moved in to take care of her. But I don't want to get too comfortable and complacent here.

She points to the screen. "Ay bendito, probecita. She lost her memory."

"Didn't Jessica also lose her memory?" I squint. How many times can they use this particular trope on the same show?

"No, no." Abuelita points to her temple. "Jessica said she lost her memory, but she was *pretending*."

"Ah, si." This makes all the sense in the world to my grandmother.

"This way, she can stop the divorce from Manuel, the only man she has ever loved." She clasps her hands to her chest. "He can't divorce her when she doesn't *remember* anything."

It's entirely possible I got my romantic streak from her. I still believe in true love even after my latest disaster. My parents had the greatest love story. He brought her flowers every day, called her "mi amor" and I caught them more than once dancing in the kitchen without music. That's what I want. Nothing less than true love. The love of my life. I refuse to settle.

Even if my parents' love story ended tragically, I've always wanted what they had together but without the sad ending. It's the reason I write romance. Everyone in my books gets a happy ending.

I watch the rest of the telenovela with Abuelita, and promise her I'll come back later to eat dinner with her and Eddie. But I need to settle in to write my daily word count on my latest vampire book. I've reached the proverbial soggy middle so it's time to bring in more obstacles from the plot outline. These books are such fun to write that I'll usually produce several pages before realizing it. Once I turn this book in, I'll get the next royalty advance and be able to finish paying off the late fees on the wedding venue we didn't cancel in time.

After getting halfway through my word count, I check email and find one from an agent I queried two years ago. The email, which not shockingly is a rejection, is standard for me:

Thank you for sharing your novel with me. You have a real gift for prose, and the characters jump off the page. Ultimately, I did not connect with the story the way I would have liked, so I'm going to pass. I wish you luck in your future publishing endeavors.

Traditional publishing moves at a snail's pace but this is ridiculous.

At writer conferences I've learned this is agent-speak for: I don't know *how* to sell your book. Even if I'm better off without an agent who can't do what I need her to do, the rejection stings, even with compliments. It always makes me think there's something I'm missing if the prose is good and the characters are fleshed out. Maybe I'm the problem. It's the story of my life.

Maybe what I'm missing, ironically enough, is *inexperience*. I'm told by one of Desdemona's former ghostwriters who quit to self-publish her own books, that rather than help, ghostwriting is something to overcome. Now that she's self-publishing with some success, she's had interest from New York. Apparently editors do not have a lot of faith in someone who writes a book when given existing characters with a back story, a decent plot, and a built-in audience.

Or maybe they'd just like us to stay in our lane.

The most frustrating part of ghostwriting is the non-disclosure agreements. No one can know anything specific about the book I'm writing, or even that I'm often writing bestselling books. For me, ghostwriting has paid the bills in an uncertain publishing landscape. Sometimes I think I've traded security for my dream but I'm comfortable with anonymity. My nightmare scenario would be a huge book tour and television appearances. Yes, the sales and peer acknowledgment would be nice but only if I can enjoy it from the comfort of my home.

There's another email from my best friend in the writing world, Holly, whom I met years ago at a romance writer conference. She's arguably my friend even if we see each other via the screen most of the time. It's always been tough for me to make long-lasting friendships and it's been a while since we connected because I'm feeling self-conscious about my background being a shed.

Like me, Holly has been writing for years without any success. Unlike me, she's never tried ghostwriting and makes her living as a high school teacher. She lives in Missouri, so we only see each other at the occasional writer conference, but mostly online when we both celebrate the little wins. She knows I'm a ghostwriter but keeps pushing me to write more of my own books. I've written the one, and with all the rejections I worry the thing agents are not telling me is that my work is derivative and I've yet to find my own voice.

To: theghostwriter@hotmail
From: inthequerytrenches@yahoo
Hope you're doing well. Just checking in. What's your progress? Any more revisions done or have you started something new? Remember, start something new, and that way if you sell this one, another one will already be in line. I wanted to tell you I'm halfway through my latest and entered a contest. Fingers crossed because I'll get in front of my dream agent if I final in my category.

Too bad I have nothing of note to report. Holly is always way ahead of me, filled with inspiration and a sense of confidence I envy. Imposter syndrome? That's not a thing to her. She works all day, is mother to three, wife of one, and writes late into the night. She's a powerhouse and I know one day soon she'll be published due to her tenacity alone.

What am I supposed to tell Holly? As writers, we always present our best self to the world. On social media, we're happy, joyful, and busy. Real life is another story, where you can often find me in a fetal position, munching on chocolate after my latest rejection. Nobody wants a photo of that.

Should I tell her my wedding is off? If I do, she'll send me all these sad face emojis. I've had enough pity from my family.

To: inthequerytrenches@yahoo

From: theghostwriter@hotmail

All is well, though wedding preparations are certainly taking a lot of my time! Funny, I just got a rejection today from an agent I queried two years ago. Um, guess she's been busy. All the usual lingo about how great it is but just isn't for her.

Do you think they're just lying to me? What's the point?

It's hard to feel too sad when I am getting married to the love of my life!

As I've said before, Chris is the perfect romance hero. I'm pretty much writing every book about him. I have so much material, it's hard to narrow it down.

Is it lying, or is it fiction?

Sometimes I don't know the difference.

CHAPTER 2

In the first week of work, five more people come by to interview for the position of research assistant. Mr. Brady now makes *me* answer the door and tell them the position is filled. I admit I don't mind doing this as I'm much nicer about it than he is.

"So sorry, the job is filled. But good luck in your future endeavors!"

Once, a university student looking for work was so upset she cried.

"If I'd gotten here sooner I could have had this job."

I hugged her. "Oh hey, hey. Did you know they're looking for baristas at The Drip? Tell them I sent you; I used to work there."

"Thanks," she said, wiping away a tear. "You're so nice."

That time, Mr. Brady looked up from his work, his mouth once again refusing to give in to another smile.

"Maybe you're a little too nice."

"There's no such thing!"

"Whatever," he said. "Kids need to get used to disappointment."

I work for him in the mornings and depending on the day, I have my afternoons free. I'm also able to work from home but Mr. Brady would rather I work in close proximity. He claims it keeps him on track because he wouldn't feel comfortable taking a nap while I'm here. Apparently, he's prone to those when on deadline.

He's not *horrible* to work for. I mean, I've had a lot worse. He does answer the phone in an interesting way.

"What?" is his preferred way of greeting people who deign to interrupt him with a call.

It's the reason I didn't argue about answering the door to inform interviewees the position is taken. And happily, the block is working. I can appreciate his male hotness in *theory*. Like the way I stare at a rainbow or a glorious sunset and appreciate the vibrant colors. I don't want to *make out* with the rainbow or the sunset. It's just very beautiful. Ryan has fallen into this "hot block" area in which I appreciate his objectively good looks while, in fact, they are not even slightly affecting me.

The day he hired me I searched online for Ryan Brady books. He's written four World War II historical fiction novels for a major publishing house. There have been awards and distinctions but no bestseller status. The point is, he's reviewed without fail in the major places and they're always positive, raving about his prose and suspenseful plots.

"Professor." I interrupt him now.

"*What?*" He sounds annoyed, then shoves a hand through his hair and turns to me. The ends stick up, glasses slightly askew.

Click.

He blinks, then scowls. "Did you just take my *picture?*"

"Why yes, I did. And you look great. Adorable and more importantly approachable."

"What are you doing with that?" He points to my phone.

"I'm posting it on your socials with some pithy and cute comment about how hard at work you are on your new book."

"*Why?*"

"Before the end of the month, I bet we double your followers."

"But I didn't hire you to up my social media game."

"You don't *have* a social media game. Look at this as an extra service I provide." While I have his attention I reach for several notes gleaned from the City of Richmond's website. "You aren't giving me enough work. Should I pick up where I left off yesterday, or do you have something I could read?"

"What I need now is a list of California area surnames from the nineteen forties. Focus on the Bay Area, people with Spanish heritage."

"Yes, I'll get to that."

Rather than working in separate rooms, he decided we should work together on the dining room table, where our books and papers mingle. I sit several seats away from him to give him plenty of elbow room. Mr. Brady is a messy writer. He tends to stare off into space a great deal, which I recognize as the mark of a writer, but occasionally he tightly grips a worn baseball while he does, which makes him…confusing.

After organizing his notes, I fall down several rabbit holes on the internet. Two days ago, I wound up on a gardening site, which had nothing to do with the Richmond Shipyard except that a rare wildflower had once been spotted nearby. Right now, I'm going back to the site to identify which flowers are natural to the area.

"What the hell is this?" Ryan spies over my shoulder. "Did I ask you to research *flowers*? What does gardening have to do with my book?"

I guiltily shut the lid of the laptop. "You know what? Setting is awfully important to a story!"

"Please, just follow directions."

But I've learned far more about ships and factories than I ever thought I would. I wonder how much of this information will actually make it into the book. I *have* read my share of historical fiction. Those authors are talented, weaving a world based on the research they've done, grounding but never boring the reader.

Privately, because he's supposed to be kind of a big deal in so-called "highbrow" literary circles, I'm reading his first book. And while the prose is fine, it meanders on and on. One entire scene on a blue jay the main character observes taking flight while stationed at Pearl Harbor. *Really.* Probably some foreshadowing of how he, too, would soon take flight. Maybe a metaphor. But I almost fell asleep while reading.

"Um, I want to make a suggestion?" I say now, accidentally phrasing this as a question. That makes me sound insecure, as if I need permission.

Anyway, he knows I'm a ghostwriter so I hope he realizes I know story.

"About?"

As a native, I know quite a lot about our area, and I've remembered something about the beach town of Santa Cruz south of us.

"About your book."

He narrows his eyes. "You have a suggestion about *my book*?"

He says this as if I've just suggested he should strip naked and run around the block a few times to get the blood pumping. The tone almost makes me back down, but something about Ryan's quiet nature is pushing me to be challenging. Bolder. It's like nature, seeking balance.

"Yes, if…if that's all right." I thrum the pads of my fingers on the table.

He studies me several seconds, like I'm a student he can't decide he should let pass his course on a technicality.

Finally, he nods. "Sure."

"Well, did you know that the Cocoanut Grove in Santa Cruz was quite the attraction during World War II? All the big bands came through to play."

"Is it still there?" He squints. "If so, we should take a field trip."

This is where I swallow hard, knowing what Mr. History might say about what I have to say next.

"Well, part of it's been converted into an arcade, but—"

"An arcade. They couldn't find any other place to put that?"

"You didn't let me finish. The ballroom can still be rented for events. Anyway, there's mention of the history of Santa Cruz during the war. All very interesting. At least, I remember being interested at the time."

Mr. Brady rubs both temples like he has a headache coming on thanks to me. "This is going to help me…how? My book is set in Richmond."

"Pacing. I thought maybe your main characters could have a diversion there for a day. Maybe there's a big military ball and something pertinent to the plot happens there. You *do* have a love story in your book, right?"

He gives me a look as if he can't believe I've asked *him* that question. Like the very idea is ludicrous.

When he doesn't speak, I keep talking. "Seriously, a love story is a great way to up the stakes and give your character something to fight for. Something he or she can't stand the thought of losing."

He seems greatly offended by this idea, given his furrowed brow and the set of his jaw.

"My characters are already dealing with a *war*. Separation and isolation from family. Danger to life and limb. Look, I know you're trying to help. But…don't." He puts up a hand. "My brain doesn't work that way. Don't you have some research to do?"

Well, fine. If he doesn't want my help he won't get it. But I've certainly read enough plots to know a character needs to risk personal loss, or the reader won't care about the story. I go back to my research on surnames, determined to push my agenda on him at some point.

Bent over a book, deep in reading, Mr. Brady doesn't seem to notice when his cell buzzes. He doesn't even move. If only he could bottle and sell his powers of concentration. They are enviable.

"Mr. Brady?" I prompt and he looks up at me. "Your phone? Should I? Should I get it?"

He hasn't assigned me telephone duties and we let the house phone go to voicemail whenever it rings. It's never anyone important on the landline since this is his mentor's house and everyone knows he's on sabbatical. A few days ago, he called Ryan on his cell and I could hear him laughing and then more quietly, "Yeah. Working out fine." And then also, "No, I don't think that's a good idea."

Now Ryan picks up his cell, gives it a glance, and stands. "Great. It's my agent. I have to take this."

Okay, okay. I get it, Mr. Big Shot. You have an agent.

He leaves the room but you'd think he wouldn't be so loud if he wants privacy. I hear every word he's saying.

A few minutes later he's increasingly frustrated. "Are you *kidding* me? I thought we had more time. But…what are we going to *do* about this? Look, I don't need this. Honestly, the advance was more than enough. It was all I wanted. Yes, yes, it's good but also very very bad."

Seriously, there's no point to leaving the room if I can still hear him. He isn't exactly disguising his frustration, but that's Mr. Brady for you. He can be grumpy and not just when he's interrupted. On the first day of work, I'd gotten his coffee order wrong, and he sulked all morning. I proudly stood my ground and refused to offer to go back and get the right drink because the coffee delivery was a perk and my way of being nice. Did he still drink it? Why, yes, he did, a scowl on his face the entire time.

"I understand, but…you said I could…then why did you *say* that? Damn it, this is getting out of control. Remember, none of this was my idea!" This he pretty much shouts, which is unusual enough that I startle.

"I'm beginning to wonder if it's worth this!"

He has my curiosity more than peaked. Something wrong with the book? The contract? I don't know much about the inside of the published author world but have heard a few things here and there through the querying author grapevine. I know all too well deals can fall apart.

"Not sure why you're asking me, then, if you're not going to listen. Do what you have to do!" He storms back into the room and has apparently forgotten I'm here given by the way he does a double take when he sees me. "Sorry, bad day. You can go home early."

It's Friday, so I'm not going to argue. My cousin Sofia is coming over later for girl talk and mostly to make her infamous mojitos. She's been trying for months to get me to go out but I can't afford fun right now.

"Bad news?" I ask while gathering my laptop and papers, slipping them inside the satchel.

He's obviously already checked out, staring out the window as if it's an abyss, his hands steepled. I think he likes to see himself as this tragic creature, forced to live in this modern age where people like to talk to each other and share information via the black magic of technology.

I cough, so he remembers I'm standing here.

"Good and bad," he says, stands and walks me to the door. "But mostly bad."

It's a good thing he doesn't write the way he talks.

"Well, I'm sorry for the bad but happy about the good."

Two can play this game.

I leave wondering if there's anyone he can call later for moral support. There's no ring on his finger and no photos he brought with him. I've snooped a little, so I've seen some of the mail he brought. Stuff like bills and such. He charges way too much coffee to his Amex card and apparently gives generously to a literary foundation.

The truth is I know very little about the man and beyond the work I do for him, he's none of my concern.

All in all, the block is working.

CHAPTER 3

The next morning, I have a headache the size of Texas, if Texas multiplied itself overnight times one hundred. My mouth doesn't feel like it's filled with cotton, it smells and feels like the place where cotton goes to die.

Last night, Sofia and I may have overdone it with the mojitos. We found a bottle of Absolut Vodka Chris left behind and I felt zero guilt cracking it open.

I let Sofia make her mojitos with his precious vodka, and what was left of it went down the drain.

All those lowered inhibitions reminded me of a couple of things:

I was practically left at the altar!

I have a second job, which might get me out of the shed faster, but I'm still no closer to my dream.

My current life is horrible. I mean, I haven't asked the universe for much. A place of my own, someone to love. Satisfying work that means something.

All *I've* ever wanted was to be successful. And the funny thing is, I am, but I can't tell anyone. I can't brag about the books I've written or that one of them made the *New York Times* list.

Luci Santana can't seem to write a book worthy of publication. But Desdemona Hill writes bestsellers. In a way I *am* Desdemona Hill for all practical purposes, which means I can write bestselling books. Just seemingly not with the stories I choose to tell. My own four-hundred-page opus sits in my desk drawer. I should be dying to get back to revisions, but I find a million excuses to put my own work last.

I'd hoped being around a working author would inspire me. Maybe I'll figure out how Ryan does his plotting and characterization. Maybe I'll get the key into the big boy's room. But so far, he hasn't let me read anything. He keeps me at arm's length, hiding his work like it's top secret. It's only been a week, so I can still hope he will let me into the inner sanctum.

Later that morning after coffee and a shower at the main house, I check my email and find one from Holly.

To: theghostwriter@hotmail
From: inthequerytrenches@yahoo
Subject: chocolate news
Hey, lady! I'm sorry about the rejection, but at least she loved your prose. Remember that you need a lot of "no's" to get to one "yes." Look at me! I'm sure before long you will get picked up by a publisher. In the meantime, you know you can write, or you wouldn't keep getting hired for whatever secret book you're writing.

At least the wedding is keeping you busy and joyful.

I'm SO excited because I'm officially a finalist in the contest I was telling you about! They liked it, they liked it, they really liked it! This means it's going to three agents, one of whom is my "dream agent." Was just thinking about you and wondering how revisions are going. Remember, you can't ghostwrite forever. You deserve to be recognized for the rock star you are! How about a zoom session next week? I'm available in the evenings.

xo

Holly

I mentally crack my knuckles and prepare to write more fiction.

To: inthequerytrenches@yahoo

From: theghostwriter@hotmail

Re: chocolate news

That is SO exciting! Am so happy for you. You're probably going to be under contract soon. I'm a little busy lately, what with the wedding, and ghostwriting (which face it, pays the bills). Last week I picked up a little extra work as a research assistant for a literary author. I guess he's kind of well-known in his own circles, so that's nice. Maybe I'll learn something. I don't think I can do zoom next week but let's circle back soon.

xo

Luci

I've left open the tab of a deep dive on the history of Santa Cruz during the war, which isn't what Mr. Brady's asked for, but it's interesting stuff if he'll give it half a chance. I firmly believe he needs a romance to raise the stakes but he won't listen to me. Why would he? I'm simply a lowly ghost-writer and research assistant.

In a new search engine tab, this time I type in Ryan's name. The page populates with quite a few Ryan Bradys and eventually I find the author. His boring website comes up listing all his books and awards. No photos of him, which is probably a mistake. His looks alone would drive readers to his site. There are a few videos I find, most of them by readers and other influencers who've reviewed his books. And then I come across a video dated three years ago, which for all intents and purposes is almost buried. It jumps out at me because of its name:

Professor Reveals the Unvarnished Truth About Publishing.

I hit play on a YouTube link to find Ryan speaking at a

podium for a conference listed as the New England Guild of Authors. And damn it all, he's actually wearing a tweed jacket with elbow patches. For a moment, shock pulses through me. He looks like a different person, sporting a *beard* of all things. It definitely makes him look older. He's not wearing the "man of steel" glasses, but some ugly tortoise shell square ones, and his wavy hair is combed back.

When the video starts, he's clearly finished a lecture and is taking questions from the audience.

He calls on a young woman who stands, her back to the camera. "Why are your books so depressing? Can't you ever give us a happily ever after? A little romance wouldn't hurt, so even if they lose the war, they've at least got each other."

Preach, I want to shout! This is what *I'm* saying, sister.

"Happily ever after?" Ryan smirks and clears his throat. "Well, as I believe a respected author once said, if you want *happy* books, you can find those at your local grocery store. Or the airport shop in the same place you pick up snacks and gum before your flight. Romance, the big bully in the room. Yes, it is a behemoth. But whenever you can find a book for ninety-nine-cents, or *free*, for God's sake, you have a publisher or author who doesn't *value* their work. And romance books, as a whole, have devalued the entire publishing industry. They've bastardized lists and destroyed them in some cases. Sure, they sell a lot, but as we know, what's popular is often not necessarily what's *well-written*."

The room thunders with applause. He takes his seat. I'm shocked. Shocked, I tell you! How dare he.

I want to wipe the smug smile off his face!

Mr. Brady might be stuck-up and in his own little world, but this is outrageous. Thankfully, people who disagree with his elitist opinion, and dare I say misogynist remarks, fill the comment section and find his attitude as revolting as I do. His comments are clearly against all the *female* romance authors who dominate the publishing industry. And when women lead anything, men will find a way to make it seem insignificant. I've been dealing with this attitude since even before my MFA program.

Why don't you write a real book?

"This *is* a real book! And this makes me happy!" I shout to no one now. "Because it makes a lot of people very, very happy!"

Well, I obviously can't work for the professor any longer. He should have been canceled for this but maybe he's not famous enough in the first place. So, I'll resign from my position, but not before giving him an earful.

I discovered that my employer feels romance writers have…what was the word he used? Oh yes, *bastardized* the publishing industry. That one still hurts, like someone hit me with a two by four, then left me in the desert to die of dehydration.

If Ryan thinks I can work for him after hearing the drivel that came out of his flapping jaw, he has another think coming.

Pushing the brain cobwebs away, I try to figure out how best to do this. My resignation has to make a bold statement. He has to know *why* I'm leaving a good paying job that, face it, I need. It's a chance for him to learn something. My quitting will show him (and the world) that money is insignificant when it comes to values and beliefs and I can't *work* with him. No matter how good he looks on the outside, his insides are rotting like a soft brown banana.

I think about texting him but I don't do well when I rage text. I sometimes rage write but it's too easy to say the wrong thing behind the safety of a screen. Monday, I'll show up with the proper speech, which I'll write today. I'll give him a point-by-point analysis of how and why he's so wrong about romance books. There are testimonials I can quote and speeches I've personally heard, like the one Julia Quinn gave at the Romance Writers of America in New York City in 2015. She told the story of how a mother and daughter were reading one of her regency romance books together, during the mother's chemo treatments. The daughter buried her mother with the book. I was there among all the others who shed tears listening to that speech. Men just don't understand what women mean to each other, how our books feed our souls and are connections. I can't tell every man, but I can tell the professor and I will.

I go to work on my speech right after my brain wakes up, but I'm interrupted by the phone buzzing. *Ryan.* It's Saturday, but we did say I'd be available and on call for emergencies. I consider texting him, asking him what he wants. The phone finally stops ringing. Let him leave a voicemail. Then it starts ringing again. Still Ryan. Super.

I answer the phone with my raspy "I'm sick" voice. "Hello."

"It's me, Ryan Brady, your employer. You sound terrible. Are you okay?"

I roll my eyes, as if he needs an introduction and I need the reminder I'm his subordinate.

"I'm fine. If you need something today, it will have to wait."

"I'm not worried about work. Are you sick? Do you need anything?"

"I don't need anything from *you*, Professor," I say in my snarkiest tone.

"You should call me Ryan. I've been meaning to say that." If he gets the message that I now hate his guts, he ignores it. "If you're sick you need soup, decongestant, cough drops."

"No, I'm not—"

"I'm coming over to bring you some chicken soup."

"That's not—"

"You should have chicken soup. It's no problem, I'm in the area," he says. And then after a beat asks, "Where do you live?"

"Honestly, you don't need to come by. I've got soup."

"I'm coming by."

"Don't."

"Why not? Do you think I'm trying to put the moves on you? Luci, I'm not. I would never make you uncomfortable. I'm a professional."

A professional *what* I want to ask. A professional asshat?

But not only do I hate every fiber of his being, I haven't finished the speech. I don't really want Mr. Bra—*Ryan* to know I live in what amounts to a hovel. He'll think my giving up the generous salary he's paying me foolish, given my situation. Maybe he's right but that's hardly the point.

Then again, if I ever want to be on even footing with him, I'll be more at ease in my own place. Small and efficient, but *my* territory. I'll give him the speech and then hustle him out the only door. No need to come in Monday, giving me more time to hit the ground running for a new job. Maybe Desdemona's estate will give me a raise. I've never asked so it's worth a try.

"I need to talk to you about something. It's urgent and time sensitive," Ryan says.

"Is this about work?"

"Well, yes. In a way. Let me bring you soup. Please."

"Okay, fine, but just for a few minutes. Come in through the side gate of the backyard and don't bother anyone in the main house. You may as well know, I live in a garden shed."

I quickly give him directions and while I wonder what could possibly be so urgent, I rush to tidy my corner of the world. I've worked my magic to make the inside of my space cozy, filling it with bright colorful prints on the walls and flowery pillows on the faux love seat. The one bookcase I could fit in here is stuffed with papers and books of all genres.

Ryan arrives sooner than I anticipated, and I've only just completed the second draft of my resignation speech. I could use another read for proper word choices. When resigning from an award-winning author, I'd like to use the strongest words. Irritation pours through me, but I open the door and there he stands with a plastic bag from Chef Chu's.

"I have your soup." He hands it to me, then gives me a long look, like he's seeing me for the first time. "You look… different."

Maybe it's because I didn't primp for this meeting. "Of course I look different."

"Yeah, that's not it." He cocks his head, studying me. "Something's changed. You're not, you know…" He draws his arms in a circle to encompass all of me. "Happy."

He doesn't think I look happy because I'm wearing ratty jeans with holes in the knees and a loose gray T-shirt? This is a new setting, so naturally I look different. Perhaps more fearsome and intimidating and in full control. Like a lioness in her den. It occurs to me I should have dressed properly for the speech I plan to give him, but I've spent all the time on the speech itself. It's good, too, and I think I'll get all the points across. I've started with a brief history of romance since history is his jam, including Jane Austen, often believed to be the first romance novelist.

Ryan scowls. "You remind me of war-torn France. Kind of sad and…defeated."

"Gee, *thanks*. You sure have a way with the ladies." I wave him inside. "It's good that you're here. We need to talk."

"Yeah, no doubt about it, someone punctured a hole in your happy bubble."

Oh, he has no idea. Two of his kind have popped *my*

happy, but at the moment he will bear the brunt of it all. For *all* of the patriarchy. For all mankind.

"What's this emergency? What's so urgent about *research* that it can't wait until Monday?"

"It's…another type of emergency." He drags a hand through his hair.

I wonder when he stopped combing it back like in the video and whether I should tell him the beard makes him look older, more seasoned. Now that he's clean shaven he looks younger.

"Are you stuck in a scene? A bit blocked?"

"I wish it were that easy of a problem. That's not it. This is something…well, it's something I can't do. I couldn't do it in a million years. It's…impossible."

I smirk. "I see…and you think, of course, that it's possible for me. Because I'm a *woman*."

"Exactly!"

"You better *not* need help with your dry cleaning." I cross my arms.

He blinks. "Why would I need help with that?"

"Never mind. I'm glad you're here. You and I have a little problem." I gesture between us.

Closing the distance, I place one hand on each of his shoulders.

This near to him, I realize that though of average height, he looms over me. I stand on tiptoes and strain to meet his eyes. They are an interesting shade of dark and icy blue and I'm determined to ignore the fact there's a deep sadness in them.

"You said some terrible things and I'm having a tough time forgiving you."

"When? I don't think I cursed, but the last time you were in, when I was arguing with my agent…it's because this… well this problem I have is primarily *her* fault."

"*What's* her fault?"

"The reason I need a woman."

I quickly remove my hands from his shoulders and quirk my eyebrow. "*You* need a woman."

"No!" He throws his hands up. "Not like that! I don't *need* 'a woman.'"

"You better not. At least not around me." I shake my finger at him.

"So." He runs a hand down his face. "I can see this isn't going well."

"You're a genius. Nope, not so far. And it's about to get a *whole* lot worse."

"Would you please tell me what I did to you that was so horrible?"

"I don't have to tell you, I'll go ahead and *show* you." I grab my phone, open the app, scroll to the video, and hit play. "*This.*"

The video plays and the moment it does, Ryan's entire demeanor switches. He closes his eyes, slumps, and rubs the back of his neck. He's never looked happy, but now he looks like someone who's been given a few months to live. He becomes, for lack of a better word, *gray.*

"We...we tried to have that taken down but it's still out there."

"Yes, of course it is, and you owe an entire industry a huge apology for being such...such a...*dick!*"

I gasp at my foul language, which is uncommon for me. This is why I prefer to communicate through the written word where I can revise each word in each sentence until it's perfection.

I hold up my finger and reach for my speech. I've memorized part of it:

Mr. Brady, you offend me. Love stories are about far more than romantic love or sexy times. They're about hope, rising stakes, and growth, and how falling in love with the right person can actually help you find the best version of yourself.

"That was recorded three years ago when I foolishly thought I'd made it." He holds up air quotes. "I'd just separated from my wife and I was probably not in the best of moods to think of romance as believable. Okay, so I was an idiot. A jerk. And *of course* I apologize. I can't apologize enough. I'll never be done apologizing. Will I?"

"Well, probably not."

Hearing that he once had a wife sets me back momentarily with some sympathy for the devil. But this blue-eyed demon won't get off that easily. I flip through the pages to find my speech.

"I'm actually glad you found that video, because that's what I need to talk to you about."

"You were going to tell me about this video? Why would you do that? You had to know I'd be angry and want to quit working for you." I hand him my handwritten speech.

"What this?" He flips through the pages, five all together, his brow furrowed in confusion.

"My resignation."

"No! You can't quit. *Please* don't quit."

"I can't work with someone who has such low opinions of romance writers. That's my tribe, sir. You have no respect for me if that's how you feel. You *know* I'm a ghostwriter and although I can't say much more, I write romance. Does that surprise you?"

"No, your regency period answer spoke volumes. And I have complete respect for you. Didn't you hear the part about how I'm sorry? About all of it?"

"You're only sorry because you've been caught." I twitch my finger in the air.

"I don't *hate* romance. Well, not anymore. In real life, sure, yes. But I think it's the hardest thing in the world to write convincingly and the people who do are...pure genius."

I tap my foot, not knowing what to make of this seemingly sincere apology. The words work, and his demeanor has the air of desperation. For the first time I notice he's wearing a wrinkled button-down shirt and it's partially tugged out of his slacks. He's got beard stubble on his chin and there's a coffee stain on his shirt. But the things he said...

"Why should I believe you've changed your mind?"

"Because...well, because I wrote one."

I lower my notebook. "I'm sorry, you wrote *what?*"

"I wrote a romance novel, and it nearly broke me. It's the hardest thing I've ever done. Oh, it looks easy, like anyone could do it. Like all you have to do is sit down and write about two people who after a few obstacles fall in love anyway. But that's not even the beginning, is it? Romance novelists don't get enough credit."

Now he really has my attention. "I don't understand. Why would *you* write a romance novel? Was it on a dare?"

"That's right. I thought it would take me a few weeks. and almost two years later I finished."

I smirk. "Harder than it looks, isn't it?"

"Frankly, I pride myself on word choice and even I can't come up with the right words for how difficult it was to write. Unfortunately, I made the mistake of sending it to my agent, as a joke, you know? But I'm not funny, and she didn't get it. No one understands my humor."

"You sent it to her as a *joke?*"

He nods, lowering his head. "Yes, and then she...liked it. She talked me into revising and submitting it to publishers and told me that we could always use another pen name."

"You must have been so pissed! Was all the rejection *soul crushing?*" I hope for that though he probably didn't care if this had all been a massive joke to him.

"I got some rejections, yes." Ryan won't look at me and shifts from one foot to another.

What does he mean by "some" rejections?

"Sit down, would you?" I point to the faux love seat which, let's just face it, is a chair. "Is this a long story?"

"I'll try to make it brief."

He finally sits and tells me everything.

CHAPTER 4

"Your book sold at *auction?*"

"Yeah," Ryan says, hanging his head. "For a good deal."

He's actually quoting from Publishers Marketplace, my bible for years. A "good deal" means a *six-figure* deal. Something much like bile rises in my throat, followed by an out of body sensation, as if I'm floating on a cloud of garbage, watching the landfill below. I fight to keep my composure.

I've forgotten my resignation letter because now there's been an unexpected real life plot twist. I still don't know why Ryan is here or how I can help him. It does not explain why he'd been headed over here to tell me this before he knew I'd even found the video.

He's written *one* romance book. I tell myself his success is probably because he already has a solid reputation in the industry of someone who can deliver a book. But his first romance book selling at auction? This is rare.

"I didn't want any of this to happen, remember, or all of this *attention.*" He says the word as though he smells garbage.

"But then my agent got the deal and…and all that…you know, *money.*"

"But…I looked up your catalog and didn't see any romance."

"No, you wouldn't have seen it."

"Why not? When did it come out?"

"Two months ago." His voice lowers to just above audible range. "It made the *New York Times* list."

All the air goes out of me. "*Seriously?*"

He nods, but sadly, as if to apologize.

"What's the name of the book?"

"They called it *Soulmates.*"

Soulmates. I'd heard about it but it mostly hadn't been on my radar since my TBR pile is about two feet tall. But I seem to recall the author was a woman. I must have that wrong. It could be initials and I simply assumed.

"Well, gosh. I guess…congratulations. That's just amazing. From someone who derided romance to someone who wrote one. I'd say that's truly an epic hero's journey."

"Believe me, I honestly didn't think I could write romance and certainly not that it would *sell.*"

This isn't helping. I still wonder why he's rushed over to tell me all this like a show-off. What he probably will need, and soon, is crisis management. Because the minute the book comes out, the video will resurface if it hasn't already, go viral, and he'll be called out on it. There will be a few potshots, especially from his existing community of literary snobs who will make fun of him. Romance writers everywhere will skewer him. A good publicist could smooth the road ahead, and spin this somehow, but I hardly have the skills.

"I'm not sure how I can help you with all this. All you have to do is apologize when the video resurfaces. Admit you were wrong because, you know, you *were.*"

"Yeah, well, that's where this gets complicated."

"Why?" I shove my hands on my hips. "You're *not* willing to issue a public apology?"

"Of course, I am. I actually already did, not that anyone saw that video." He shakes his head. "A while ago we decided to publish the romance under a pen name. To keep my works separate. There was never any intention I would write another book like it."

"Ah, I see. But word will still get out, pen name or not. You have the same face."

"Which is why I thought it much safer if I chose a woman's name. Elizabeth Brogan."

Now the pieces were coming together. The sheer audacity. Okay. A woman's pen name. It isn't like this kind of thing hasn't been done before, though in reverse and usually by women trying to make it into a man's world. There are many more examples going back to Shakespearean times.

"I can see how this has complicated your life. All this attention and you don't even have a face to put with the name. Honestly, I'm surprised your agent hasn't helped you with this."

"She has but I don't like her ideas. I don't want to hire an *actress* to do this."

So, apparently no girlfriend or significant other who might step in. Words aren't coming as easily as they usually do, the information overload having a clear effect on my bandwidth.

"But it all might have been okay because I should have been able to stay under the radar, except…here's where the *real* problem comes in." He sighs. "The book was selected as the morning show pick on that new segment the insipid former reality star started. That's the phone call I had yesterday from my agent."

I have to sit down, so I plop down on the small end table,

leaving two feet between us. The shed is small, but it's a good twenty feet from one wall to another. I've tried to keep a few feet between me and Ryan at all times. Now, in this small space, I'm having trouble taking in a breath.

Last week I'd read that Carla Hopkins, one of the former contestants on *Love Line*, a reality dating show, and a cover model now married to an NHL player, wanted to share her love of romance books with the world. A major streaming service started their own book club for her to compete with GMA, Reese, and Jenna's picks. She'll be doing one a month and it sounds like Ryan's book might be the first one.

"I didn't know this, because I've never been in this position, but the size of the advance my agent negotiated meant the publisher made the book a lead title. They proposed several books to the show, including mine. Carla got an early copy and she chose the book because it reminds her of her love story with Mark." Ryan runs a hand through his hair. "Apparently they hated each other when they first met."

Enemies to lovers is one of my favorite tropes, right next to Grumpy Sunshine, but after pretend relationships. I have a numbered list somewhere.

"My agent wants to make the most of this temporary sensation. Trends come and go, and we happened to hit gold with this one. If only they hadn't chosen the book, this might not even be a problem."

Cry me a river, sir, I want to say. I think of Holly, who's been querying for ten years without the slightest interest. She's talented and has great ideas and plots but no one will give her a chance.

"So, of course you have to do it. The only problem is they usually have a live interview with the author. I've seen GMA do it on zoom, so the author doesn't have to travel unless they want to or can." I snap my fingers. "I guess you have no choice at this point but to hire someone. It's either that or reveal the truth. You have to go all in with this deception."

"I don't like the word 'deception.'" He makes air quotes.

"Riiight."

I lower my gaze and stare at him from under hooded eyes to give him my "are you for real?" look.

"Okay, fine. Deception is the correct word, under most circumstances. But Elizabeth Brogan will eventually fade in popularity when there are no more romance books from her. From me. Problem solved."

"Quitting at the top of your game? Gotta say, not many would do that."

"This book was a fluke, and I don't have another one in me. I write historical fiction and I'll die happily in obscurity. Believe me, this is not what I wanted. I'm going to divorce Elizabeth Brogan like I divorced my ex-wife. *Soulmates* was Elizabeth's first and last book."

"And that's your final answer?"

He nods. "The reason I'm here is…well, the moment I met you I thought…and so did Henry, by the way, and that's why he thought I'd be an idiot not to hire you. Seriously, it's like you just stepped out of the pages of my book. So maybe *you* could pretend to be Elizabeth Brogan…as part of your employment."

Is this what he meant by being flexible? By "other duties"? I'm definitely not being paid enough for *this*.

"Just the web meeting they'll broadcast later on the show. I'm sure you've seen those. You'll pose for some photos holding the book, that kind of thing."

Without saying a word, I swallow so hard I think maybe the people next door can hear me. He doesn't know he's asked me to do something so far out of my comfort zone it may as well be set on another galaxy. Is it because I'm already a ghostwriter so he thinks it's easy for me to slip into the skin of someone else? I don't want to believe it, but he's probably right. After all, I already write other people's stories.

I still haven't answered so he keeps talking.

"Of course, this all has to be approved by my agency and the publisher. We never pictured or planned on doing anything this public, hence the pen name. If the publisher is okay with this, we can go forward. You're already a writer, so you'd be perfect. You know this world. Our world."

If he's trying to flatter me, it works. *Our* world. As if I share even a slice of that world with an author whose book debuted on a major list.

"Of course, you couldn't tell anyone about this. You'd have to sign an NDA, which I'm sure you've already done for your ghostwriting."

I nod because of course I have. "But I've never been on TV before."

"That makes two of us."

I've always been in the background where I'm comfortable. I don't participate in author panels the way Ryan has. No one has ever asked. This is like asking the backup singer to headline the show. She might have the vocal chops, but she doesn't have the stage presence. I can't possibly do this. I'm not ready for prime time.

But Ryan is still making his case. "You'd make the perfect Elizabeth Brogan."

"Here's the thing. I like being in the background. Sure, I want to get my own book published some day, but all this… it's scary."

Ryan nods as if he totally gets it. Most writers, after all, are introverts who would rather stay home than go to a party. Some of my best days are when plans are canceled and I can just stay home.

But Sofia's words to me come back, how I sometimes

make myself small to accommodate others. She thinks it's what happened with Chris. I gave him so much room he walked straight out of my life. I've never wanted to challenge the status quo. I go along with the way things are because it's easier than fighting.

On the other hand, if there ever is a time to ask for the moon…this might be the moment. He's desperate. He needs a woman all right, but not just any woman. Someone who can fake being the writer of his book because oh let's see, she *is* a writer. Someone who will keep quiet about the deception because she understands the need for privacy and confidentiality. He needs someone special.

Someone like me.

A few minutes ago, I was ready to part ways with Ryan forever but that would have been shortsighted.

I tip my chin, projecting my voice. "Naturally, I would need to be appropriately compensated for this project."

"Whatever you need."

A long silence stretches between us.

"So…let me get this straight." I put a hand to my chest. "You want Elizabeth Brogan to be *my* pen name. And you want me to pretend I wrote the book you did."

"Exactly."

"And I obviously can't tell anyone. I've got to tell everyone that I wrote the book. My friends, my family."

"Right."

"The most popular book in the country."

"Apparently."

"So, it's like the reverse of what I usually do." I gesture to him. "You're the ghostwriter."

"That's one way to put it."

"It's the only way to put it. You did the work. I take the credit. I know the drill."

Ryan is quiet, just closing his eyes and pinching the bridge of his nose, and a long silence stretches between us.

"When is this interview being filmed?"

"Monday," he says miserably.

"Monday! Monday as in two days from today? Monday as in the day that comes after Sunday, which is tomorrow?"

He groans. "Why do you think I'm here? This is the emergency."

"Give me a minute," I say, holding up a finger. "I need to think."

Behind his spectacles, Ryan's eyes are wide and dare I say hopeful. He can see I'm considering this.

I should just let him sink. I'm not sure he deserves to be saved. He might not deserve my help.

The irony of this is not lost on me. I've never been able to brag about my achievements as a ghostwriter.

And now I'm going to take credit for something I didn't do.

.

CHAPTER 5

I step behind the wood panel divider I use as a mock closet and take a good long look at myself in the mirror I've hung on the back. My hazel eyes are bloodshot from the mojitos last night. Dark blotches on my cheekbones suspiciously resemble mascara smudges. Purple circles ring my eyelids. I notice a stain on my shirt. I'd managed to locate a pair of old jeans in the dirty clothes pile before Ryan dropped by, so I wouldn't have to answer the door pant-less. I hadn't planned to let him *inside* but then…those down-turned puppy dog eyes… I folded.

Truly, I'm a delight. I've probably never looked worse in front of a man. Or single person. Ever.

None of this is fair. *One* book. Ryan wrote one romance book and has the kind of success most authors could only dream about. I should just *let* him deal with the fallout of this deception. Screw him and the patriarchy, moving into *my* territory. Taking a woman's name, for the love of God. Is nothing sacred?

But if I *don't* do this, if I'm not the one to help, his agency will find someone else.

There's a lot about publishing that is pure luck. I remember something I once heard said about luck. A teacher quoted the Roman philosopher Seneca when he claimed *luck* was nothing more than opportunity meeting preparation.

And I have been prepared for *years*. Now, maybe, just *maybe* opportunity has arrived. This could be fun. This could be life altering. Afterward, I'll have some contacts. Maybe Ryan's agent, or even his editor, would be so grateful they'll be willing to read my manuscript and help me fix what's obviously wrong. They're all going to owe me, but none more than Ryan.

I can do this. After all, I'm already a chameleon in many ways. Easily adaptable. Whether in a condo or converted shed in the yard, I survive. Hell, I thrive.

I can *be* Elizabeth Brogan. She isn't even real so she can't step out and scream, "Sit down, you impostor!" One television appearance, for the fans. Romance readers deserve this. It's not necessarily about helping *Ryan* but about his readers. He might be a literary snob who's taken full advantage of the voracious romance fans, but he has one thing going for him.

He can help me.

It will be the highlight of my rather turbulent year to step into the shoes of this type of success, and see what it feels like. Anything can happen. I'll read his book. I'll read the hell out of it. And not just read it but absorb it. I do this with any breakout book, no matter the genre. I *have* to know what made it so exceptional.

Sometimes I believe if I look inside a book, if I read and absorb every word and let it attach itself to my soul, I will somehow find the key. *The secret sauce.* The holy grail. I don't have to wonder anymore, do I, because the man who created bestselling words sits in my shed waiting for *my* answer. If I do this right, by the end of this experience we'll both have what we want. I'll be able to dig myself out of my financial hole and move out of my she-shed far sooner than planned.

Emerging from behind the divider, I march back to give him my answer.

Ryan sits, arms crossed, looking up at the ceiling. It shocks me a little, to be honest, that he's worried I might actually refuse. This, more than anything else, makes me realize he knows exactly how badly he blew it on that video.

I step in his line of vision. "I can see you've learned your lesson. You've got a deal."

When he looks up and smiles, it changes the geography of his face. And his is a *good* face. It's one of those faces people remember. When he smiles, all those looks flash like the sun and it's a little blinding.

Ryan sits up straighter. "Thank you. I'll make sure you're generously compensated for this."

"Yes, you will."

"There might be a few other minor things the publisher suggests. I want to be fair and come up with a good offer."

"You're an author, Ryan, and since you're not James Patterson, you can't exactly be a billionaire." I fiddle with one of the holes in my jeans. "Maybe part of your advance?"

"Well, that's…mostly gone."

Six figures all gone? His agent gets some, and I know it's not cheap to live in California, but it seems like a lot of money to go through.

"But since the book has been chosen for the morning spot…" Ryan says.

"You'll make more money for the publisher."

"I'll give you half of all of my next quarter royalties from the book, whatever they are."

"That sounds a bit too lavish."

"Not at all. It's my reputation you're saving."

As if I would forget. I consider how much money a

publisher can make off a deal like this, but I also realize it isn't the publisher who cares whether or not Ryan reveals he's Elizabeth. Even negative publicity sells books though it isn't the best path to a long-lasting career. I assume this is solely about Ryan's publisher not wanting to be at the apex of what might become a huge conflict among readers and other romance authors if the discovery is made that the man who disparaged the whole genre in that video is the author of their new bestselling romance. It is vitally important that no link between Ryan and Elizabeth ever be made.

Might as well go for broke. "Do you think you can introduce me to your publisher, or agent?"

"I can't promise you anything in the outcome, but I'll introduce you to some people in publishing. The rest will be up to you."

"I can't ask for more than that."

"I'll tell my agent, Kate. We'll work up an agreement. You've made my day. No, my *year*." Ryan offers his hand.

I shake his warm, strong hand, surprised by the strength, and together we solidify this deal. On a handshake.

"I think it will be fun."

"*Fun*." He says the word as though it's foreign. "I guess it could be."

"Of course! Haven't you ever pretended to be someone you're not?"

He rubs his temples. "*Yes*. That's the point."

I'm about to ask him why he picked a woman's name for a pen name when someone knocks and I see Eddie is at my door. I've never called him Tio Eddie or Uncle Eddie. He's just plain Eddie, my father's oldest brother and the one he was closest to. After my father died, he easily took over the role of pseudo-papi. Single, he's never had any children of his own and his nieces and nephews are like his own kids. He'll walk through fire for any one of us.

And there are a lot of us.

"Mija!" He opens his arms wide, his expression tender. "Guess what? It's Satur-yay!"

I go into his arms and accept the loud smoochy kisses he lays on first one cheek, then the other.

"Ah ha," he says, noticing I have company. "And who are you?"

"Ryan Brady, sir." Ryan offers his hand. "Pleased to meet you."

Eddie does what he always does, whether he's known you for a lifetime or two minutes. He grabs a hold of Ryan's shoulders and plants a kiss on each of Ryan's cheeks. It's a European thing, but also big in Puerto Rico, and Eddie lived there pretty much the entire time my parents were married.

Still, take it from me, American men are not used to the kissing thing. Chris couldn't stop talking about it for days.

"Your uncle kissed me! What's up with that? My father has never even kissed me. It's just...weird."

One more thing I won't miss about Chris. I smile, hoping by now he's been kissed by many men in South America. They are going to be grateful for all those orphanages he and the Peace Corps are building.

"He's my *employer*," I say to Eddie, giving Ryan an apologetic smile.

"It's good that you're both here." Eddie turns to me. "We're having a party tonight."

I moan. "No, Eddie. No."

"Just a little one. I invited everyone!"

"Why won't you believe me? I'm fine!"

"Ay dios mio, no. Does she *look* fine?" Eddie, hands on both of my shoulders, twirls me to face Ryan.

It's been six months, but my family behaves as if I'm still heartbroken over Chris and they must be the ones to save me.

"You're right." Ryan appraises me, eyes lingering on the holes in my pants. "She does not look fine."

"What do you expect when her fiancé abandoned her? The wedding is off! He *never* deserved her. *Nunca.*" Eddie's hand makes a dramatic slash through the air.

Once upon a time, he would have made a fine telenovela male lead, but instead dentistry called. Also, his father would not have allowed him to become an actor. Not a stable or honorable profession, and practicality ran deep on my grandfather's side.

"I'm sorry. I didn't know," Ryan says to me. "No wonder you look like France."

"Don't worry. We know how to make the happy over here." Eddie smiles. "Tia Carmelita is coming over with the food, and Diego is bringing the karaoke machine."

"No! Not the *karaoke machine*!" I clasp my hands together, prayer-like.

My family loves nothing more than embarrassing themselves with their knowledge and affection for Cher and Bon Jovi. Most of them have never heard of any artists more current than the eighties, when according to Eddie, music experienced its most glorious era. And if he and some of his friends get going, they'll sing in three-part harmony.

Really *bad* three-part harmony.

"Well, it was good to meet you. I should get going," Ryan says. "See you Monday, Luci. We have some planning to do."

Eddie moves his body to block Ryan's exit. "I would love to have you as our honored guest tonight."

"That's a great idea," I say. "Ryan is an author researching his novel set in Richmond. He writes historical fiction."

"I've been to Richmond! We have *much* to talk about." Eddie claps Ryan's back. "You must tell me *everything.*"

CHAPTER 6

The party is in full swing by six o'clock, with Tia
Carmelita and her sisters supplying trays of arroz
con pollo, fried plantains, and arroz con habichuelas. I
change into a buttery yellow dress I find in one of my packed
moving boxes and introduce Ryan to everyone. My abuelita
meets him and gives him the Santana nod of approval. At
times like these the absence of my own father is felt like a
gaping open wound. He died when I was ten and Mami
dropped me off with Abuelita a few months later, claiming
she couldn't handle me on her own. She said I needed more
stability than she could provide. She settled in Los Angeles to
pursue acting and came around to visit a few times a year,
only to leave again.

But I never left Seven Trees, the town of my father's
family.

I keep track of Ryan, making sure his hands are always
filled with either a drink or a plate of food as Abuelita taught
me. The women swarm him, as is typical for single men at
these family functions. Eddie is usually one of the few single

men at family weddings, dancing with every woman who comes without a date.

Sofia shows up late and grabs me in a hug. She's brought someone, good-looking in a GQ sort of way.

"This is Kyle," she says.

Instead of a hug, he fist-bumps me. "Dude, nice to meet you."

He lopes off to get them some drinks, and then Sofia turns her full attention to me. "Is that the professor?"

It's not tough to find the only other young white male in the crowd who is not related to any of us. I glance back to see Ryan shaking his head at another plate of food from Abuelita, finally relenting when she pushes it straight into his stomach.

Sofia whistles softly. "Not bad. You didn't mention he's totally hot."

"Didn't I? Is he? I don't know." I shrug.

"He's cute and you *know* it. He looks like Henry Cavill and Indiana Jones had a baby."

"Well, that's not possible but I see what you're saying."

We both turn in unison to watch him a few feet away from Abuelita, who is still talking to him. He nods and half-heartedly takes a bite of a fried plantain.

Eddie moves to the karaoke machine and sings his rendition of "All By Myself," the Eric Carmen version. You might think this especially cruel, given my relationship status, but you would be wrong. One of the best ways I get over myself is to laugh until I cry. Eddie performs the hammy, campy version of the song, stretching out the long notes and waving his hands around with his exaggerated dramatics. He's always known how to make me laugh.

Though I can't say the same for everyone else. They don't laugh so much as cringe.

"Is he all right?" Ryan joins me when Eddie throws his head back and croons, "anymore!"

"Eddie?" I smother another laugh. "Oh yeah. He's fine."

"Did he also just go through a bad breakup?"

"No, Eddie's always been notoriously single."

There was a time, family lore says, he had a college sweetheart but that ended badly. No one talks about it. He's never been serious about anyone else.

Ryan turns to me, and his dark eyes shimmer in the moonlight. "Hey. I'm really sorry about the breakup. You should have said something before you let me go on and on about my problem."

"Your problem is bigger. I should have known when my ex left for the Peace Corps that we were breaking up. He didn't have the cojones to tell me to my face that he wanted out. And he's always wanted everyone to like him."

"Well, *you* don't have to."

Eddie finishes to a round of applause, most of it because he's finally done. He nearly gets hauled off the mike by my cousin Diego, who takes over the sound system as strains of Shakira pipe through the speakers. This is more like it. My cousin Isla and Sofia grab me with an "excuse us!" and drag me with them to the center of the covered patio.

They've always promised, when we do these embarrassing shows for the family, that I can be on the side and barely noticeable. In a million years I'd never do this in public except for my family, who is quite forgiving (see Eddie, above). I learned a long time ago how to shake my hips to the music, and we have our routine. We grew up together and spent many an evening learning the moves. Of course, we liked Brittany and Christina too, but Shakira's music sounded like the salsa we'd grown up around. She felt like home in many ways and, for me, it helped that she was blonde. Another blonde Latina. I could kid myself that I fit right in and didn't necessarily look like *my mother*. Only later I learned Shakira dyed her hair.

Either way, I always get lost in a Shakira tune, imitating Sofia as she tosses her hair, licks her lips. As the song ends, our families applaud dutifully. We're not great, but they love us anyway.

Ryan comes up to us. "That was amazing."

"Thank you!" Isla says, blowing on her manicured fingernails and licking her lips. "We've been practicing for years. We call ourselves The Three Primas. Get it? Like prima donna, but we're actually cousins. Prima means cousin in Spanish."

"C'mon! Tia needs you." Sofia hooks an arm through Isla and hauls her away.

"Your family," Ryan says. "They're so—"

"I know. They're loud and annoying, but you have to admit, the food is great and there's never a dull moment around here. This isn't the first time Eddie's pulled off a party with only a few hours. He's dangerous since he bought that karaoke machine."

"I was going to say…they're great. You're lucky." A speck of pain crosses Ryan's gaze.

"Honestly, I know they're a little much sometimes but they mean well."

Looking for privacy, I walk toward the shrubs and overgrown trees that shade the brick paved walkway, beckoning him to follow.

"Tell me about *your* family."

If there's one thing my abuelita taught me, besides making sure to wash and soak beans before they're cooked, it's to honor all family. She's never said a bad word about my mother, even if she has plenty of ammunition.

"What do you want to know?" Ryan asks.

"Are you still separated?"

"Divorced."

"I'm sorry."

"Look, I don't want to talk about this." He stuffs his hands in the pockets of his jeans and studies the ground.

"Just one question and I won't say anything more on the subject."

"Somehow I doubt that."

"What did *she* think of you writing a romance? Is she a fan of the genre?"

Not all women are, I'm keenly aware. In fact, Holly and I once joined an online writing chapter and left when the leaders derided the entire romance genre as being "predictable and plebian."

The question I've asked, which isn't all *that* personal, seems to make Ryan particularly uncomfortable.

"No, not a fan, but she knows I wrote this one. What did *your* ex think about you writing romance?"

I sigh. "He was…not supportive. After a while, he got impatient with me for always complaining I could never get my own work published. The thing is, I had to keep my ghostwriting work confidential so I couldn't even celebrate any of my successes."

"That has to be tough, not being able to celebrate your success."

"Something tells me you understand something about that."

"Right."

"I do have a book I've been revising forever. Sometimes I think I've written the heart right out of the book."

"It's time to stop, then."

"Easier said than done."

"I'd like to read your novel," he says.

"You *would*?"

"When you're ready. It's the least I can do. Even if I'm not the intended audience, I could give advice on voice and point of view."

Yes, especially now. What he wrote is successful. Suddenly, the thought of Ryan reading my work… I feel a little squeamish. I've had a few alpha readers, mostly Sofia and Isla, who love it, but they're my cousins. I've entered it into a few contests, which only require the first three chapters, and it always does well. But once it gets to an agent, the rejections inevitably follow.

Maybe I am too derivative and that's the problem. Ryan reading one of my love scenes would feel like grocery shopping naked because maybe he'll think that, too. Maybe he'll think it but he'll be too nice to say anything.

"I…may take you up on that."

A slice of moonlight beams through the branches of our family oak tree. One nice thing about the shed is I occasionally get to feel like I live in a shady forest thick with shrubs and trees.

I wander toward the swing set my abuelo set up long ago for all the grandchildren. We're all grown now and ready for the next generation. It will be my cousin Diego first, I assume, because he's been dating his high school sweetheart for years. Hopefully the swing will hold up.

Either way, life goes on because a memory never dies. You can count on it. And if you're lucky, you have plenty of good ones. I think of my papi and how he pushed me on this very swing, laughing and telling me to let my toes touch the clouds. I think of my mother, and wish the memories were better. But I have to reach far back for those, to the times before my father died.

I kick off my sandals, take a seat in the empty swing, and push off.

Ryan sits on the swing next to mine. "Your breakup is recent. I should ask how *you* feel."

I pump a little harder, and the soles of my feet graze the top of the garden fence. "He…he made it sound like he wanted to join the Peace Corps to give back, but only later did I find out he followed a woman there."

His coffeehouse crush, Nadia. We used to bump into each other from time to time but he never gave me the slightest hint he was interested in her.

A few seconds later, I stand and my toes graze across the short damp grass. "I have to confess something. I'm sorry but I haven't read your book. I meant to, but I've got a TBR stack two feet high."

Ryan shakes his head, smiling. "I'm happy to meet someone who hasn't."

"I'll download it to my e-reader tonight."

"Not necessary. I should be able to get ahold of the digital file for you. Just give me a day."

"Because I can't go on the morning show without at least reading half the book if not the whole thing. I'd feel like a complete fraud. Ever hear of impostor syndrome? I'm about to live it."

He shakes his head. "You're a writer even if you didn't write *this* book."

I know he's right and I'm going to go ahead and claim that belief.

CHAPTER 7

On Monday, I'm sitting on the living room sofa in Ryan's rental, quietly finishing the last few pages of *Soulmates* before the online interview with the morning show. He's conferring with the photographer his publicist sent over with several hardcover print books, which he's setting up as a backdrop.

A box of books arrived with the photographer this morning, and I finally got to hold the book in my hot little hands. The special edition cover is gorgeous, spray-painted blue edges, a silver foiled and white aesthetic photo of a flower and a ship hovering in the distance. A book you'd want decorating your bookshelf.

I've been reading the digital book, but I'm a slow reader and haven't been able to dedicate twelve hours a day to read. However, I did stay up late last night because Ryan had me more than a little intrigued. I did not see how this could end well for the main characters. I almost committed the cardinal sin of skipping ahead to reassure myself. The book is mostly a love triangle, not my favorite trope. And while I'm rooting for whom I believe the story has clearly told me *is* the best man, I don't see *how* he's going to get the girl.

Since there are only a few pages left, the happily ever after or happy for now will no doubt be rushed. I'm already not crazy about this book, but apparently I'm greatly in the minority according to Goodreads. The book has close to a million four- and five-star reviews with an average of four and a half stars. This will not be the first time I disagree with the majority on a popular commercial book and surely won't be the last. It's a book I'm going to pretend I've written, so I wanted to like it but I'm afraid…I don't.

When I finally finish the book a few minutes later it's official. I drop my e-reader. Literally drop it to the ground. This is worse than I imagined. I think every reader has had those times when they finish a book with a lousy ending and are so upset they wish to throw it against a wall. I've never done this, though I've been tempted. No, it doesn't have the same satisfaction, but I drop my e-reader on the floor. Hard. I literally *hate* this book. What in the hell was Ryan thinking? What was his agent thinking?

The sound is loud enough to make Ryan turn and stare at me. Stare at the floor. Back at me. He must guess my response to his book is *not good.*

I throw my hands up. "Why? Just…*why?*"

"Why *what?*" His brow is doing that furrowed thing it does.

This is outrageous. No, it's disgraceful. Brazen. Inhumane! Reaching for one of the hardcover books, of which we now have way more than we need, I flip through the pages to the end and point.

"Um, *you* don't have an ending."

"Of course I do. The ending is…up for grabs." He shrugs. "That's what made the book unique."

I don't know if he's being serious or messing with me.

"Look, at least no one died," he says.

"But it's not finished!"

He wrenches the book from me, opens to the last page, and taps it hard several times. "Right here. Do you see how the words just stop and there's all this blank space? The. End."

"But…unless I'm missing something, and maybe I could be since I, you know, didn't write it…you don't make it *clear* that Lula chose Grayson over Derek the idiot."

"You feel that way but it doesn't mean every reader does. What I've done is let the *reader* decide." He tips his chin like he's proud of this.

"Let the reader…let the reader decide? C'mon! What are you talking about?"

"The reader will decide who Lula winds up with. It's their choice. It will be clear to some that she obviously picks Grayson. For others, not so certain. One of the men represents security and safety and the other adventure. It's a metaphor."

I can't accept that this book has been categorized as a romance. It's not a romance in the truest sense of the word.

"This is also called in some circles a *cliffhanger*. No wonder readers want a sequel."

It was the one complaint I saw on reviews. The expectation they'd find the next book on preorder.

"Excuse me," the photographer who has finished setting up interrupts. "We're about ready to take a few shots with the books."

"We will table this discussion for later," I say, pointing to Ryan.

But my stomach is churning because I hate this book. The book I will have to sell to the American public in a matter of minutes. I wanted so badly to like Elizabeth's book, just like everyone else did.

I've been prepped for the morning show interview by Pepper Monahan, who is Ryan's publicist. He gets one of those. Since she's in New York, we met on a video call. She's about my age with short dark hair and wears dangling earrings in the shapes of books. I liked her immediately.

"It's really great that you're doing this. We're *so* grateful. You can't imagine what Ryan's work with *Soulmates* has meant to us. I think it's great! Brilliant! And don't worry, we're going to talk you through this. Walk you through, step by step. Okay, do you have any questions for me?"

"Is your name really Pepper?"

She laughed. "Nope. But everyone calls me that because I'm spicy."

Count on me to ask all the redundant questions, but I've had second and third thoughts about all this and all before I discovered I hate the book. I've never pretended to be somebody else except for that time I was twelve, called a boy Sofia liked, at her request, and pretended to *be* her when I asked him out—or she asked him, though not technically. Whatever. He fell for it, and they dated for a while, but I don't think this will be quite as easy.

It's so public. A couple of days ago, it all sounded simpler in theory even if every moment since then I've been terrified. It's ever so much worse now that I hate the book. I read romance to lift me up, to make me happy, to inspire me. Not to make me want to cry and sob and hide under my blanket all day eating ice cream.

I'm terrified I'll ruin this for the publisher by somehow revealing my utter disdain for the popularity of this book. But now, I've signed a non-disclosure agreement and in a few minutes, I'll have an interview with a former reality TV celebrity.

I've agreed never to disclose I'd worked with Literary

Dimensions on the Elizabeth Brogan Project. Sort of like the Manhattan Project, but more literary, less harmful.

When I signed, I did so knowing Ryan had no intention of writing any more Elizabeth Brogan books, which was fine when I believed the book had a tidy ending.

We've all decided Elizabeth is going to be a happy and cheerful author. The publisher wants people to be inspired when they see Elizabeth, to want to *be* her. When Dan, the photographer they've sent, agrees on the dress I picked, I know I've made the right choice. It's a bright and colorful yellow and royal blue polka dot dress which almost matches the cover of the book. I've never worn anything quite this… loud.

Dan has artfully arranged dozens of copies of the special edition on a shelf. My instructions are to sit to the side of all these hardcovers, holding one of them, smiling into the camera. My legs are crossed in some, uncrossed in another. Head tilted to the left in one, to the right in the other. Smile. No smile. Eyebrow quirk. No eyebrow quirk. A few hundred or so poses later, we are done. Dan sets up a separate monitor where I'll sit for the call. The roll-up backdrop behind me is one of French double doors and resembles a home in any corner of the country.

"Don't be nervous," Dan instructs as he fiddles with the monitor setup. "You look *scared*."

How ironic. I look scared because I'm going on national TV pretending to be someone else? Lying to the entire country about writing the book everyone seems to want to read?

"Are you okay?" Ryan asks.

"Pretending I wrote a book without a real ending?"

I try a laugh but it comes out like a scream. "Look, I've pretended to be impressed with my date's car, pretended to be thinner, pretended to be happy, and pretended to enjoy dry chicken. I can do this."

But pretending isn't really the issue. I pretend all the time since I'm a writer and lie for a living. The problem here is that I'm showing my face to the world. I've been told in the past I should never attempt to play poker. Everything I think and feel is apparently reflected way too easily on my face and Sofia tells me I have a smirk that apparently tells the world, "yeah, right." Today it's my job to wrestle that smirk into submission. The world will believe I'm proud of this book.

"No one can question you, remember," Pepper says from the other monitor nearby, a hovering face. "As far as we're concerned, you *are* Elizabeth Brogan."

"I think what she's trying to say is that just because *we* all know this is a deception, don't think for a second anyone will doubt you," Ryan says.

This is supposed to somehow make me feel better.

"Sure, I mean, why would they?" I laugh. "Who would do something like this?"

We all exchange nervous smiles and laughs. *We* would do something like this.

As we wait, Ryan stands a few feet behind me and out of camera range. He's alternately wiping his brow and swiping away the lock of hair that consistently falls over his glasses. It's almost a comfort to know he's worried, too.

"I'm here if you need me," he reminds me.

"Perfect," Pepper says, reminding us she's still the face behind a monitor nearby. "Just be sure not to be seen, and if Luci gets stumped by a question, you scribble down the answer fast and hand it to her. Just make sure you *always* remain off camera."

"She won't get stumped," Ryan says, giving me more credit than I deserve.

But he adds shoving a hand through his rumpled hair to his routine of adjusting his frames. He's worried.

Seconds before we go live on the web cam, I turn to Ryan, a slice of fear quaking through me like a tsunami.

"Ryan, I changed my mind."

"No, you *didn't*. You can't."

"How am I supposed to *do* this?"

He simply stares at me blankly with those magnetic midnight blue eyes. "Fake it."

I reach out and give him a little push. "You're not helping."

And then three, two, one...

"Hello, Elizabeth! Welcome to the show!"

And with those few words I begin my tenure as Elizabeth Brogan.

CHAPTER 8

arla, the reality star, is wearing blood red lipstick and beaming a toothy smile when she appears on the call. She's just as beautiful as you'd think a former model married to a professional athlete would be.

"Now, don't be nervous. I can see you are. This isn't live and we'll edit anything that doesn't work. Just roll and relax those tight shoulders and let's talk about your wonderful book!" She shimmies her shoulders and rubs her hands together, her long straight dark hair fanning over her shoulders.

She makes introductions and we chat a little about the weather in the Bay Area, where we've all decided Elizabeth Brogan resides. Convenient for me.

Then she asks the *question*.

"You had such courage writing the entire novel from the male character's point of view. How did you come up with the idea? Who was your inspiration for Grayson?" Carla asks.

Behind me, Ryan stops pacing, grabs a piece of paper, and scribbles on it.

Don't answer that!

Oh, helpful. Really. And what should I say? Sorry, I have no idea what possessed me? I glance at him out of the corner of my eye, smile, and gently shake my head.

I've got this.

"Grayson is every man."

"Well, except when he isn't. He's not your classic romance hero. Wouldn't you agree?"

Nothing like being corrected about your own book. I squirm, then somehow slide off of the stool before I quickly right myself.

"Oh, crap!"

She laughs. "Don't worry, we'll edit that out."

"Well, um, what I meant by every man is, um, he's the kind of man we all secretly adore. Strong and a little grumpy at times, but also kind and protective of Lula even when it's not needed. She can take care of herself. He means well."

It's like shooting a blurry moving target, but I nail it.

"I laughed out loud at the scene where he intended to help Lula but wound up making a mess of everything. The kitchen scene! You'd think the guy never cooked a day in his life."

"Ah yes, but we love him anyway, don't we?"

I try to swallow but discover I have no saliva left. It's all gone to my palms and become sweat by way of some odd body malfunction.

"Grayson is what my husband is like, which is why I love this book so much," she says. "Mark has ADHD and dyslexia and he can't follow a simple recipe to save his life. That's just not how his brain works. He can still cook delicious meals, however, his own way. I think it's time we have a hero who doesn't fit into any of these alpha male, toxic masculinity roles often assigned to romance heroes. Those heroes who throw around their good looks and sexual prowess like it's a gift to humanity. It's why I selected *Soulmates* and why I want everyone to read about a hero like the one in your book. Good for you for going beyond what we expect to read in a romance."

"Um…yes, well. Thanks. Thanks for noticing."

Thanks for *noticing*? I want to face palm.

We talk a bit about my writing process, which is the easiest thing for me to fake. I use my actual process, changing it up a bit to sound far more effective. Yes, of course, ideally I too would isolate myself for several hours a day away from social media and other distractions. I too would not stop until I reached my daily word count goal. Heh, heh.

"No spoilers here, of course, but I'd say the ending was… well, unexpected. I was surprised, as apparently were so many others. So *courageous*."

Courageous? How about a complete cop-out?

"Yes, well. Thank you. It's…sometimes you have to do, uh, you know, the unexpected."

"It certainly caught my attention! Tell us. Did you write it with anyone in mind? Because I obviously saw a real bent toward Grayson. But was he always the obvious choice?"

"I…I also feel it would be Grayson. But I do look forward to hearing what everyone else thinks."

"What's next for you?" she asks. "More books like this one? Because if so, you've got a fan for life."

"Well…"

I've got nothing. I think about the book sitting on my hard drive and backed up in a cloud waiting to be ready to fly. I think about the hours I spend writing for someone else. But we aren't here to talk about me, Luci Santana. We are talking about *Elizabeth Brogan*, an author who debuted on the *New York Times* bestseller list. My heart stops beating in a regular pattern, and my palms can be called sweaty in the same way Lake Superior is a pond. I'm certain the next words to come from my mouth will sound like a baby's babbling. Baba-dada-doo. What are words?

"I have an idea," Carla says, finishing my sentence. "Why not next write a sequel! There were so many times I just wanted to slap Lula upside the head. Like, what are you thinking, girl?"

"Oh, absolutely! Can I tell you something? So did I! I wanted to just slug her a few times."

And I'm not even lying.

I'm on a roll. The thing to do is agree with everything she says. I'm golden. Then I say something for which I worry Ryan might never forgive me. It's an honest mistake, born of nerves, insecurity, and my borderline neurotic need to please.

"Something special is coming next. And I think you're going to like it."

"Sounds like a sequel." She squeals and claps her hands. "Please give us more Grayson! Let Lula choose him or at least give him someone else. He deserves to be happy."

"I'll see what I can do!" I hook my thumb in the air.

I actually point, wink, and make an awful clicking sound with my tongue, which isn't something I've done before or *will ever do again.* It's as if I've stepped outside my body and become a used car salesman.

"*Come on down! We got what you need.*" Point, wink, point, annoying tongue click.

"I'm thrilled. You'll have to send me an early copy."

"Of course, of course."

Finally, thank you God, it's over. She lets me know that the program will air next week during the last hour of the morning show.

I wait for the recording to end, and slide off the stool, this time with something resembling a hint of grace.

I find Ryan on a stool in the kitchen, head in his hands.

"I can't *believe* you did that."

I throw my palms up. "I'm sorry! I folded. I didn't mean to. It just…it just came out of me."

"You made it sound like there will be *another book*!"

"You saw what happened! She had me on the ropes. All the pressure got to me. I just couldn't take it."

"But I *told* you I was done."

"Look, you wouldn't be the first author to get writer's block and never be able to write another word. Let's say that's what happened and why there won't be another book."

He stood. "Don't wish writer's block on me!"

"Not *you*, Elizabeth Brogan. It's just fiction. Remember fiction?"

"Hello? Ryan?" The disembodied voice of Pepper calls to us from the other room. "Luci?"

I've forgotten all about her. Apparently, so has Ryan.

"Do you think she *heard* you promise another book?" Ryan runs a hand through his hair.

I follow him back into the living room.

"Oh hey, Pepper." He strolls in casually, hands in the pockets of his jeans. "We were just conferring. About how it went."

"That's right," I say, giving the face of Pepper on the monitor a little wave, hoping my cheeks aren't as flushed as they feel. "We were discussing and conferring."

"So…did you hear the entire interview?" Ryan says. "I think it went well."

"I saw it more than *heard* it," Pepper says. "The sound wasn't the best. From what I can tell, it went smoothly. I'm sure I'll hear soon. What did you two think? Exciting, right?"

"Exciting." Ryan gives me the side-eye.

"Very much so," I lie.

Honestly we are both much better on paper. Pepper will eventually hear the entire interview and know then that I've promised Ryan will deliver another book. The publisher will rejoice, I imagine, and so will his agent. I bet if they throw enough money at him, he will do it. Miserably, but he will.

Pepper points from the screen. "Remember I'm only a phone call or an email away. And though it's not official, it looks like *Soulmates* is already gaining ground and may take another run at the list!"

"Great," Ryan says, not convincingly.

Pepper disconnects and for a long moment we simply stare at each other.

Two placements on the list. For a book without a real ending. Sometimes life isn't fair.

"I'm no longer feeling guilty that I practically promised everyone another book."

"You shouldn't have done that. Now we have to deal with those questions all over again."

"Yes, I know! We'll have to figure something out if you continue to refuse to write another book with an *actual* ending."

Ryan shakes his head and I know the discussion is over. For now.

CHAPTER 9

When I get home later that afternoon, there's an email waiting for me from my mother.

To: theghostwriter@hotmail

From: Geneva.Santana

As I said before, I would very much like to come and see you and help choose your dress. I've been to so many award shows and galas and I know which dress will be most flattering for your particular body type. Please don't tell me you've already decided on one. I will pay for the wedding dress; money is no object. I know Christopher's family has money, but don't forget I starred for years in Desperate Hearts. I couldn't have lived in Los Angeles for all these years without money, could I?

Ladies and gentlemen, my mother. The soap opera star. The woman who inserts herself into my life whenever there's drama to be had because she doesn't leave the histrionics for the screen. I've been avoiding her and haven't told her about my broken engagement, not that we have the kind of relationship where I'll cry my heart out on her shoulder. She went off to pursue her dream of being an actress in Hollywood, wound up in Puerto Rico for a time on a telenovela,

69

then graduated to soap operas in Los Angeles by way of New York. However, she was killed off *Desperate Hearts* a few years ago and there hasn't been much success since then.

But even if I'm only a short plane ride away, I haven't seen her in five years.

Unlike me, my mother remains the definition of cool. I'd hoped to have her level of sophistication, but I've never fully understood fashion. My idea of style is to wear the latest trends and hope they flatter my particular body shape. This happens about two out of ten times so the odds are never in my favor.

The *Geneva* Santana shape was always in style. Mami was long legged and slender, with the kind of shapely breasts that accentuate but don't take over the landscape. Later I would learn how much surgery she had in order to look the way she does, even before turning forty. Eddie said she was beautiful, like me, before all the "plastic stuff" ruined her, perhaps ever so conscious of how much I resemble my mother.

The last time I visited her I'd boarded the plane to Los Angeles as a thirteen-year-old unaccompanied minor. I hadn't seen my mother for a year, and I had so much to tell her. My body had changed, was still changing, and I'd been indoctrinated into the society of monthly menses. Fun times. My moods shifted from Texas hot to Alaska cold and Eddie, with whom I'd always had a close relationship, avoided me, as if I was a creature from another planet. My abuelita and tias did their best, taking me to the pharmacy and instructing me as to the particulars. As luck would have it, I was the first of the female cousins to "become a woman" so I became the practice they would need for their own daughters.

As I boarded the plane that summer, and said goodbye to my cousins, I knew that I'd come back a much hipper version of myself. Mami would be so happy to see me she wouldn't notice all the extra weight that had bunched on since last year. For reasons not quite clear to me, most of my clothes didn't fit, and I kept going up in sizes until my tias shopped for me in the women's section. I thought that since I was a woman, like Mami, we would talk like besties, stay up all night, and she'd give me tips on hair and makeup. We'd go shopping for the best designer clothes and have lunch in Beverly Hills.

But instead, my mother picked me up at the airport with her new *husband*. Sebastian "Seb" Caballero, a telenovela producer. He was the first man I'd ever seen her with besides my father. Not that I would have ever loved him anyway, but I found him oily, loud, and hairy. Privately I'd always expected Mami would never remarry because she'd loved my father too much to compare to any other man. Seb was the evidence my mother had moved on, and I hated him for that in the way only teens can. That first encounter with Seb was the first time a man spoke Spanish in front of me expecting I didn't understand a word of it simply because my hair was blonde.

"Ella esta muy gordita," he'd said with a chuckle as he drove us out of the airport lot.

"My daughter speaks fluent Spanish, *Seb*," Mami said.

Her new husband had just called me "very chubby." It wasn't the first time I'd heard myself called chunky, but not by any member of my family. Seb wasn't my *family*, not technically, and by the sound in my mother's artic-freeze tone, I knew she would defend me. Any minute now she'd chime in and explain I was her daughter, therefore, this had to be simply a stage I was going through. She would take me to find clothes that would flatter my figure and then hairy Seb would see I was gorgeous, no matter the size.

Instead, Mami muttered, "I can only imagine what they're feeding her. It's not her fault. Believe me, if I ate the way her father's family does I'd be big too."

And the way she looked at me…it wasn't disappointment in her eyes. I knew disappointment. This was shame. Her mini-me was not living up to potential.

There almost wasn't enough room in my still-growing body for the agony that pierced and pulsed through me. My own mother, embarrassed of me. She didn't disagree with Seb when she had a chance, only offered her feeble explanation of why I might not be thin, like *her*. The subject of the shape of my body, or anyone else's for that matter, was not a common one in a Latina household. In our culture, we ate good food, danced, and enjoyed life. Some people were bigger than others and this did not concern us.

That evening, we had salad for dinner. A green salad with *five* croutons. This was the summer for me to discover carbs were the devil. My mother nearly starved me, even taking me to her doctor for the "stars."

"She's a beautiful girl as you can see, is there anything we can do?" my mother asked, wringing her hands, sounding like I might be dying, and he should for the love of God, *save* me.

I thought the doctor would disagree with my mother and tell her I was fine and still growing. But they put me on a diet. There's nothing quite like having your caloric intake restricted to make you crave everything in sight. I ate even when I *wasn't* hungry, which wasn't often.

When she took me to a soap opera taping, I hung by the food table and grazed all afternoon when she wasn't looking. Sandwiches with ham and cheese and mayo on crusty bread, cookies, cake, and soda. All food never allowed in Mami's presence. Never allowed in her home.

I ate so much I wasn't hungry that evening for my green salad.

"See? Your stomach is already shrinking!" Mami said.

No matter how she hurt me, I still loved her. For a young

girl, that love became toxic when it was mixed with a heavy shot of contempt.

"You realize I'm doing this for your own good, don't you?" Mami said, "You'll thank me some day. Wait and see."

Here's the funny thing.

I'm still waiting to thank her for that. It's not going to happen.

My life feels like fodder for a women's fiction novel some days, but maybe that's why I write romance to take me away from real life. Most people are familiar with the peculiar burdens of family, the way obligations pull and push until they break you in half. Family love and devotion can splinter and crack. Some say real love is unconditional, but that's also why it hurts. Because love is not *always* healthy. Even when it should be.

It's time I tell Mami the truth. I no longer need a wedding dress, or her help shopping.

I'd hoped planning the wedding would be a way we'd connect. We could repair our relationship. But she was often too busy to talk about invitations and favors. The dress, however, was of interest.

There's still so much I want to say to her, but the timing has to be right. I thought the time would be on my wedding day when I'd be glowing and bathed with the happiness of marrying a man who loved and accepted me for who I am.

I have a speech, which I've written and revised about a dozen times over the last few months:

This is something I should have said long ago, but it took being a little bit older and wiser to find the right words. You are my mother and above anyone else, you should accept me as I am. Instead, you let a thirteen-year-old girl feel inferior because I didn't match the version of me you had in your head. Guess what? There are many versions of me. I've been a size twelve and I've been a size six, but I've never changed the person I am inside. I still love books and reading and castles and unicorns. There is nothing wrong with my body, or anything that needs fixing. But for a while, you made me think there was. It took years to fix what you broke in one summer, but now I'm happy and whole. No thanks to you.

Oh, by the way, thank you for coming.

I planned to say this to her at my wedding, but I'm honestly not sure that speech will ever be given. I'm beginning to think the entire speech was just like everything else I write—fiction. My issue might not be my weight anymore, but I'm still falling second to others.

I need to let her know the wedding is off, but I don't need to see her in person. A simple email will do. I've been putting it off because of the phone call it might provoke. She might think I need her comfort, or some little life lesson about love. I don't want to hear any of it.

At one time, I needed her. Not anymore. I have Eddie, Abuelita, Sofia. My family.

Later that night, I compose an email to my mother:

Dear Mami,

I thought you should know there isn't going to be a wedding. Chris and I broke up. You're probably curious and want to know why. Maybe you won't be surprised he found someone else. Yes, she's thinner than me. Big deal. The point is, it's over. Dress shopping is unnecessary. By the way, I wear a size eight in case you were wondering. A very small size eight.

Best regards,

Luci

In a way, what I'll miss the most about the wedding is the fact that I won't give her my little speech.

CHAPTER 10

Two days later, I haven't heard from my mother and I consider this a good sign. She's aware she won't be able to consult my fashion choices and she's moved on. Now, it's time to tell my family that soon I'll be broadcast on national television pretending to be someone else. I'm going to explain that I've written a book and used a pen name.

I don't expect it to go over well.

Generally, my family isn't cool about things they don't understand and I could fill a book with all they don't know about publishing. The first person I tell is Sofia. I have no time to build this up, to make it believable. She knows I've finished a novel and I've been shopping it. But that novel, which she's read, is nothing like Ryan's book. Add to that the guilt that pierces me at the lie I'll be telling and this isn't easy.

All at once, she learns my book is published and it's going to be on the morning show. Fortunately, Sofia knows even less about publishing than I do. She thought the comedy show about a woman who dropped off her unsolicited manuscript at Simon & Schuster, wound up with a million-dollar deal and a fully funded book tour was something that could really happen until I set her straight.

Sofia gasps at my news. "Is this the one I read, the book about time travel?"

"No, it's something new."

She's only read one of my books because officially that's all I've written. Since she knows I ghostwrite, she's always wanted to know how she can read those books. But she knows better than to ask me for any details. From time to time, I try to trick people into reading my work by suggesting a Desdemona Hill book I've written. Since Sofia was into vampires for a while, she read a few of my books without realizing it. She claimed they were good, but "not as good as your book," which I found hilarious and proof of why we're told not to let our family be our first readers.

"Finally! I knew it would happen someday," she says. "Why didn't you tell me?"

I've had to work to come up with a plausible explanation for why I'd keep something like this from my bestie. My ride or die since I was a kid. The ghostwriting is one thing, but this wouldn't make any sense to her. I do some of my best work and spin a tale of many late nights writing a super-secret project over the last year, and the shock of getting an agent, and a deal.

"I'm sorry I couldn't say anything sooner, but the publisher asked me not to. It's kind of like my ghostwriting stuff in that it had to be confidential until it was time to release," I say, coming the closest I can to the truth.

"But now you wrote it *and* get credit for it!"

I cringe. "Um, yeah. I'm going to tell Abuelita and Eddie tonight. Wish me luck."

They think ghostwriting is wrong and unfair but they don't understand it no matter how many times I try to explain I get paid to do it.

"You wrote a book for someone else?"

"Why can't they write the book?"

In Desdemona's case, she's long been dead, so she can't very well write them anymore. But ghostwriters are never truly appreciated for all they do.

THAT EVENING, the succulent smells of Spanish rice and chicken waft through the air of Abuelita's modest-sized kitchen.

We've been eating for several minutes, when Eddie begins discussing his patients' horrible flossing habits. He tells us we wouldn't *believe* the food he finds in their molars. This is common at our table, where no disgusting subject is off-limits because Eddie has a stomach made out of steel.

Abuelita glares at him. "No talk of teeth at the table!"

I use the opportunity. "I have an announcement to make."

They both turn to me and I clear my throat.

"No!" Abuelita says, setting her spoon down. "You are not!"

Eddie reaches for his mother's hand, stilling it. "Tranquila, Mami."

"She cannot take Chris back!" Abuelita pounds her fist on the table. "I will not have it. Not in my house."

I shake my head. "Nope, not taking Chris back. He's still somewhere in South America with the Peace Corps, and I don't care."

"Good," Abuelita says, then mutters several curse words in Spanish under her breath.

"Will you let the girl talk?" Eddie says and then waves at me to take the floor.

"Thanks." I fold my hands together. "Well, you know how I ghostwrite books for authors?"

Both of them nod.

And so, I lie about everything. How I've finally written a book that New York wants, and that I'm sorry I had to keep it a secret all this time. Unlike Sofia, they don't wonder why I haven't told them sooner. Writing is my thing and something we rarely discuss. I tell them I've written this book under a pen name because it's unlike the other books I write, and for privacy reasons.

"Many authors do this, you know."

"I don't like it," Abuelita grumbles. "You should be Lucia Milagros Santana and proud of it."

I sit up straighter. "Don't worry, I promise my next book will be published as Lucia Santana."

I know how important it is for my grandmother to have her son's name live on in me.

"The good news is the book is successful and I'll make enough royalties to be able to move out of the shed soon."

Abuelita scowls. "Don't rush. Save your money and take all the time you need."

"And also, I'm going to be on a morning show next week, which is exciting. It's national."

They glance at each other with a quick nod, and I see the pride flash in their eyes.

I only wish we were actually talking about a book I wrote.

THE FOLLOWING TUESDAY, I wake and open the app to the streaming network for the morning show, which I've been watching religiously since we taped the episode.

Glancing at the screen now, I see the anchor reporting distressing news about the world and weather, so I mute him while I go to the main house and brew myself a single cup of coffee. Next door, I hop in the shower, and dress for my low-key day. Ryan has given me the morning off and my plans are to get words down on my Desdemona book. For the past two weeks I've spent so much time with Ryan between research, and becoming Elizabeth, that I haven't spent enough time on the manuscript due next month. I'm so close and all of the threads are coming together for one epic showdown between two vampire enemies.

Back in my shed, I try to get into the zone, but first I check my email.

One is from the new editor assigned to me at Blushing Publications, which manages all the Desdemona books. This is the first book we've worked on together and from the beginning she's treated me a bit like a drone, or a bot, even suggesting the way I should rewrite a sentence.

To: theghostwriter@hotmail

From: Dee@BlushingPublications

I was shocked to learn you've published a book under the Eliza-beth Brogan pen name. Your contract states you are to let us know ahead of time of any new project with which you're involved. You have violated our terms and therefore we're going to have to let you go. Send over everything you have, and we'll take it from here.

Wait. What? No, they've misunderstood. They think I actually wrote the book.

I've already written three-fourths of the current Desdemona book. Besides, her information is incorrect. I'm not *writing* as Elizabeth Brogan. I'm a ghostwriter, but in reverse. Ryan is the ghostwriter. I hit reply and began to compose my email when my cell buzzes, my landline rings, and someone knocks on the shed's door.

All at the same time. I'm not accustomed to this chaos before noon.

A text from Ryan simply reads:

Call me.

Always a man of few words. Ironic since his historical fiction books are huge doorstoppers. I set my cell down, let the landline go to voicemail, and go to the front door because it might be a package. The UPS guy is always confused when Abuelita asks him to deliver it to a shed.

Not a delivery guy. It's Sofia.

"Congratulations!"

"Thanks?" I say as she slides past me. "What for?"

"It's official. The book selection! Did you miss it?"

I *have* missed it. I pick up my phone, then hit rewind until I see the cover of the book appear. Sofia looks over my shoulder.

And there I am in a photo holding the book, smiling into the camera. The host describes me as a debut author whose book holds a unique premise. The emotional, heartfelt, and funny book written entirely in the male's perspective has been praised by early reviewers. Kirkus Reviews calls it "lyrical" and "soulful." Publishers Weekly has given it a starred review.

They splice the press junket skillfully and use snippets of the interview in which I've talked about the hero. In the end, they use just three minutes of the thirty-minute interview and cut out the part where I nearly fell off the stool.

"I can't believe you're not more excited than this," Sofia says, plopping down on the love seat. "You're on TV! And you looked *great.*"

"Thanks. You think I looked okay? Did the camera add ten pounds?"

The smile slides off Sofia's face. "We're not going there, chica."

Then I remember the email and face palm. "It's not all a bed of roses for me. I just got fired."

"What? They can't do that! It's too late." She points to the monitor to make her point.

"I mean from my ghostwriting gig. They said some foolishness about violating my contract because I published under a pen name."

"Well, that's a bunch of bull. You should be able to do both."

"I was just getting ready to compose my reply when you came over."

"Tell them they can't do that. Plus, they owe you money, don't they?"

"Yes! For everything I've already written. I was supposed to get my last installment on this book when I turn it in."

I don't want to tell Sofia that this won't be the first time a ghostwriter has been stiffed, because companies often go out of business. But Desdemona Inc. has a rock-solid reputation. They won't do this to me after all the years I've spent with them helping build their brand.

"Oh, Ryan! I nearly forgot. He texted me earlier." I pick up my phone and call him.

He sounds cloudy and gruff. "You're finally calling me back. I'm sorry."

"What? Why? They did a great job, even cut out that part where I slid off the stool. Didn't you see it?"

"See what?"

Oh, for crying out loud. Leave it to Ryan.

"The *morning* show. Carla announced the book this morning and they played some of my interview."

Silence on the other end and I begin to think Ryan is sorry for something else entirely.

"So, you haven't heard?"

My stomach does a little roll and pitch. Surely there's no more bad news. I hold up a finger to Sofia to indicate I'll be right back, and step outside my shed.

"Heard what?"

He manages a cross between a moan and a groan and a sigh. What a talented man.

"Yeah, so listen. Here's the thing. Because of the secrecy

behind our agreement, we had to tell your other editor at Blushing…”

“Spit it out!”

“My publisher had to tell her *you* wrote the book when she asked. Because they couldn’t very well tell them the truth. Telling them you didn’t actually write the book would lead to questions and rumors. That would defeat the purpose of all this.”

I close my eyes. I suppose that makes all the sense, so therefore, I *have* violated my contract. If I’d only had the time to tell them beforehand, it *might* have been okay.

“I guess that explains why I just got fired this morning via email.”

A beat of silence, then, “Will saying sorry again have any effect?”

“I know you’re *sorry*, it just doesn’t change anything.”

There goes my safety net. Desdemona books are always a surefire way to earn money writing. I will never get rich off them but she’s the reason I’ve been able to call myself a working writer for years. Some would say I should burn that bridge, so I’ll never be tempted to cross back into the security and safety again. But I’m different from my mother in that way, too. I don’t take big risks. Until now. And it’s made my skin prickle and sting with worry, which I should have seen as a sign.

After the Elizabeth Brogan project, I will have nothing. I’ll join the ranks of the unemployed. Sure, there are plenty of possibilities but no guarantees. I can’t assume they will like and buy my time travel book. A stepping stone would be nice, but I have no desire to jump off a cliff.

“Those books were my livelihood. They kept me writing.”

“Listen, you don’t need them. Once enough people read *your* book, and know that it’s you behind the keyboard, that will all change. Your life is about to change, and way beyond me and Elizabeth."

"I don't see how you can say that when you haven't even read any of my own work."

"Whose fault is that?"

The words stop me short. How could I have the man who's written the book that everyone loved so much judge *my* work? Uh-uh, my brain says.

Holy shit, my heart says.

I can hear Sofia telling me to "snap out of it" and *answer the question.*

"Um, you're serious?"

Look, every author understands what a big deal it is to ask a colleague to read for you. No one has the time to read anymore, ironically. I understood from the experience of my colleagues that most established authors only read the first three chapters of a book when asked for endorsements. But those were usually given through referrals by a shared agent, editor, or publisher who were lending their credibility. There were only a handful of enormously kind and generous authors who would offer to read for a virtual stranger who simply asked. But clearly, Ryan owes me. Big time.

"It would be an honor."

An honor. It's hardly an honor. Now I feel like I'm being set up to fail.

"You shouldn't expect too much. I haven't been writing as long as you have."

"I'm familiar with what you're doing. Don't do that."

"Don't do what?"

"Belittle your work. I *know* how hard it is to write romance. That's why I don't think I can do it again. I prefer writing about war, which should tell you something."

"You don't seem to realize that makes it even worse. Only

one book and look at the success you've had right out the gate."

Ryan clears his throat. "My publisher put a lot of publicity into the book. They probably wanted to earn back the generous advance my agent negotiated. The idea of writing from a male point of view was unique enough there weren't any other books quite like it. Sometimes you run into some luck. That's all this was."

I appreciate his modesty but it's not helping.

"You should at least give me a chance to find out what Luci Santana writes," he says. "You've watched me bleed all over the pages."

I hang up and step back into my shed where Sofia is waiting for me.

"Everything okay?"

"No," I say. "But it will be."

"Is the professor helping you with all this?" she asks.

It's a reasonable thing to assume, and I can answer this honestly.

"Yes, he's been a huge help."

CHAPTER 11

Dumped by my fiancé.

Living in my abuelita's shed.

No more ghostwriting gig.

When I wake up hours later after a nap, the shadows of the dipping sunlight are dappling through my only window, but nothing else has changed. I'm still pretending to be Elizabeth Brogan, and I'm no longer writing for Desdemona.

There's something I'm in the habit of doing every time I'm too upset to read or write.

I drive to a bookstore and browse. And then I browse some more. For hours. Doesn't everybody? Maybe I'll pick up a book or two, maybe five, because I have the store discount. But I always make myself stop at ten.

Grabbing my keys, I drive to the local bookshop an hour before they close. Yes, I'm grumbling while I do. Something along the lines of how no good deed goes unpunished or other cliches, which exist for a damn good reason. They're true. I no longer have a secure and stable writing job due to a *favor* I've done for my employer. Fine. That's okay. I live in a shed in my abuelita's back yard, so expenses are low. The

85

salary Ryan will give me for becoming Elizabeth might actually be enough to carry me for a year if I'm careful.

And after this summer pretending to be a published author, I might find other ghostwriting work. I can copyedit, find another research assistant job, teach, or go back to work as a barista. There are options. None of these are ideal, but even if I've relied on the Desdemona books to make me feel like a "real" author, this doesn't mean my world has ended. I still have *my* book. The book I've been revising for what feels like forever, and maybe it's time to finally start another round of querying agents. All I need is a little inspiration.

Inside the bookstore, I take a deep breath of the inky, slightly dusty smells of my youth. I haunted this shop as a child, hiding in the cozy corners filled with chairs and strategically placed soft pillows. A few years ago, the shop changed ownership and the pandemic nearly put them out of business. But the new owner bounced back, pulling in on each one of her many resources. She hired young people and asked them to curate sections and advertise the books they love.

I find my way to the rows of romance books, sliding my finger gently down the spines, taking one out and reading the back cover copy, then reverently putting it back. In honor of Ryan, I move from my usual contemporary fare to historical women's fiction. Picking up a Kristin Hannah book, I reread the back cover of *Nightingale*, a book I devoured years ago, and I decide this edition needs to go into my keeper collection. There are some periods of history too important not to be tragically memorialized. The book made me cry but it also stayed with me for weeks, and even to this day.

It doesn't go back on the shelf.

Maybe I can convince Ryan to try his hand at a historical romance, merging together the best of his two worlds. I don't understand his resistance to writing another romance, considering how well received his debut has been. Unless of course he fears, as so many authors do, that he'll never be able to replicate the first success. Even in my position, I understand this. I have a healthy fear of both failure *and* success.

I've been so intently reading the back copy of another French resistance romance book with an amazing cover, that it takes me a minute to catch the image of a figure in the periphery of my vision. But there's no mistaking the man sitting in one of the chairs the owner has deposited in various corners, his attention riveted to the book in his hands. His legs are crossed, a man deep in another world. I recognize the look. Once more I find his powers of concentration enviable.

For a moment, I enjoy watching this man who is at once so puzzling and yet also somehow so familiar. As if he senses being watched, Ryan glances up from the book. His brow furrows in confusion and it's almost as if his mind is swiftly making connections.

"Oh hey, I know this person. Maybe I need to stop reading and be a human. Converse. Relate."

I can practically hear his synapses firing and I can't stop smiling.

Still gripping the book, he uses a finger to hold his place. "Hey."

"Hey yourself. You come here often?"

His lips quirk. "Almost never. Actually, this is my first time."

"Well, let me be the first to say 'welcome in.' I see you found a book there." I nudge my chin in his direction. "More historical fiction?"

"Guilty." He shuts the book. "I should probably be trying

to expand my horizons, but when I'm feeling out of sorts, I go to the familiar."

"Same." I hug the book to my chest. "You can probably guess why I'm here, too, seeking comfort."

He nods. "And I'm sorry again."

"It was just a ghostwriting gig." I shrug.

I try to minimize it, the way I do with everything. No big deal, move on.

"But you enjoyed it. The work *meant* something to you."

"Maybe. Or maybe my sense of pride was misplaced."

"Not at all. They might not be your characters, or your world, but they were *your words*."

I know he's right and I'll miss giving my own voice to that world. But it has never been mine.

When I don't say anything, Ryan asks, "I looked up Desdemona Hill's catalog. How many have you written?"

"Ten."

"Impressive." He nods. "I know I shouldn't really be asking this question, but my book was a complete fluke. Maybe you can tell me. What is it, exactly, about romance books? *Why* are they so popular?"

Funny to have to answer this question for Ryan, but I'm up for it.

"I think each of us are sixteen years old again when we first fall in love. Yes, as we get older there are further complications of becoming an adult. But hearts are always, always young." I have much more to say on the subject. "And connections. It's the human condition. These books represent the life and relationships we all want but are afraid to demand. Family, love, friendship. It's easier to just say they're about sex and demean the genre as nothing more than mommy porn."

Ryan winced at the term. "I wish critics wouldn't make fun of those love scenes. They're difficult to write. I feel like every writer should have to try at least once. It's an education."

"Preaching to the choir, buddy." I elbow him.

It's meant to be friendly, casual, but when my body buzzes at being so near, I really wish I hadn't touched him at all.

Ryan gives his usual half smile but he doesn't seem to be as thrown by the touch as I am. "So, what are you going to do next, now that you've lost the ghostwriting gig?"

"I'm making a new plan," I say, because this is mostly true. "Still evolving."

He quirks a brow. "Does it involve writing your own books?"

"Without a safety net," I say, borrowing from the phrase of earlier this afternoon and turning it into a metaphor.

His lips quirk into a smile as if I've spoken in his secret code. "That's the very best way to write."

little magic sometimes happens while inside a bookstore.

Ryan and I have been staring at each other for several seconds. I don't know what he's thinking, but I'm once more inappropriately noticing the way his deep-set dark blue eyes tip downward at the corners, giving him the look of both sorrow and annoyance at the world. There's an unnerving desire in me to know him better, to find out how she hurt him, how it ended. Why. He's been hurt and his entire body seems to carry some of the weight of that. It's in his eyes, and in his shoulders.

We've never gone over the line of being professionals, but I wonder if it counts when we're not technically at work now.

I break the stare fest first to look over his shoulder when the store clerk pushes a cart filled with books toward the front of the store.

"Look." I point.

He turns to follow my gaze.

The clerk is stocking *Soulmates*, dozens of the special

edition hardcover copies.

"Should we tell them we know the author?" I elbow him. "*That* might be fun."

"No." He takes my arm and stills my forward movement.

His grip is stronger than I would have guessed, but I still shake him off. "You're right. It's better if we're here incognito. Undercover."

"You know what this means." He gives me one of his serious professorial don't-mess-with-me looks.

"Yes. We can listen to people talk about the book."

"And they won't feel like they have to lie to…us."

There's a lot to unpack in that sentence. It appears I might not be the only one who's not crazy about the book.

We stand for several minutes, watching quietly from a distance. The clerk stacks the books in a gorgeous center display with signage that might as well be fluorescent red blinking arrows ordering, "Read me!" and "Don't get stuck being the only idiot that hasn't read this book."

Clearly, one of the booksellers loved this book, too.

I sidle up to the display, leaving Ryan behind me. "New release?"

"Yes, it's a debut with high praise," the clerk says.

Ryan joins me. "I've heard it's a pedantic approach to story. Not that I've read it."

The clerk, a young woman, gives Ryan the look you'd give someone who's just insulted your best friend. "As *booksellers*, we get early copies and I've read it. I disagree. The writing is lyrical. Poetic."

Ryan clears his throat. "Seems my information is wrong."

I give her a wide smile. "Huh. So, *you* don't think it's a pedantic approach to writing?"

She straightens. "I wouldn't hype anything I felt that way about!"

A middle-aged woman elbows her way into our conversation. "My book club is looking for a new selection. Do you recommend it?"

"Highly," the bookseller said. "The book is written entirely from the hero's point of view. He's neurodivergent and suffering with PTSD. In his case, he's grieving the man he used to be. We read and talk so much about grief as the loss of a loved one, but not as much about the grief we feel for another version of ourselves. This is far more than a love story. It's truly a hero's journey."

I don't like hearing it quantified as "far more than a love story" as if that itself isn't *enough*, but I'm going to be the bigger person and let that go.

I take a copy from the display. "I think I'll give this a read."

"You'll love it. It's funny, too. I love my books to have a good balance of funny and tragic. There's plenty of both." She walks away with a smile and a finger wave.

The middle-aged woman follows her to the register with a book.

"What a nice lady," Ryan says. "Get her name, would you? I'd like to put her in my will."

"High praise for a book that doesn't have an ending." I tuck the book in my arms.

"I'm going to buy it."

"No, you're not. You've already read it and have dozens of copies available. Put it back."

"Nope. I'm *buying* it."

"Buy something else. Someone who needs the sale." He waves his arm to indicate all the books surrounding us.

"You are rather dominating the square footage here. I'm sorry, are we feeling a tad guilty?" I cock my head. "Poor wittle bestselling author."

"We're not *feeling* anything at all. *We're* thinking it's time to leave now." He reaches for my elbow.

"Not until I buy this book."

"I can get you as many copies as you'd like in case two dozen isn't enough," he hisses.

"That's not the same thing and you know it. I'm the face of this book. There's an experience here I'm not going to deny myself."

"Put it back, and that's an order."

"An order?" I snort. "Don't you even dare."

He straightens, taking his height advantage. "I'm still your employer."

"And we're not at work. I don't take orders after hours."

"You don't take them *during* work hours."

Seriously, just because I wouldn't go back to get his coffee order right, or immediately jump when he gives me an assignment. The point is, I always get to it.

Now I pull on the book, and he pulls back.

Like we're children, for several minutes, we grapple over the book. Every time he tugs on it, he brings me a little closer, which is not entirely a bad thing. For one thing, he smells like leather and sunshine.

"This is ridiculous." He smiles through gritted teeth.

I'm about to agree because people are beginning to stare. They have probably never seen two grown adults haggling over a book when there are so many of them. I let him have it, then grab another one. He tries to take that one, too.

I give him a little half-hearted kick in the shins. "Give. Me. This. Book."

He lets go of the book because maybe he's also noticed that we've definitely attracted some undesired attention. Unfortunately, due to my kick, I lose my balance. I try to regain said balance by grabbing on to the tower of books on the display, not a good idea. Books, as much as they add to the richness of our lives, aren't intended to hold the weight of a human being.

The display goes down, scattering copies everywhere.

"Look what you made me do!" I'm laughing but set the book down and start to pick up all the others.

"You're ridiculous. This wouldn't have happened if you hadn't tried to kick me," he says, chuckling and shaking his head.

"This wouldn't have happened if you'd just let me buy the damn book."

The clerk has joined us, but so have a few other customers, and they are not only picking up the book but reading the back cover copy and heading to the register with it.

"I've been hearing a lot about this book," one of them says. "I don't know why you were fighting over it. There's plenty of them."

"I'm going to recommend it to my sister. She hates everything," the first woman says.

They all head to the register with a copy.

"See?" I say in a hushed tone. "This is so classic. All it takes is for a few people to be highly interested, leading to even more people. When you get right down to it, we humans are pack animals and we never want to be left out. You're welcome. I got them to buy your book."

"You must mean *your* book." He gives me a warning look despite my whisper. "They don't already have several copies at home. *You* don't need to buy the book."

"But I want to support you…us."

"You already are."

In the end, we reach a détente. I absolutely *don't* buy the book.

Ryan buys it for me.

A FEW MINUTES LATER, we walk together toward street parking, and I'm holding tightly to my copy of the book. It must be surreal to find one's book in a bookstore, especially given such star treatment. Tonight, maybe I'll practice signing my fake name. I haven't done that yet. The publisher might at some point set up a book signing and I should be ready. Elizabeth Brogan needs a signature and I have to come up with something. It should have a nice flourish. Maybe I'll add a heart to the *i* like I do with Luci when I want to be super whimsical. Should it be legible, or should I do one of those authorly things some do where the name is little more than a scribble no one can identify?

"I've been thinking and I agree with your offer of a field trip to Santa Cruz for the uh…" He clears his throat. "World War II history you suggested. It might be the distraction I need."

I pause by my old reliable clunker car and clutch my chest. "I'm shocked."

"I doubt that. You've made your case and, yeah, maybe a single date between the two protagonists might be helpful. Otherwise, how else are readers going to believe there's a love interest?"

"When should we go?"

"Soon. I need to start writing this book. Sometimes I get too caught up in research. It's time."

"But has it been nine months? The baby comes when it's time, and not a moment before." I open my door, setting the book down. "See you tomorrow, professor. Bright and early. I'll bring the coffee."

Ryan takes a step toward me. "In case I haven't said it enough…"

"I know, thank you. And you're welcome very much."

"We'll figure out what to do about the sequel later."

"You mean the one I may have accidentally suggested?" I wince.

Naturally, the show didn't cut *that* part out of the interview.

He meets my eyes. "I won't lie. Kate saw the interview and she's onboard, already pushing for a second book."

"If I haven't said I'm sorry enough…"

"I know. You meant well but that book took a lot out of me. I can't do it again. I've told Kate but I doubt she'll listen."

This is my chance but I'm still too kind to tell him the entire truth. I hate the book.

"At least it would be a chance, you know, to improve on what you wrote in the first one."

He quirks a brow. "You didn't like it either, did you?"

I can't admit to this. I've always believed in supporting other authors and this even includes Ryan.

"What? Did I say that?" I press a hand against my chest.

He quirks a brow. "One can't improve on something that they like, can they?"

"Well, the ending…"

"Not this again."

"You left him at sort of a crossroads. Was it Grayson? The other guy?"

"We've been over this. I think you know. We all know."

"But it's not *clear*." Even to my own ears, my voice sounds like a whine. "I don't like the vagueness. Besides, the other guy was a chump."

"Did you ever stop to think that we don't always pick the right person? That sometimes we live to regret our choices?"

I resist telling him that we both know this is true. We've both lived this. But fiction is supposed to be the one place where justice reigns and happiness is assured. Forever, amen.

"You can clearly see that the other guy can't possibly love Lula as much as Grayson does!"

"Did you ever stop to think that maybe Lula doesn't think so?"

"What? Of course she does! She's no dummy. You didn't write her that way."

"Then she chooses Grayson. Happy?"

"Not really."

We're arguing over imaginary people, but for me, it's not the first time nor will it be the last.

Ryan shakes his head, holding up hands like, "I can't win with you," and we part ways as he walks to his car.

I'm home before eight, turning the key into the makeshift lock Eddie has devised for my security. Since I'm back here in the yard among overgrown trees and bushes, he sometimes worries it's the perfect place for a thief, or someone worse than a thief, to "lie in wait." Honestly, my family comes by histrionics the natural way.

The sound that comes out from near the bushes, however, does make me jump and I reach for the pepper spray Eddie makes me carry.

"Why do you live in the shed?"

I turn to the sound of the voice in the dark.

Mami.

CHAPTER 13

"**W**hat are *you* doing here?"

My first instinct is to protect the neck. No idea why. Must be my lizard brain.

"You sent me an email, *despondent* over your breakup with Chris."

"I am not despondent! And that was months ago."

"Well, I didn't know but I'm here now. I can't let you go through this alone." She opens her arms wide.

This is where I'm to fall right into those arms like when I was a little girl. I know the drill. I don't so much go into her arms as I take a step, and then another, until inevitably she has her arms around me. She's smaller now, or maybe I'm taller. Grudgingly I accept the maternal hug, expecting it to do nothing, but surprised by how warm and genuine it feels. With Mami, I never understand what's real, and what's an act. That's always been the problem for us.

"You look thin," she says, utter amazement lacing through her tone, and I stiffen.

I'm not *thin*, but simply no longer overweight.

"A small size eight for some time now, actually."

I hear the defensiveness in my voice, and I don't like where my thoughts go. I try to remember my mother grew up in an age of body shaming, first done to her by a model-thin mother. Next, by a career she loved.

"You were a thin child, just like me. And how much do you weigh now?"

"Have you seen Abuelita?" I ask, purposely ignoring her question.

I vow that in my lifetime, I will redefine my relationship with her, and it will not include any talk of my weight or size. Or *her* weight for that matter.

"Yes, and Eddie." She sighs. "He'll never change, will he?"

"Still the same amazing man he's always been," I say, because I know she's never liked my father's older brother and she better not cut him down in front of me.

She'd met both brothers at San Jose State University where they all attended but said Eddie always thought himself "too good for her." Where she got this idea I'll never know because Eddie is one of those people who loves everyone.

Reluctantly, I unlock the door and wave her inside. "This is temporary. I couldn't afford the condo on my own."

"How incredibly cruel of Chris to do this to you."

"Well, he joined the Peace Corps…"

"And abandoned his fiancée."

She's not wrong.

Mami glances around the tiny space, her lips tight, and I can feel the judgment coming off her in waves.

"*Why* are you not in the main house with your family?"

"Abuelita has a small house, stocked to the roof with decades of memories. Plus, I like my privacy. This is pretty much like my bedroom. I eat dinner with them and use the restroom, shower, anything else I need."

When she takes a seat on what I still creatively call the

love seat, I'm happy that at least there's no way she can stay here with me. Yay me. Not even a couch she can crash on. My bed is too small for more than one person. She and Seb will have to go find a hotel room and, unless Mami sleeps on the couch, there's no room for her in the main house either.

"Have you ever thought of doing something different with your hair?"

"With my *hair?*"

She makes movements with her hands. "A layered cut with your type of natural wave would be so flattering."

The unspoken message, I suppose, is that my current cut is *not* flattering. Ask me if I care.

"I like my hair the way it is," I say between clenched teeth. "Where's Seb?"

I hope he's getting them a hotel room, the sooner the better. Mami crosses one lean sculpted leg over the other one. Naturally, she's dressed to kill in black pumps that have partially sunk into the dirt on the way to my she-shed. She should have considered that before she walked across the lawn. Her crème pantsuit is tailored to her slim figure and her naturally wavy hair is straightened so no hint of a wave will show. I, however, am a ball of frizz because while we might have the same hair, I don't spend much time on mine.

For a moment, the silence between us is heavy, the way I worried it would be at my wedding. I planned to see her on the best day of my life, not on one of the worst. But even if she's here for sympathy, I don't want any. I'll be fine. I always have been. Okay, so I might have to give up my firstborn to the real estate gods if I ever want to own a home in Seven Trees but otherwise it's all good.

She reaches for my hand and squeezes it. "I have some news. It's not good and I wanted to tell you in person."

My breath hitches when worst-case scenarios come to mind. While she looks smaller, she's also noticeably thinner.

Even for *her*, which says something. She's paler than normal, so either she's finally stopped bed tanning, or she's seriously ill. For a moment I wonder what I'll do if my mother is dying from some horrible disease.

"W-what is it?" I brace myself to hear the dreaded C word.

"Seb and I divorced weeks ago." Her lower lip quivers but unfortunately I recognize it from her soap opera days. "It became final last week."

She could turn tears on like a faucet. It was her greatest skill. Bravo! I almost whistle and clap. What a performance. It's just like my mother to make her divorce from Seb a production. She'd sell tickets if she could.

I slump in relief. "Dios mio, I thought you were *dying*. Well, I'm sorry to hear it. Why didn't you tell me before?"

She blinks in surprise and her hand rises to her chest. "And ruin your *wedding*?"

"Oh. Right. That was very…um, considerate of you."

"And when you told me about you and Chris, well, I *wanted* to tell you right then and there. But I knew you'd be hurting, too, over your own breakup." She pats my hand as if to show her motherly concern.

It falls flat. There must be another reason she didn't turn up the drama earlier. She wants me to believe she's put my feelings above her own. It doesn't seem likely, and I won't fall for her machinations. She wants to be mother of the year now, and I can't let her get away with it. I'll be nice, but I won't embrace her second act. Or believe it.

"I'm doing great, actually."

"You've always been stronger than me." She sniffles.

"I'm not stronger than you, but I don't let a relationship status define me."

I threw the dart and it hit the target. But if I've hurt her, I haven't penetrated the outer shell.

"You're *young*, mi amor. Wait until you're my age. The parts dry up, or they all go to Meryl Streep. The men want someone twenty years younger and they always get what *they* want. It doesn't matter how much work a woman gets done."

"Not *all* men want someone twenty years younger."

"Just the best ones," she says.

No. The worst ones.

Mami and I still see the world in opposite ways. Maybe if my father hadn't died she wouldn't be in this position. Everyone in the family says my father truly loved her, the way I remember, and I doubt he would have judged her for having the audacity to get older.

"What I had with Seb fizzled. So, I had to let him go." She moves her fingers as if shaking off dust.

"You divorced *him*?" I want to believe that my mother has finally set an example I can follow of choosing to be with the right man or choosing to be alone.

"You better believe I did. But let's not talk about me anymore." She shifts in her seat. "I want to know all the news. Give me the latest updates. Are you still writing your little books?"

My little books, she calls them, still not in touch. The dialogue she memorized for her soap opera was written by talented writers. Years ago, Eddie shared a rumor Mami lost her job when she attempted to rewrite her dialogue to something more "believable."

"There's something I have to tell you." I clear my throat. "You might hear about this at some point, but I was recently on a morning show with my new book."

"Querida! I'm so happy for you. It's what you've always wanted. You finally wrote the book!"

I finally wrote the book?

She's forgetting all the ghostwriting I've done. A little

pride in what her daughter has accomplished would be appreciated.

Although not the worst moment of my life, I believe it will surely be in the top ten when I tell her about Ryan, the real talent behind the curtain. Hang on a second. I *can't* tell her. It's in the NDA and pretty sure it includes mothers. Anyway, she won't be here long and will need to go back to LA and the endless cycle of auditions.

"I wrote it under a pen name. Elizabeth Brogan."

There. The words are out. I've just lied to my own mother and the ground didn't open up and swallow me whole.

She gasps. "What a *beautiful* name. Great choice! I wanted to name you Elizabeth, after Elizabeth Taylor, but your father wouldn't allow it. He wanted something Spanish. Sometimes a name really matters and can mean something. The name Geneva has suited me well all these years."

"Anyway, just in case you want to look up the book. It won't be under Lucia."

"I'll go and get your book right away. I'll buy five of them and send them to all my friends."

"That's not necessary. Not to brag, but it's already sold *a lot* of copies."

It's odd to boast about something that is not my accomplishment, but…that's what Ryan wants me to do. He *hired* me for this purpose. I refuse to feel guilty about any of this.

Besides, looks like I've finally made my mother proud.

THE NEXT MORNING, I'm up earlier than normal for my shower.

The main house is quiet, Eddie already gone because he leaves early for his commute into San Francisco. All is per the usual, except for finding the sleeping form of my mother on the couch. Her suitcases surround her, and there's no less than *five* of them taking up a whole lot of square footage in Abuelita's modest home.

She stirs and removes the eye mask, sitting up. "Querida. Buenos dias."

"Why are you still here?" Hard to believe she couldn't find a single hotel room in Seven Trees, Mountain View, or Menlo Park.

"Eddie insisted I stay the night. It was late when we were done talking." She smooths a stray hair back into place. "It's been years but we will never stop being family."

That's convenient after she's left Seb and apparently has no one else. Now suddenly *we're* her family again.

I hear pots and pans clanging in the kitchen, which means Abuelita is up and cooking. She's close to eighty and not fond of my mother, but she's been raised never to turn anyone in need away. Once, she served lunch to an unhoused man who showed up at her doorstep. When Eddie arrived, he escorted the man to the front door. Then he'd had a stern talk with his mother about the fact not all strangers are created equal.

I leave my mother and join Abuelita in the kitchen.

"What are you doing? You don't have to cook for her."

"I'm cooking dinner early. It will be hot today so better to do it now."

I'm not convinced this is true, or that she won't offer to cook my mother huevos rancheros or anything else she wants.

My mother appears in the doorway of the kitchen. "Buenos dias. Is there café?"

I shouldn't be surprised but she appears to be wearing some fancy negligee. At least she has the decency to cover up with an equally slinky robe. Her slippers, of course, are pink furry little bunny ones with heels. I refrain from telling her that the eighties called and want their outfit back.

"Aqui." Abuelita gestures to the coffeepot she's already brewed with fresh coffee for her guest.

"I'm going to work so I can't eat with you," I explain.

"That's alright," Mami says. "I'll have breakfast with Abuelita."

"Really? You're going to *eat*?"

Coffee in hand, my mother nods on her way out of the kitchen. "I would love to."

I glance between the two women, who are different as salt and sugar, two ingredients that should never be substituted for one another. Abuelita barely glances up from the pan where she's heating one of her homemade tortillas, but we exchange a significant look. She's not going to skimp on the butter or salt.

"Your mami is going to stay a while," Abuelita says.

"What? Why?"

"Because she's your *madre*."

"But she lives in LA."

She shrugs. "As long as she's here, my door is open. This is the way my Antonio would want it. It's done."

Nothing I say will change her mind. The lines of hospitality run deep in my grandmother. Besides, I know my mother will be gone as soon as she hears of an audition for a woman of a certain age. Maybe I should ask about her plans, but I don't want to know.

When I leave, I overhear Abuelita and Mami eating at the table, and neither one of them appears to be ready to sock the other one. I think it's safe to go, and I do, heading over to the coffee shop on University Avenue where they serve the best dark roast beans. The line is out the door, and I take the time to scroll through my phone for any updates. There is one from Pepper, advising she's added photos from the shoot and links to the morning show to Elizabeth's social media profiles but would like me to add personal photos as I see fit.

I'm told I should fixate on a funny object that will serve as brand-adjacent, such as being a coffee aficionado (though that's been done) to a dog lover (done) and a bacon enthusiast (also done.) Pepper thinks branding me as a boat lover would fit nicely given that *Soulmates* features so many sailboats.

I've never even been on a boat.

Next, there's a disconcerting email from Holly.

To: theghostwriter@hotmail

From: inthequerytrenches@yahoo

Subject: WTAF

Why didn't you tell me you had a contract? When did you write the book? I'm insulted you didn't think to tell me, while I've been sharing news of my dumb contest finals. You must think that's so cute. Even so, I will be buying and reading your book today.

Holly

What am I going to tell *Holly*? I want to tell her the truth, because she knows if I actually wrote the book I'd have told her about it. We've been close enough to share our queries and rejections. But I absolutely cannot tell her the truth.

Now I need to come up with some excuse why I had to write it in secret. One that an actual writer would believe.

I'm so preoccupied with my thoughts it isn't until I'm second in line that I look up and notice him.

Ryan.

No doubt about it. It's Ryan. And he is not alone. He's sitting at a booth with a brunette who looks like she just stepped out of the pages of *Glamour* magazine. I'm shocked enough to nearly bump into the person in front of me as I strain to get a better look.

Ryan and the woman appear to be deep in conversation, and she's *stroking his hand*. He doesn't pull away even though if I'm being honest, I recognize the appearance of a man completely uninterested. The rigid posture, the body turned away. All things I saw in Chris in the last few weeks before he left, and which I only now recognize as the kiss-off.

I'm not surprised someone of this caliber is interested in Ryan, because he's objectively good-looking by almost anyone's standards.

Once I receive my order, one for Ryan as I've been doing since he hired me, it takes everything in me not to stop by their table and offer a quick hello. Not surprisingly, I'm the curious type, but interrupting feels like a violation of privacy and I talk myself out it. I appreciate having the separation of both worlds more than most.

Ryan once gave me a key to the house so I could come in if he's too preoccupied to get up and open the door for me. I've learned such things are extremely bothersome if he's in the flow. His powers of concentration are a thing of wonder. The house could be on fire and he might miss it.

Usually I knock first, but now I let myself in, knowing for the first time with certainty that he's not here. Longingly, I look at the closed bedroom door where I might do some of my best snooping. If he brought a photo of anyone with him it would be in there. But no. If Ryan wants to tell me who that woman is, he will.

Setting his coffee down on the dining table where he usually works, I open my laptop on the kitchen counter. I go to my new Facebook page and log in with the email and password Pepper sent. Her email says:

Add some photos in everyday situations so you appear to be a genuine person. Please be careful not to give too much information. When it comes to sales numbers and the like, no statements are preferred to going on and on about your enormous success. Readers like a down-to-earth person. People who are far more grounded and self-deprecating are preferred. In other words, no bragging, though I'm sure I don't have to tell you that. Simply thank readers at every opportunity. Everyone is a fan. Respond to every comment.

The part about appearing to be "a genuine person" makes me chuckle. Yeah, I get it. But Elizabeth Brogan isn't real and I'm not likely to brag about something I haven't earned.

My new profile page includes a header graphic, a cover of *Soulmates* with some of the rave reviews. I upload some of my personal photos, including older ones like that time I tried making homemade tortillas. A mini-disaster and I burned most of them. Very "real" and authentic. No bragging merits here. There are already comments and I do my best to respond to everyone. Then I see that Holly has left a comment that makes me cringe:

I know the author personally! I'm super jazzed at this kind of sudden and meteoric success!

I'm not sure how to handle this latest wrinkle. I've composed three different responses to Holly's casual comment, deleting each one by the time Ryan arrives alone. He quirks a brow as if surprised to see me but I've become accustomed to this by now and don't let it phase me.

"Got you a coffee." I nudge my chin toward the desk.

I say nothing about the fact I spotted him in the coffee shop, *not* alone, and know he's already had coffee.

"Thanks," he says.

"Did you already have some this morning? Since you were out, I wondered," I press, hoping he'll volunteer information without me having to yank it out of him.

"Can never have too much coffee," he says, not actually answering the question. "I've been thinking. How about the field trip to Santa Cruz today?"

"Yeah?" I perk up. It's a weekday so it won't be quite as crowded as the weekend. "The Cocoanut Grove?"

"Sure, or whatever else you want to show me." He's digging through his messenger bag. "Maybe what I need is to walk away from all this paper and see some of the real world for a change."

"I couldn't agree more, professor."

I have no idea what's brought about his change of attitude, but I like it. Within a few minutes, after we've argued over who will drive and I win, because it's still difficult to get in a car with someone else driving, we're on 101 on the way to the Highway 17 interchange. Once I get to 17, I slow my roll. I'm particular about driving the curvy mountain twists and turns and I prefer to be in the driver's seat. I have my reasons for this and they go way back and are extremely valid. Yes, my hands are shaking a little on the steering wheel but it isn't like I haven't driven this treacherous road before.

It isn't long before Ryan has to pipe in, "Hey, Dale Earhart, Jr. Slow down."

The sarcasm runs deep in his comment, since going any slower might get me a ticket from the CHP.

"This road is dangerous." He doesn't know the half of it. I usually drive to the beach completely out of my way avoiding 17 and instead taking the much longer Highway 1. "I prefer to take it slow."

"Any slower and we'll be going backward."

"No more comments from you, Mr. Backseat Driver."

"I'm sure we'll get there eventually."

"Yes, we will. And you can count on me to get us there safely." I clear my throat. "So, have you met anyone since you arrived in Seven Trees?"

"Besides you? When would I have the time to meet anyone?"

A blatant lie. Maybe the woman from this morning is an escort and he isn't proud of the situation. But an escort at the coffee shop? Not likely. Perhaps an escort he couldn't shake from the previous night? I'm dying to know about this woman but I'll have to admit I saw them together. My mind is spinning with possible scenarios.

I try again, because maybe it was a professional meeting. Maybe it was Kate? However, stroking the hand? I don't think that's something an agent would do, no matter how much she likes Ryan.

"Have you, um, heard from Kate? I mean, about the sales numbers."

"No."

"Okay, so are you going to call her for the sales numbers?"

"Eventually."

A zippy BMW illegally passes me even though there's a double solid yellow line. Someone is in a hurry to get in an accident.

"If it were me, I'd be dying to know."

"Don't worry, you'll get paid."

"That's not why I'm asking. Aren't you at all curious?"

"Maybe I don't want to know."

Ah, suddenly I understand the need to be away from his desk. He's worried, or concerned, or maybe just…out of sorts. A feeling of protectiveness washes over me, because I'm truly my abuelita's granddaughter. I can't help but feel compassion where it is clearly needed. Ryan is the most unlikely of love story writers. He's got to feel as if he's wearing his skin inside out. Now, tens of thousands will read his words and while he might be used to great reviews and awards, *someone* will hate his book. That tends to be the way of extreme popularity. You either love a book or passionately hate it. There are some books that stir up powerful emotions and I think this might be one of them.

Finally, we secure a parking space and begin our stroll to the boardwalk. The roller-coaster rumbling sounds and screams of riders greet us as we approach the entrance. It's free to get inside but the rides and food will cost you. The first thing is to lead Ryan away from all the noise of families enjoying the day, and toward the Cocoanut Grove to paint a picture of what life might have been like for a couple in the 1940s during war time. It isn't going to be easy but I expect he has a good imagination.

"You see how it isn't too long of a drive over the mountains to the ocean and why Bay Area residents wouldn't have thought of it as too far for a little nightlife. Especially back when there was less traffic."

My imagination fills with thoughts of couples on their way to the dance, the women wearing tea dresses with puffed cap sleeves. The men in slacks or suits with ties, dressed for a night on the town. They'd be worried about so many things. The war overseas, the economy, their jobs.

I can almost see the big band thrumming from the stage as everyone gives in to the music. I wonder if Ryan can see it, too.

The entire time we walk I recite facts about the boardwalk I've carefully researched. When an investor's casino burned down in 1904, he rebuilt it in 1906, and that casino is now the present-day Santa Cruz Beach Boardwalk. Both the Looff Carousel and Giant Dipper are national historic landmarks. Families come out in droves all year but tourists are more frequent in the summer.

Ryan walks beside me, an unreadable expression on his face, that deep divet in between his eyes. I can't decide if he's irritated, worried, or distracted. Perhaps he's thinking of the beautiful lady from this morning. When his phone buzzes and he glances at it, I can't help but wonder who's texting him. Ryan is vulnerable even if he fails to show that side of himself. I catch it in his guarded and hooded eyes. I feel it when I get closer to him to show him something I've found in my research and he makes an almost exaggerated attempt to put distance between us.

I lead him to the framed historical photo, hanging in the raucous area of the Cocoanut Grove. This is now an arcade and it turns out the most historically accurate part of the Grove is closed for an event. We both stare at a photo of the present Grove superimposed over a historical photo. The main difference is that in the older photo, the white-clothed circle tables are closer to the wall, each table surrounded by a short rail. There once was a second level, and tall palm trees were part of the décor.

I can picture it now. Me, wearing a long glittery gold gown, my hair in an updo as I dance with gentleman after gentleman. Ryan, standing against the wall, dressed in a suit, his dark wavy hair slicked back. He's staring at me but not making a move to interrupt and take his turn on my dance card. I wonder who the gentleman is and why he won't make a move.

"Sometimes, I think I was born in the wrong time," Ryan says, startling me out of my daydream.

I can't exactly agree, because I'm a woman. But it might be nice to be at an event without the distractions of a phone that could buzz or ring at any time. Nice to know if you slip and fall no one is going to make a reel or boomerang of it and plaster it on social media for all eternity. How amazing, too, for a chance to get to know someone without the constant chatter. I can barely picture such a silent world.

"I'm getting a feel for the place," Ryan says. "After all, geography doesn't change much. All it takes is a little imagination."

"True, the ocean has always been right there." I point.

We pass by the Looff Carousel, which has been here for decades and seen generations of children make the rounds. Their parents now stand by with phones in their hands, scrolling. A few take photos before they go back to their scrolling.

Ryan treats me to a waffle cone and we walk through the covered concrete walkway, the crowded beach to our right. There isn't a place for privacy, or quiet, so we finally settle against the rail that separates us from the concrete steps leading to the sand. I hold my cone, facing the beach. It's a cloudless day, the sun bright and punishing. Children are running, laughing, splashing at the water's edge, and building sandcastles while their parents rest in the shade underneath huge colorful umbrellas. I would imagine a scene like this one transcends time and place. The only difference is the clothing. There's a woman wearing a string bikini getting ogled by the men.

I think of a game I've only played with Sofia, but Ryan will be a worthy opponent.

"You see her?" I point to the woman hauling an umbrella, carrying towels, sand toys, *and* a baby on her back. A toddler follows close behind, a man holding his hand. And nothing else.

Ryan stiffens, mutters a curse word and I know, were we not several hundred yards and crowds of people away, he'd rush to help. So would I, but that's not the point. I chose her for a reason. She has a story.

"I think she's going home to tell him he either steps up or she wants a separation. This is just a slice of what happens between them every day."

"Ah, I used to play this game but it's been many years." Ryan leans over the rail, splaying out his arms. "See those two over there?"

I see a young woman on the edge of the surf, a young man beside her. There's a healthy distance between them. Either they don't know each other or they're not happy with each other. Funny how both might be true.

"They just met. She's not too sure about him, or even men in general, because she just broke up with someone and it was traumatic. The groom stood her up at the altar, but she took the honeymoon by herself. That's why she's here, alone. She's not at all ready for this, but he is extremely interested. He just leaned in."

I scrunch up my nose and take another look at the couple. "What do you mean?"

"Yeah, the lean. What, you don't know the lean?" He cocks his head.

I'm drawing a blank and a little ashamed to find that my first thoughts run to how lean and fit the young woman is, which shows in many ways I'm my mother's daughter.

"I think I know what you mean but I'm not sure," I confess. "In this context."

"The *lean*," he says.

Actually, I need to hear his explanation because something tells me it will be delicious.

"Explain it to me like I'm five."

"I think you know." He smirks. "There are different kinds of leans. There's the friend lean, where you bend slightly in interest. Like I'm doing right now."

"I see."

"And then there's the lean away." He exaggeratedly leans back. "This is when someone is definitely not interested."

"Like I haven't seen that one before," I say.

"Lastly, smartass, when a guy is interested, this is the lean."

When he closes the distance between us, all the breath leaves my body. He's right. The lean is powerful, especially when it's him. His eyes are the deep blue of the sky at twilight and I've absolutely stopped breathing.

"You're r-right," I say. "That's powerful."

Ryan returns to the healthy distance between us and we're back to the way we are every day at work.

"Before revisions for the book, when I was actually trying to write a love story, I devoured a dozen romantic comedies. The lean is from *While You Were Sleeping*."

"One of my favorite movies of all time!" It's time for a rewatch.

"Writing a love story forced me to take a hard look at the unspoken physical language between two people. A lean is just the start."

We're quiet for several seconds, simply watching the couple as they start off on a walk in the other direction. I catch the lean this time, when he laughs and says something to her. She also laughs. She's giving him a chance. Good for her.

Sometimes you have to take a risk.

"Are your parents still together?" I ask.

He nods. "Over thirty years and still madly in love."

"Really?"

"Don't sound so surprised. Divorce doesn't run in families like genes for eye and hair color."

"I know." I chuckle. "Plenty of couples stay together for decades but are miserable. It's just…the in-love part surprises me."

"Sounds like a good thing, right? Instead, they set me up for unrealistic expectations. Do you want to know how you stay in love for over thirty years?"

Naturally, I nod. Doesn't everyone want that?

"You ignore your children and stay in your own little world with each other."

"That's not the best way, I'm afraid." I shake my head.

My parents never ignored me and I never got the idea that they wished for time away from me. Devoted to each other, rather than ignore me, they put me at the center of their love. It's one of the things I miss most about my childhood. When I was between them, they were a cocoon for me. Rather than feeling squeezed I felt utterly and completely loved. I can't imagine a world in which they would have ignored me for each other.

"It worked for them. My brother and I were like accessories. You get the older one to watch the younger one. I bet they only had children because they were expected to reproduce."

"What do you mean *expected*?"

He sighs. "More soldiers for the spiritual battle. Basically, we lived in a cult for the first few years of my life."

"If that's a joke, it's not funny."

"Cult is too strong a word but we were raised in a highly regimented religion. They raised us in a micro world where love was merit based. The better you obeyed the rules, the more you were loved by your family, and ostensibly, God. I didn't manage well, so I wasn't very loved."

My heart pinches imagining a little boy who went unloved. I don't know if there's much worse. My family has often been my salvation when it feels like nothing is going my way. It's the one place where one should feel accepted.

"It sounds like you made your own way."

"It took a while, but I found my tribe at college. I don't have much to do with my parents anymore, but I'm close with my little brother. And he's still close with them. What about your parents?" Ryan asks.

"Theirs was a great love story. There was never anyone else, could never *be* anyone else. It's what I want someday. I think that's why I started reading and writing romance. That amazing love story, the once-in-a-lifetime love."

"How did they meet?"

"San Jose State University where my father was studying when my mother arrived from New Jersey. They met, love at first sight, and married young. My father died when I was ten and she went off the rails. Maybe it was her chance to do everything she'd wanted to do while they were married. So, she dumped me off with my father's family and went off to audition for acting roles. She was actually pretty successful. After that, I only saw her about once a year when she or I visited. She remarried."

My heart is a raw and pulsing beat remembering those empty years when she chose Seb over me. I push back the tears with the pads of my fingers. I'm too old to feel this hurt but maybe Ryan and I have more in common than I realized. I have Sofia, Eddie, and Abuelita but I don't have a real mother. Not one who listens to my heart, who accepts me for who I am, who dries my tears.

Ryan is still looking out at the ocean as if he thinks he'll find the answer to the mysteries of the cosmos.

"I'm sorry about your father," he says. "And I think when you really love someone, you're not going to hold them back from their dreams. You're not going to chase them."

I wonder who he means or if he's talking about himself.

"So," I say. "Since you're not going to share those sales numbers yet, *I* have something to say."

He turns to me, but dark shades conceal his expressive eyes.

"I saw you this morning at the coffee shop with a woman. She's pretty, but if I can give you a bit of unsolicited advice… it's not a good idea to get involved with someone when you're on the rebound."

"Rebound? It's been three *years*." He cocks his head and there's the hint of a smile and amusement laced in his voice.

"Yes, well, maybe a long-distance relationship is not the best idea, either."

One corner of his mouth quirks up. "You're right. After all, you're the romance expert."

"If I was writing this book, I'd say you're in an opposites-attract situation with that woman."

He nods. "That's true. You're very observant."

"Where did you meet her?"

"In Pasadena, but she moved out here a few years ago for her work. She's a software engineer."

I don't know why that hits me like a punch. They obviously have history. This woman means something to him.

Ryan throws away what's left of his cone in the nearby receptacle, then turns to me with his full attention. He takes off his glasses and props them on his head like he wants me to see his eyes. They squint against the sun but they're still every bit as blue.

"The woman you saw me with this morning is my ex-wife."

CHAPTER 15

His *ex-wife*. His ex-wife in the coffee shop in Seven Trees, stroking his hand. He's rented Professor Henry's home while he's on sabbatical, but maybe it's not a coincidence this is also where his ex lives. I don't know why I should care, except that I've started to feel protective about Ryan. It has nothing to do with my picturing him at the ball in the 1940s just watching me from a distance with a look of longing as I danced with the others. Nothing to do with the way his dark hair glistens in the sun and when he smiles it feels like a gift.

I don't have a thing for Ryan. I can't. The blocks always work like a charm but in this case slivers of desire are threading through.

I need to change the subject. This is none of my business.

"Um, I forgot to mention the Loma Prieta Earthquake of 1989 hit this area hard. Lots of rebuilding. But you don't need to know that." I wave my hand. "It's past the era of your novel."

"That's it? You're not going to ask me what I was doing

having coffee with the woman who tore my heart out by its ventricles?"

"It's none of my business."

"But you make everything your business. Don't think I didn't catch you looking through my mail."

Busted. I rub my sweaty palms against my jeans and bite my lower lip.

"I was…I was looking for something you asked me for. Don't give me that look. You're drowning in paperwork and asked me to organize you!"

"Uh-huh." But he seems to be fighting a smile, his eyes twinkling. "I understand. You were curious. I can't say I haven't felt the same way about you."

"You have?"

"When you left me alone in your shed so you could consider my offer, I took an inventory of every book you own."

Inexplicably, I feel the start of a tingle in my belly. I've been seen.

"And…how did I do?"

"I'd have to say eight of ten if I'm grading. More romance that I would like, but with a generous showing for the classics."

I have to smile at this. This is the man who's written possibly the year's bestselling romance book. Eventually, I will ask what possessed him. I assume it's the money but with what I've learned about Ryan, there's more to it.

"And speaking of romance, we were talking about your heart when you changed the subject. I mean, you've been warned. It's not like I have to tell you about the high failure rates of a second marriage with the same person. The problems you had before will still be there."

"From what I've read, the failure rates of a second

marriage in general are bad, so I'm screwed any way you look at it."

I tip my chin. "Not with the right person. Those statistics are *skewed*."

Ryan breaks into a smile, and it's the most relaxed and authentic one I've ever seen on him. "You're making that up."

"I am not. It just makes sense that your outcome will be different with someone new. Two different people with differing backgrounds and histories make for a completely different situation."

He lifts a shoulder. "I won't argue since it seems to put me on a more even playing field."

"So…you're not trying to get back together?"

Another smile. "I thought you said this was none of your business."

Now, I'm done with my waffle cone so I throw it in the receptacle. "It still isn't, but *you* brought it up."

"The thing is, maybe it *is* your business."

My heart jumps. He says it's my business, too, but I can't imagine why. Maybe Ryan is beginning to have some slight, and by slight I mean *minimal*, interest in me beyond being Elizabeth.

"W-why is it my business?" My voice sounds shaky to my own ears.

"She knows about you. I had to tell her."

This is more serious than I thought. I'd like to say it's fear that strikes me but unfortunately it falls far closer to excitement. She wouldn't know about me for any other reason than he's talking to her about *me.* This worries me because I'm dangerously on the cusp of what I might describe as giddy.

"How does she know about me?"

This is where my imagination runs wild. He could *lean in*

close and say he told her there's someone else. He can't stop thinking about me. Since the night of the spontaneous party Eddie threw and I danced with my cousins, he can't stop thinking of my legs and the way I gyrated my hips. The way I threw back my head and let the music guide me. Like Shakira.

But he doesn't say anything remotely like that. He simply drags a hand through his hair. "She's heard about the book and she knows everything."

Oh, the book. We've switched gears and now segued to the book. It takes me a minute, but I'm now on track.

"She knows you wrote a bestseller with a pen name. A woman's pen name."

He nods. "It couldn't be helped."

I'm having a tough time keeping up here. They've been divorced three years. It's like Ryan has left out important information.

"*How* did she read the book? Did she get an early copy?"

"In a manner of speaking."

"In *which* manner of speaking?" Now, I'm the one who's annoyed.

"She had the earliest version, because in a way, I wrote it for her."

I'm stunned. Shocked. My ability to speak is temporarily gone. I'm probably gaping so big a seagull could make a nest in my mouth.

"You wrote the book for your *ex-wife*?"

"No, not exactly. And she wasn't my ex-wife at the time. We were separated. But remember I told you that I wrote the book as a joke, a lark? Just to see if I could do it? That was a lie."

I pointed. "I *knew* that didn't sound like you!"

"You were right. It's too humiliating to admit, but I don't see how I have much choice now. I wrote what amounted to a short story, a love story left open to see who she'd choose.

Me, or the other guy. So now you see why it isn't standard romance fare." He shrugged.

It makes sense now. The book is written from a male's point of view because it might as well have been a diary. No wonder the book read like the writer bled all over the pages. He had. Even I'd never do something like this. I doubt any romance author would. A poem or short story? Sure. But devoting an entire novel, tens of thousands of words within a plot, is too much work to simply be a gift never intended to see publication.

"And…if it was just intended for her, when did you decide to try to get it published?"

"I didn't. It wasn't a book."

"I'm lost."

He works his jaw. "I never had plans for this to be a *book*, much less be published. But she took the liberty of sending my *unedited* pages to my agent."

I take a step back as if he's slapped me. "She did *what?*"

I'm outraged on Ryan's behalf. Just the idea that someone would send off unedited pages is anathema to my brain. It's unthinkable to do this without the author's permission and particularly with such a private matter. I'm furious on his behalf.

"It's…it's a breach of privacy, of intimacy."

My heart is racing and pumping. I feel the pounding beat in my *eyes*.

Ryan nods. "Anyway, my agent read the pages. She assumed I was okay with it, or this is what she tells me, since it came through my wife at the time. You can imagine my response when she said she loved the premise and wanted to talk about making it into a book. She tried to sell me on romance, and how it's a bestselling genre. I had no idea what she meant by my pages and when she explained, I hung up on her. We didn't speak for three weeks."

"I don't blame you. But at some point, you decided to do this."

"After Kate wouldn't leave me alone I eventually agreed to *consider* publishing a romance. Kate promised me a great deal of money if we worked hard to tailor it to the market. But it took a year of back and forth, revisions, cuts, with Kate always promising me more and more. By then Millie and I were divorced." He lowers his shades, shaking his head. "I thought I'd get an advance, sell a few copies, move on. I had no idea it would all blow up like this thanks to a reality star that somehow saw her husband in Grayson and loved the book. Believe me, I don't understand any of this."

"Gosh, if you'd just been honest with me from the start, I would have had more sympathy for you. It's been tough to feel sorry for someone who has met with your success almost accidentally."

"And that's just the point. I never wanted you to feel sorry for me. I would have kept this from you forever. Keep in mind, I'm used to writing in anonymity like most authors. Despite what Kate promised, I thought this book would be forgotten. But readers of love stories are voracious and dedicated and…we don't give them enough credit."

I smirk. "We've established that."

"Anyway, I'm not allowed to be angry. This book changed my life. It was good therapy, too."

"As you recently said to me, 'you don't have to like her' and you're allowed to be mad at your ex."

"It feels like forever ago when I wrote the book. I barely recognize that man. And the truth is the final version is entirely different from what I intended."

"But…you were saying your ex knows about me?"

"That's the reason she wanted to meet." Ryan turns to face the ocean and the gray color of the waves. "When she asked about the book, I told her it was being released under a pen name and that we'd hired a kind of reverse ghostwriter to play Elizabeth."

I consider this. It seemed inevitable that the ex would have to know everything. But I feel somehow exposed and seen in a way Ryan's publisher didn't prepare me to face.

The fog is set to roll in as it does nearly every afternoon. It's hovering in the distance, waiting to cover us with gray.

Ryan keeps talking. "She wanted to meet because she somehow thinks this book means more than it does. For me, the book has become a product I was able to sell. For her, it's our love story. Let me assure you, it's *not*."

Ryan's reluctance to fully embrace his book, his desire to keep a distance from it, makes more sense than ever.

Publishing the book kept a tie to his ex-wife that he no longer wants.

CHAPTER 16

*I*f I was the one writing *this* story, I'd choose a different twist. Definitely not the ex-wife returning. Not that it matters.

"Are you getting back together?" I ask.

He laughs. "No. There's zero chance."

My heart feels like a pulsing vein, centered right on my forehead. I like this answer more than I should. This has nothing to do with me nor should I care, but apparently my heart isn't getting the message.

"I can't believe you'd ever speak to her again. She…she sent in something you wrote for her. It wasn't for public consumption."

"No one else understands it the way a writer does. But look what happened. It led to a big payoff for me when I've barely made a living as a writer until now. Should I be upset?"

"Of course! Just because the outcome is good, that doesn't mean the original intent was honorable."

"I know."

"I'm sorry, but you'd be crazy to try again with someone who betrayed your trust."

"I would be, and don't worry, I'm not crazy."

"Worry? Well, yeah, I'm just concerned about you, Ryan."

"Clearly." He rolls his eyes.

On the way back, I notice Ryan is throwing concerned looks in my direction as we once again traverse the Santa Cruz mountains on Highway 17. I might be going a little slow again but I've got this. It could be he's noticed my hands are trembling and that I'm pretty much white-knuckling it, but I'm perfectly fine and I'm glad I took this drive. I can't even recall how long it's been. As a rule, the entire Santana family as a unit chose never to drive Highway 17 again. There are other ways to get to the beach even if they take longer.

"Okay," Ryan says. "Did something happen to you on this road?"

"What do you mean?"

"Did your car break down here and you have bad memories? It would be a difficult place for a car to break down. No real shoulder to pull over as you go up and down the mountain."

"It's fine, really. Don't worry."

"Consider it dropped. I just sense you're terrified."

"Hmm. Maybe I should assign you a higher rate on the emotional IQ than previously."

"Excuse me? You don't think I rate high on the scale? I will blow that scale. I'll have you know I'm off the charts."

"Hmm. Let's start with your greeting. You answer the phone with, 'what?' Did you ever think people might have their feelings hurt by your attitude? It gives 'why are you bothering me?' vibes. How about 'hello.'"

"They *are* interrupting me, and if I say hello I'm encouraging them," he says with a slightly offended tone.

"Listen, after reading the book, I see you're an emotional guy but—"

"But nothing. As a writer, I use emotion. And I put it on paper where it *belongs*."

I wonder if that's true. I wonder if Ryan purposely revised the book to be what the publisher wanted: more of a romance, more of a love story. Pulling on the heart strings. Slaying the emotion. Maybe he wasn't as heartbroken as I imagined. Maybe it's just…fiction.

"Okay, I'm finally going to ask. Why didn't you just write her a *poem* instead of a short story?"

"I can't write poetry." He sighs. "But if I'm any good at expressing my feelings, it's always on paper. I think that's why Kate encouraged me to write a romance. I'd love to be able to express the way I feel out loud, but I'm not built like that. It's just not in me. When we were having problems, I ignored them. I retreated to my work. So, she had an affair."

I can't help but gasp. "Oh, Ryan."

"I didn't know this when I wrote to her, of course, or we wouldn't even be in this position. But the truth is, I saw how I'd failed in many ways. I made a commitment to her, and if I agree with anything my parents taught me, it's to honor those. So that's why I put my feelings down on paper."

"Did you learn anything from the experience?"

"I learned that a person could fool themselves into thinking they love someone when all they really love is an idea."

"Hey, that's a line in the book, but it's Lula who says it to Grayson."

"You do realize I'm Grayson, Lula, *and* the other guy." He snorts.

I love the way he won't even name his faux rival.

"But the 'other guy' is a brute. He's mean and obnoxious."

In the business, we refer to that hero as an alpha-hole.

Sexy in a dominating and obnoxious way. He's the arrogant male main character who realizes he's handsome and is prepared for women to fall at his feet as they so often do. He's good with his hands, he's tall and fit, and has a big you-know-what. I can't believe Lula fell for someone so… obvious.

I now see exactly what Kate saw in Grayson. It's the same thing I do. I might not like the book, or the ending, but I loved the hero. Grayson is a classic cinnamon roll hero, the antithesis of toxic masculinity. He's emotionally available. He's vulnerable.

"I'm also all of those other things. Mean. Obnoxious."

"No, you're not. You're grumpy, sure, and distracted, but not like Der— um, the other dude."

"Chalk it up to hyperbole, a writer's toolbox."

This makes me laugh because I've been accused of relying on this one tool far too often. *But* I write romantic fantasy.

"It happened to me, too," I say.

I think of Nadia, a dark beauty, so elusive and mysterious the few times I saw her at the coffee shop. Then I wonder how many times they met together in private, while I was home pulling the strands of my hair out one by one, trying to write my book.

"That was his mistake," Ryan says.

A warm blush rolls over me. "We were supposed to get married and I had to cancel the wedding venue and pay for the penalties."

"Damn."

"At least he didn't leave me at the altar. That's…that's why I live in a shed. The rent on our condo was too much for me alone. Wait. Forget I said that. I don't know why I'm telling you this."

If this was a text message, I could edit. Delete, delete, delete. But it's too late. It's out there. "It's not like I want you to feel sorry for me. I have a wonderful family, you've met them, and I could live in the main house but it's small and crowded. And this is just temporary."

"You should have said something. I'll have a check for you on Monday."

That's not why I'm laying my heart bare right now, and I wish I hadn't mentioned money. It's never been important to me or I wouldn't be a writer.

"Don't worry about that, I'm fine. I'm letting you know I understand what you went through. Being abandoned is tough. The thing of it is, once someone leaves you, if they come back, I think it's impossible to believe they won't leave you again. And they usually do."

"Is that another warning about giving my ex another chance? Because that's not happening."

I'm actually thinking of my mother because even now I'm wondering how much longer it will be before she takes off. I saw her rental car this morning, parked on the curb. Abuelita is not going to ask her to leave and Eddie will follow her lead. My mother will be here as long as she wants to be. Historically, it hasn't been more than a week. I'm tired of seeing her walk out the door but it's what I've come to expect.

"You deserve better."

"Would you take your ex back? What if he grovels the way Grayson did?"

"No. I'd have to take my own advice, or I'd be a hypocrite. The same issues would still be there. I thought Chris was different but he's an entitled...*jerk*!"

"Tell me what you really think."

"I was actually editorializing what I really think. Want to know what I think? Chris joined the Peace Corps to break off our engagement because he didn't have the courage to do it any other way."

"And maybe he didn't want to hurt you. Speaking for my species, men, we're a little stupid sometimes. We don't want to confront our feelings because they could lead to *dis*comfort. We're creatures of comfort."

"Don't defend him." I'm irked by how close he hit the mark with Chris, who doesn't even like to get caught in the rain without an umbrella.

"Sorry, just being devil's advocate. I'm trying to understand how any red-blooded male would ever choose anyone but you."

There's silence for a beat as I absorb the words. They send a new thrill running through me but I remind myself Ryan is trying to cheer me up. He's being nice to the woman who's literally saving his career.

Nothing more.

THAT EVENING, I settle in to write. This time, it's my book. I pull it up again and I imagine even the file looks tired and worn. It's been through so many edits, revisions, and changes I'm not sure it's my book anymore. Maybe I've lost the heart.

It's my opus, a romantic fantasy set in a world where time doesn't exist. Two people from different positions of power love each other beyond and across time. I don't think it's ready but hey, as Nora Roberts famously said, "you can't edit a blank page." I'm not sure what she'd say about someone who keeps editing the same pages over and over. I suppose that's what happens when you don't have a contract, or a deadline, and you've collected dozens of rejections along the way.

As I read, I find the good parts I can't believe I wrote, and then the cringy scenes. Something is missing but I don't know what it is. There's a reason dozens of agents have turned me away, many of them saying, "Love the premise, but I couldn't connect with these characters."

Inspired by Ryan, I too decide to write something different. Sometimes this gets the juices flowing. Ryan wrote a romance. I can certainly write a short thriller portraying Chris as a serial killer I must murder to protect the world.

Picture, if you will, Stephen King's *Misery* meets Katherine Center's *The Bodyguard*. A weird mix and not my usual fare. But my idea/brainchild centers around a woman (Millie) who steals her husband's manuscript and tries to pass it off as her own. She gets a significant deal, then needs to hire a bodyguard (I cast Ryan) to protect her from her murderous ex (Chris.) But the bodyguard, who seduces her, is a friend of the ex, and they both conspire to kill her.

Meh, it's a work in progress.

And yes, I am feeling maybe a tad homicidal toward Ryan's ex-wife. If Chris had sent anything I'd written to an agent without my approval I'd be devastated. Humiliated.

Ryan is such a good guy. He didn't press me on the driving thing even though he understood something must have happened on that road. He deserves to know. Today was the first time I've opened up to him and I know far more about him than he knows about me. The thing is, I don't talk about the accident anymore, not even with Sofia. With anyone. It was so long ago now that it feels like it happened to another person. But whenever my mind lands on that event, that excruciating part of my life, an agonizing pain pierces my chest.

Some of my friends have told me it might help to talk about it since my family refuses to discuss it. And as much as I've refused therapy or anything else that might lead me to talk about the event, tonight I want to talk about it. With Ryan.

I pick up my cell and dial his number. Ryan might like to

write his emotions, and maybe that's why he's a great author. But for me, some things need to be said.

Ryan picks up, sounding distracted as usual. "What."

Now I know this is his way of saying hello and don't take it personally.

"It's me. Luci."

"I know. Hello, Luci."

Oh, a hello! He's encouraging me. I can almost hear the smile in his voice and I smile back.

"Hey there. I'm calling because I have something…something I want to tell you. I want to explain."

There's silence and I realize Ryan is simply waiting. No prompts, like "yes?" Most people would wonder what I want to ask but that's not Ryan's way. It's as if he's a character in a book who doesn't put in a word of dialogue unless it advances the plot.

"See, there was an accident on Highway 17. A bad one. But it was nighttime, and raining, and someone wasn't driving safely. Someone was speeding."

Ryan is quiet, but I can feel him…waiting. "We don't have to talk about this. It's okay."

In this moment I sense a strange kind of permission. Not from him but from myself.

"It wasn't me. My father was in an accident on that highway and…that's how he died." I swallow the sob in my throat and a tear comes rolling down my cheek instead. I brush it away.

Ryan lets out a long breath. "I'm sorry. I shouldn't have pressed you. I shouldn't have brought it up."

"It's okay, after reading your book, you might be the only one who can understand."

Ryan knows about grief, or he couldn't have written about it so convincingly in his book. Yes, maybe it was just his incredible research, or maybe just writing about the end of a marriage, but he understands. He knows what it's like to have someone ripped away from your life. It might be better, somehow, if you're prepared. But when you're not expecting it, it comes straight to your soul like a slap, tearing into you, leaving pieces of your heart tossed everywhere.

"I understand more than you know," he says.

Ryan's voice is so sweet, so calm, so endearing. It feels like a hug.

Oh God, this block isn't working!

"That was the first time I'd ever driven that road," I say, biting my lower lip to keep it from quivering.

"I wouldn't have let you if I'd known that."

"I know. That's just the point. Maybe that's why I didn't tell you. It's not up to you. Sometimes, I'm learning, you have to face your fears."

"You're a far braver person than I am."

"I doubt that's true."

"Write about it. Put all that pain on the page. It's the only way."

He's not wrong. I need to stop holding back so much because it hurts.

"Ryan? I'm going to hang up and write now."

Afterward, my new words come easily, fingers flying across the keyboard. It's taken me all this time, but I finally know what's missing from my book.

My heart.

I think of true love like my parents had once. He was the love of her life until he was taken away. I need more of that emotion to drive me.

And then I write with my heart cracked and bleeding all over the pages.

CHAPTER 17

On Sunday morning, I wake clutching my laptop, still in the clothes I wore yesterday. I haven't pulled an all-nighter like this since I was a *teenager*. I've been writing all weekend and it feels so freeing.

Panicked, I make sure everything I wrote last night was saved. Only when I'm certain every word is right where I left it, I hook up my laptop to charge and make my way to the main house for coffee and a shower.

Abuelita will already be at mass with her friends. Sometimes Eddie takes her, sometimes he does not. But either way, he's never sacked out on the couch the way I find him now. I wonder now how long this has been going on.

"*Why* are you sleeping on the couch?" I ask him.

He rolls over and yawns. "I let your mami take my room. It just makes sense."

I sigh. Of course it would make sense to Eddie. He couldn't abide having a woman sleep on a sofa when there was a perfectly good bed available.

"I'm not here all that much," he protests.

"But having a bed to sleep in is the main reason you *live* here."

He waves it away. "She needs a bed more than I do."

"*You* have a bad back!"

"This couch is actually comfortable," he says but when he winces, I know he's lying.

"Riiight."

I wish my entire family wouldn't cater to my mother but I remind myself they're doing it for me. Because she's connected to me, and more importantly my father, and that's all it takes in the Santana home.

As usual, Abuelita has left café for us. She makes strong coffee, the closest thing to an espresso I'm going to have this morning and I need every milligram of caffeine in my bloodstream. I rattle around in the cupboard searching for my "best granddaughter in the world" cup but am forced to settle for an "I'd rather be watching a telenovela" mug.

A fully dressed Eddie joins me in the kitchen and I hand him the carafe. He looks like he needs the caffeine more than I do. While he pours his coffee, he gives me a look I've come to realize means he's about to give me a lecture.

I hold up my hand. "I was up late writing. That's why I look like this."

This means he should not bother me with anything trivial or nag me about my appearance. Sometimes Eddie can be just as bad as my mother with the exception that he's never mentioned my weight. But he's of the somewhat old-school opinion that a single lady should be ready to meet her possible Mr. Right at all times. Even in her own damn house. Obviously, I disagree.

He looks confused and shakes his head. "I want to talk to you about your mami."

"Oh, that." A lecture about my mother is not going to be much better, I fear.

"Mija, she is your mother, so *try* to be nice."

"I am nice! But it's not okay that she just shows up here like she has no other place to be. She's taking advantage of our hospitality."

"Did you ever stop to think she has nowhere else to go?" He narrows his eyes.

"How is that possible? She divorced Seb and if I know my mother she got a settlement. Besides, there's all the money she made in all her years of acting. Look at the way she dresses! Does she *look* penniless?"

"Neither one of us knows the whole story. Just be patient with her. You love your mother, and you can't pretend you don't."

"She's never been supportive. I don't know if she deserves my forgiveness."

"No one actually deserves forgiveness, but we give it anyway." Eddie lowers his head and gives me his saintly look possibly because it's Sunday. "That's who we are."

It's pointless to argue and I hold out my palms. "Fine, sure. I'll try to be better."

Mami appears in the doorway and we both turn to see her, hair perfectly styled, full makeup, wearing a dress that emphasizes the straight lines of her slender figure. Like Eddie, she's old-school and must be photo op ready at any moment.

"Buenos dias. Guess what? I haven't been able to fit into this dress for a while. The best thing about divorce is the diet," she says, then takes a seat at the kitchen table. "Eddie, would you pour me a café, por favor?"

I bite my tongue before I tell her to get it herself. She's not the queen. Naturally, Eddie pours her a cup and brings it to her the way he already knows she likes it. Black, like her soul. She curls her fingers around the warm cup, her manicure utter perfection.

"What are you doing today, mi amor?" she asks me, taking a dainty sip of her coffee.

"Writing," I say. "All day. I'm on a roll."

"Fantastic. Another little book? Eddie isn't it wonderful our Luci is a *New York Times* bestselling author?"

"I'm not sure whether we—I mean I, made the list yet."

"Yes, you did," she says, stirring her coffee. "I subscribe to the *Times*, and I saw it myself last week. *Soulmates*, by Elizabeth Brogan, that's your book right?"

"Oh my God. Really? He's…I'm on the list? Again?" My voice is a squeak.

It's been a week since the episode aired and between the excitement building around it the book made the list again.

"What number placement?" I ask. "Was it number one?"

I don't think we could dare to hope.

"Is that important? I don't remember," she answers. "Isn't that nice, Eddie?" She gives him a pointed look from under her long (and obviously fake) lashes.

"Yes, yes, of course. It's very nice."

It would help if Eddie or at least my mother understood what an *achievement* this means in any author's life. She seems unfazed, as though I won first place in a local writing contest, while I'm about to scream in delight.

"I have to make a phone call." I rush right out the kitchen back door toward the shed to call Ryan in privacy. "Um, I have to tell all my friends."

I can't believe he didn't bother to tell me. But as I'm changing and slipping on a pair of sandals, I decide I need to congratulate Ryan in person. This is a huge accomplishment for any author but especially one with what is, albeit technically, a debut. He must be thrilled and I can't even imagine what I'll find when I drive over to his home. This will be a celebration of sorts, so after I shower and dress, I stop by Michaela's Bakery, but it's Sunday so they're closed.

I don't need anything fancy and I'm not even sure flowers are appropriate. I drive all over town looking for the right gift, spending hours musing over sentimental cards, candy, and flowers. At Trader Joe's, I decide a plant is more appropriate. A happy plant, of course, so I choose basil because it smells good and can do double duty as food. And ballons, naturally. I have to go somewhere else for those and finally, thirty minutes later, I shove the "Congratulations" mylar balloons low into the back seat of my sedan. Each time they pop up, obstructing my rear view, I reach to push them back down.

I ring the doorbell twice since he won't be expecting me. I start to wonder if Ryan is home even though I see his rental parked, when he opens the door, a big smile on his face.

He holds his arms out in a greeting I've never seen from him. "Hello! It's you."

He *never* greets me like this and I'm a bit unnerved. First, I hand him the basil plant, which he accepts.

"Congratulations! I just heard the news."

"Yes! Come in!" He sweeps his arm wide in a flourish. "Welcome!"

He almost looks…happy. Or high. Guess making a list, a crowning achievement for authors, has a way of doing this to a person.

"Are you okay?" I narrow my eyes.

"I'm great! Why wouldn't I be? It's official. And I'm sure this plant…" He gestures.

"It's basil. An herb, so you can cook with it, too."

He gives the plant a sideways look. "Right and those… um…"

"*Balloons*," I say, feeling stupid now. A grown man doesn't need balloons. He's not twelve.

"Are all to congratulate me on making the list."

There's something different about Ryan. He's not clean-shaven this morning, a small amount of dark stubble covering his jaw and chin. But it isn't until I notice the amber liquid in a nearly empty tumbler, and glassy eyes behind his frames that I realize he's tipsy. In the middle of the day. On a Sunday.

"I thought maybe you'd call me when you heard the official news," I say, still holding the balloons and sitting down with them. They float above me like I'm their only tether. "I guess it happened last week?"

"Would you like a drink to celebrate?" He walks to the kitchen counter where he holds up an opened bottle of Scotch. "This is supposed to be the good stuff. Kate sent it via carrier."

I can't believe I brought a dude balloons and a plant. I should have brought *liquor*, of course.

"No, thank you. I'm…"

"Not a Scotch person?"

"No."

"You don't drink?" He squints his eyes as if I've just told him I like to skip uphill.

"I don't drink before *five o'clock.*"

I hold the balloons securely because this side of Ryan seems unnatural. I half expect to find he's been body snatched and that his body pod is lying around here in the back room somewhere.

"Me either but I'm breaking with tradition." He holds up his tumbler. "This is a monumental day."

"My mother gave me the news but I don't think she realizes what a big deal this is. She thinks *I* just made the *Times* list and didn't even suggest we celebrate."

"You should go celebrate with her." He points to me with his free hand. "This is your achievement too."

"No, it's not." I shake my head.

This time draws no comparison to when I *actually wrote a*

book for Desdemona that made a list. The publisher sent me a basket of flowers with a card that said, "thank you," the only acknowledgment I received or would ever receive. I celebrated my achievement quietly with my family. They thought I was celebrating getting a new contract.

When everyone in reader and writer circles was talking about the Desdemona book that made *The New York Times* for the first time in decades, I couldn't say a word. Now, I feel like a double impostor. It's worse, it turns out, to pretend you wrote the book when you didn't. At least before, I secretly knew my book, my words, had made the list. Now I'm taking credit I don't deserve.

Ryan takes a seat beside me, the balloons between us like a barrier. I only realize how many I have when he pushes several aside and gives me a long look.

"I sent a few chapters of my new book to Kate, the one you've been helping me research," Ryan says.

"You started writing it?" He hasn't shared that bit of news with me.

He nods. "I was inspired after our trip to Santa Cruz and stayed up all night. You were right. I needed to get out of the house for some inspiration."

"That's great," I say. "What did she think of it?"

"Kate kindly told me she hates it." He laughs and for the first time, I hear Ryan's deep scrape of a chuckle. "Isn't that funny?"

Okay, so this drinking isn't only celebratory. He might be indulging in a little self-pity. I'm familiar with rejection, and even if Ryan doesn't get many, surely it never gets any easier to hear your work leaves something to be desired.

"No, it's not *funny*. Why did she say that?"

Ryan gives me a look like he can't quite figure me out. "It lacks what *the book* has. Maybe I should write another book that reads like a poor sap's diary. It's pretty clear she's going to compare all my other work to that book from now on."

"Don't say 'that book.' It's good, Ryan, you know it's true."

I might hate the book because of the ending but even I can appreciate the stylistic writing. It's witty and emotional and doesn't pull any punches.

"Maybe. But I'll never write anything that great again, which was a fluke in the first place. What does that say about me?"

Tired of shoving balloons out of my line of sight, I get up and set them on the table like a centerpiece.

When I return, Ryan is seated on the edge of his seat, studying me. I feel something uncomfortably like a tingle wash over me. He has the most intense eyes and in that one crazy moment I want to kiss him. Just to make him feel better. He should know that even though he's had crushing heartbreak, followed by a staggering betrayal, he's not damaged goods. He's intensely attractive, young, and can still find love and be happy someday. Maybe this time it will be the love of his life.

It's as if he's reading my mind and his gaze softens a bit. "Luci. You're so kind. You are a lifesaver and I don't deserve you at all."

It's my chance to make light and I chuckle, shimmying my shoulders. "Well, who really does?"

"Only a great man. The best man alive." He holds his glass as if to salute this imaginary creature.

"When you meet him give him my number." I wink and give him a little shoulder check.

There's a slight quirk of his lips and then he downs the rest of his Scotch.

"Do you know how many times in my life I dreamed I'd have a book do this well? I lost count. And now that it's happened, I can't celebrate it."

"Of course you can! They are your words."

"They're not words I wanted to write. Ironically, in a way neither one of us can." He stares at the empty contents of his glass.

I see his point. For me, it's a half-hearted celebration because it's not my book. Not even my name, but the name of a fictitious person I'm pretending to be. It might be difficult to celebrate without feeling like a total impostor, but I'm up to the task. The face of Elizabeth Brogan, after all, is mine.

"You're wrong and I'll prove it. We can both celebrate." I stand. "We're going out to dinner, my treat."

CHAPTER 18

By the time I return hours later to pick him up for our celebratory dinner, Ryan has sobered up. More to the point, he's dressed sharply, like this is a real date. He's freshly shaven, wearing dark slacks and a blue dress shirt with the sleeves rolled up. He smells like the divine cologne scent I found in his bathroom while snooping.

This feels like a date! But I tell myself, of course, it's far more like a meeting between two colleagues.

"I'm driving," he says, heading to his rented sedan. "And you're not paying. Not until I get you that check."

Even more like a date.

"Uh…"

At my quirked brow, he says, "That was hours ago. Don't worry, I'm good to drive."

He's no longer smiling hugely so I believe him. He won't be too adorable for my comfort with his lowered inhibitions. Now I won't be tempted to inappropriately flirt, or vault over those temporarily low walls. The walls are back up where they belong. We can keep it professional. I would hate anyone to think Ryan hired me for this position because he found me attractive.

I decided to take Ryan to Osteria, the Italian restaurant that serves the best crunchy bread in the county of Santa Clara. It's always warm and delicious and the butter melts into the cracks. Tasting it is like an out-of-body experience.

"I'm what you might call a bread afficionado," I tell Ryan once we've been seated. "I thought I could visit the bakery where they buy their bread. Do you know they actually bake it here, on the premises? There's no way I can get *this* bread unless I come here. And of course, they have a lot more than good bread, which is the point."

Unfortunately I'm talking too much, which is something I always do when I'm trying to impress someone.

Ryan peruses the menu, removes his glasses, then slips them back on. "Is there anything other than bread you recommend?"

"The lasagna is fantastic, but you can't go wrong with any dish here. My ex used to love the linguini and clam sauce."

The moment I say it, I regret it. I don't want to think about Chris, much less mention him in casual dinner conversation.

Ryan meets my gaze and there's nothing but curiosity in them. "Is this a place you two came to often?"

I figure what the hell, tell him the truth. Why not. The memory of Chris isn't going to ruin this place for me anymore. I haven't been back since our breakup, the memories too fresh and raw. This is where he *should* have proposed, my favorite restaurant. I pictured him hiding the ring in my salad because he knows I tend to poke around and rearrange my food on the plate before I take a bite.

And there would be a shiny ring, Chris smiling as he went on bended knee. This was the way my father had proposed to my mother, but hiding the ring in a cupcake, a story I heard many times over the years. Instead, Chris proposed by taking the ring box out of his gym bag next to his dirty sweaty socks. At the *gym*.

"Because this is where we met," Chris had said proudly. "And now you'll have a good memory of this place because you need to come here more often."

When I gaped at him, he backpedaled: "For your health!"

"We didn't come here often," I admit now, checking the wine list. "But I want to wash him away with a new memory. This is perfect. Nothing will ever compare to this. You, sir, are a *New York Times* bestselling author. And so is Elizabeth Brogan, who happens to have my face."

"And what a face it is. We need champagne."

"I'm not sure you should be drinking, but I'll allow it." I wink.

"After all, it's past five." He quirks an eyebrow. "I had no idea you were such a stickler for rules."

The head waitress, Doris, interrupts. She's skilled at being right where you need her, and nowhere to be seen when you don't.

"Welcome in, you two," she says. "I haven't seen you for a while, Luci. How are you?"

"Hey there. This is my boss, Ryan Brady. He's an author from LA."

"Pasadena," Ryan corrects, but I'm afraid there's no difference for us northerners.

"Oooh. So far, Luci is the only author I've ever met." She gives Ryan a wide and welcoming smile.

"Well, there are actually a lot of us. We seem to be multiplying." I flip open the menu.

I catch a smirk from Ryan but Doris doesn't get the joke. "Shall I recite the specials?"

The specials are recited directly to Ryan, as if he's the only person at our table. Hell, the entire restaurant. I've never seen Doris work this hard for a tip and I'm annoyed when I realize she's openly flirting. She's tossing hair and licking lips. Ryan is oblivious.

Doris brings us a chilled bottle of champagne when he asks for their most expensive bottle. She pops it open, offers the first glass to Ryan for his approval. Only when he nods does she pour mine.

"To you," I say, raising my flute. "And your well-deserved success."

We clink our glasses together.

"See? Isn't this nice?" I lean forward. "You're allowed to celebrate the success of the book. I was taught to celebrate even little wins, and this was not a small one."

"It isn't that I don't appreciate what's happened, but it's disappointing when I don't think I can replicate it in the books I *want* to write."

"Look, maybe every author feels that way when they luck into writing something so popular. You wrote the book after a bad breakup, but that doesn't mean you can't do it again once you've healed. Just try to get back to that place in your mind."

"No thanks." He pinches the bridge of his nose as though the thought pains him.

"I meant, try to get in that emotional headspace."

He shakes his head like that's not something he can do. Ryan must have really loved his ex.

I'd love to have that type of devotion from a man. The only man I can ever recall behaving with such adoration for a woman was my father. Their marriage was the goal I strive for someday. He brought her daisies, her favorite flowers, every day just because and cooked dinner often after a full day of work, so she would not have to. I caught them dancing in the kitchen without music and more than once making out on the couch. This is the epic love story I want for myself someday. My father behaved like he knew what he had and was lucky to have it.

"Would you let me read the first pages of your new book? The ones Kate didn't like. I can offer some suggestions."

His eyes soften from the hard glint of a moment ago. "I appreciate that."

Ryan tells me about his younger brother, the doctor, the "successful one." I learn he's married, living in New Hampshire with a thriving family practice. Once a season, the brothers get together for the World Series. It's a passion they both share.

"Tell me about baseball," I ask.

He often stares out the window while palming a ball back and forth in his hands, much like a worry stone. There's a story there.

"Did you play in high school?" I press.

"Yes, not that I was any good. Funny thing is, I originally played little league to please my dad. He thought I had my head stuck in a book too much and needed fresh air and exercise." He snorts. "I deeply resented being torn away a few hours every week from my comic books and graphic novels but, ironically, I grew to love the sport. As a spectator."

"My dad took me to a Giants game when I was about eight. I was bored out of my mind and only later did I learn I'd been at a historic no-hitter. That's not my idea of fun. Sorry to throw shade on your sport."

"Not everyone appreciates a no-hitter. But it takes tremendous skill."

We go down the memory lane of other things in life that are not writing or story related. Ryan tells me about his base-ball card collection and how his first splurge after his advance was on a Jackie Robinson card.

I gape. Even I know who that is. "So *that's* where your advance went."

Ryan looks sheepish. "No. I got a great deal."

It's refreshing to see this side of Ryan. We don't talk about the book.

Dinner is a feast. The scents of Bolognese sauce, butter, and garlic waft in the air around us, our entrees artfully arranged and good enough to be photographed for a lifestyle site. Our meal is decadently delicious. We toast to our mutual success, and we eat, with plenty of bread for me. In fact, I ask for another basket. We discuss Ryan's latest novel, which has dual timelines and sounds fascinating.

I don't want to tell him, but the use of time in a novel is my jam, and the book I've finished is a time traveling romance. *The Time Traveler's Wife* was a huge inspiration to me as a teenager, but I've taken the idea in a different direction. I've invented a world in which time travel is the norm and two star-crossed lovers always seem to be in different timelines.

This is the novel Holly has heard about over the years and I wonder how I'll ever explain my change of direction. My work has always leaned toward fantasy and *Soulmates* is a straight up small-town contemporary romance.

I'm in the middle of buttering another piece of bread when I see something I never thought I'd see in a million years. It's enough to suck all the air out of me. A few booths away from us sits Eddie and he's not alone. He's with my *mother*. This wouldn't be so odd by itself, but when he reaches for her hand and kisses it I feel like I'm floating outside my body in some other parallel universe in which these two secretly like each other.

"Oh my God," I say, dropping the butter knife.

"What is it? Are you choking?" He's leaning forward, as if ready to jump across the table and Heimlich me.

When I left the house earlier, those two were both having

a chat with Abuelita, reminiscing old times. Lots of talk of my father, of course, and what a great man he was.

Now this. This! What is this fresh hell?

I cough and wave Ryan away. "No, no. I'm okay. Fine."

Except I'm not. I can't imagine why Eddie kissed my mother's hand. Wait. Hold on. Maybe I imagined it. It's true that sometimes my writer's brain can get carried away, but not like this. I've never *hallucinated* before. On the other hand, maybe there's a viable explanation. Eddie was simply checking her hand. Like, maybe she cut or bruised it accidentally and he was just making sure it was okay. With his *lips*.

Oh no, I think I'm going to be sick. I don't want them to see me, and everything in me is pushing me to run out of here, but I can't do this to Ryan. This is a celebration and not a time for me to deal with my chaotic family. This latest development qualifies under the heading of highly irrational. My mother hates Eddie and he only tolerates her because of me.

"I have to powder my nose," I say like a 1960s ingenue. "Be right back."

The only thing to do, once I close the bathroom stall, is text Sofia. She will know what to do.

Help! I'm at Osteria and I just saw Eddie and my mother together.

Sofia:

Why do you need help?

Me:

I mean they are together TOGETHER.

Sofia:

And...? I don't get it.

I really need to spell this out for her.

Me:

He kissed her hand!

A long pause as the bubbles form, meaning she's composing her response.

Sofia:

Are you sure? Because that IS weird.

Me:

I know! I'm here with Ryan trying to celebrate and I have to see this. It's ruined my appetite.

Sofia:

I suggest you go back to your celebration with Professor Hottie. There has to be some rational explanation for this. I think you should just go over there, say hi, and let them know you saw them. Their reaction is probably going to tell you a lot. It's probably nothing. Don't worry.

Sofia is a genius. She's right, of course. I *can* do this. I'll handle this matter delicately and with the utmost sensitivity. In other words, I'm going to pretend I didn't see what I did. It never happened. They are just eating dinner together and that is all. That's the end of it. And they're allowed to eat dinner together. I'm fine with it.

I wash my hands, study my face in the mirror, reapply my lipstick, and smooth down a wave of hair. I'm ready. But when I reach my table, I find that Eddie and my mother have joined Ryan.

Eddie waves. "There she is! We found your friend, and he said we should join you."

There's a seat next to Ryan so now I have to sit there instead of across from him as I had been. I see they've skillfully moved my plate and silverware. I would bet this is a matchmaking attempt on their part. They've obviously got romance on the mind.

I'm looking for tell-tale reactions from either one, but I see nothing. Neither Mami nor Eddie look the slightest bit frazzled. No deer-in-the-headlights, "you caught me" looks. There's a healthy distance between them, too, which I thoroughly appreciate. It's possible I've imagined this whole thing. Yes, I saw him bring her hand to his lips but the kiss is beginning to fade in shades of gray. He might have wanted to look a bit closer at a freckle or something. Maybe she's worried about skin cancer. Eddie is a dentist, not a doctor, but he shares an office with an MD and socializes with many of them. He knows things. I wasn't *that* close to them. It's possible I could have seen wrong. I should probably check my eyesight. Maybe I need glasses. What's that they say about eyewitness statements being the least reliable of all?

"How funny seeing you here," I say, giving my mother the stare-down. "I had no idea you two were going out."

"Eddie wanted to go out, and I wasn't doing anything," my mother says. "And now I got to meet your friend, the professor."

"He's a writer," I say. "And my employer."

"We're celebrating Luci's book. The one she wrote as Elizabeth Brogan," Ryan says, gently touching my hand.

My body tingles when he touches me. It's like something out of a romance novel. I used to believe it hyperbole, but it apparently happens.

"She made the *New York Times*!" my mother says, hand to her bosom, and it's possible between now and this morning she's discovered the magnitude of this. "I'm so proud."

"You should be," Ryan says. "She's amazing."

"Have you also sold many of your books?" My mother leans in.

Hmm, she's not calling them "little" anymore, or perhaps only my books qualify as something *cute* her daughter decided to do in her spare time.

"Oh, no. Not like that."

Ryan shakes his head and I bite down on a smile.

"Someday," my mother says encouragingly.

"It's a goal." Ryan nods.

"Selling a lot of books is not necessarily what makes you a good writer. Ryan writes historical fiction set mostly during World War II," I explain. "He's won awards."

"I adore historical fiction!" My mother reaches to cover Ryan's hand.

I'm surprised she reads at all unless it's a script sent for an audition. "You do?"

"*The Nightingale*," she says. "I cried for days."

I'm surprised since I also loved the book and cried for days. Ironically, these books about World War II authored by women are too often called "women's fiction" even if they qualify as historical fiction. It may be nothing more than a way to shelve books but it annoys me. There's no such thing as "men's fiction."

The waiter interrupts, asking us if there's room for dessert. I prepare to say no to cut this evening short, but Eddie wants crème brûlée and Ryan orders the lava chocolate cake.

"Should we share one?" Mami asks me, then speaks directly to Ryan. "Us women eat like birds but I don't want you men to partake alone."

"I don't eat like a *bird*," I say in defense of the sisterhood everywhere. "I'm ordering the coconut cake and I want my own."

Mami laughs. "You always had a big appetite. Just like your father."

I'm going to ignore that jab, because it's true, but Eddie doesn't let it go. "She's healthy and that's all that matters."

God bless Eddie. Eddie, who complains all the time that his patients eat way too much sugar. Even so, he's got my back. As the desserts are served, Mami goes on to talk about all the weight she's lost lately, dropping a dress size and weighing less than she did in her twenties. How and why she talks about her weight like it's an accomplishment, I'll never understand.

I'm now determined to enjoy every bite of this cake.

"Eddie, I'm surprised at you. All that sugar," my mother scolds. "You're a *dentist*."

"Take care of your teeth and you can eat anything you want, in moderation." He smiles and licks his spoon.

It takes me a moment to realize my thigh is brushed up against Ryan's. I'm suddenly so aware of him, his leg like a weight against mine. We always keep a physical distance on the job, and it's the first time I realize how intentional we've both been about this.

My mother is talking about weight training now, and how more muscle means a faster burning metabolism. Like I haven't heard that one before. The woman is obsessed. I swear if I hear one more word, I'll spontaneously combust, hopefully into white granules of sugar, and rain down on my mother while she screams in holy terror.

Ryan gives me a sidelong glance and half smile in the midst of this diatribe and at that point I realize our knees are touching, too. The feeling and warmth of a man this close is something I forgot how much I miss. He's even closer now and I want to imagine he did this for the emotional support. We both understand rejection, both literary and romantic, but maybe he also understands this part of my life, too. He thought my family was so perfect but now he's met my mother. She is the crack in our family.

Ryan hasn't said a word but I know he sees me and that's enough.

After dinner Ryan and I part ways with Eddie and my mother. The insecurity I felt seeing them together is gone, replaced with the assurance that Eddie and my mother are simply old friends catching up. They're bound together forever for the mutual love of one man, and me, his daughter. The rest of it I was imagining and it's not surprising my overactive brain would do this. I've been under an incredible amount of stress lately.

I'm still thinking of Holly and what I should tell her. I'm sure Ryan's publisher assumed everyone who knew me would think I'd taken on a pen name to write the book. But Holly is my closest writing friend, my critique partner, and I would have had to be lying to her all this time. Even the good things happening now are stressing me out. It's as if I can't simply accept the fullness of my life because it always comes with another complication. I want to relax and enjoy this but I keep waiting for something else to go wrong.

"Do you mind if we walk a little first?" Ryan says, holding the door to the restaurant open for me.

I'm more than willing to do this, because this stretch

along University Avenue is easy walking, even if you couldn't call Seven Trees a walking city. As we walk, Ryan doesn't say a word. It's like he's left an open space. But when I don't fill it, he does.

"Want to explain what was going on in there?" He hooks a thumb to the restaurant now behind us.

I'm too embarrassed to admit what for a few moments I thought I saw. I have to be wrong.

"My mother and Eddie?"

"You, rage eating your dessert."

He didn't even notice Eddie and my mother being anything more than family, and that encourages me. I've been reading far too much into this.

"Rage eating? That's a new one." I chuckle. "Thanks to my mother, I've had a complicated relationship with food."

"Yeah? How so?"

"She likes to pretend she doesn't eat and I'm rather fond of it. I eat what I like in moderation. But when I'm around my mother, I probably eat more than I would normally. We have a difficult relationship. After my father died, I felt pretty abandoned. She took off to have the career she always wanted. Unfortunately, she is obsessed with body image and I'm not."

He nods and I remember that he also has a complex family dynamic.

"What about you? Do you get along with your mother?"

"Other than the fact she's continually trying to fix me up with the daughter of a friend?"

"Well, you're a catch. I can't say I blame her."

We walk quietly along the tree-lined sidewalks, which are old enough to have cracks in them.

"You look like your mother." His voice is soft, almost tender.

"I know."

I grunt my acknowledgment. It's the story of my life, the physical manifestation of myself so at odds with who I am inside, and who I want to be. In other words, nothing like her.

"Is she visiting? I didn't see her at the party."

"She showed up last week but I don't expect her to stay long. She tends to flit in and out of my life. This time, she's gone through a divorce." I chuckle. "You won't believe this, but tonight I thought I saw Eddie kissing her hand. But he's my father's older brother. They've always barely had a tolerance for each other."

"Enemies to lovers," he says without hesitation. "And falling for your brother's widow, not quite as popular."

I hold my hand to my heart. "No, not *those* two, but can I say I'm proud you know these tropes?"

The skies darken and the streetlights flash on as we walk down the sidewalk, past storefronts with outside seating and striped parasols. It's the weekend in a university town, so we see plenty of young people.

Seven Trees is quaint, comparatively small with San Jose to the south and San Francisco to the north. It has a youthful vibe while also being the center of tech giants. There's the hum of conversations, laughter, and live music coming from the bar across the street. We keep walking and settle into an easy silence. Ryan turns down a side street, hands in the pockets of his slacks, occasionally glancing up.

He stops walking just before we enter a crosswalk, and groups of students go around us.

"Have you thought any more about writing a sequel?" I ask.

"No," he says.

"Ryan, your readers deserve one."

"This may sound ungrateful, but I want to be able to write the kind of book that moves people the way *Soulmates* did.

Without writing a sequel. And without writing any more romance."

It must be why Kate's remarks about his proposal cut him deeply.

"You'll do it, if that's what you want."

"Careful," Ryan says, taking my hand.

A bicyclist passes by us, coming out of nowhere, and Ryan pulls me toward him. It's just an instant, a moment of his touch, but I'm in the crook of his arm and a little surprised by the way my pulse quickens. Something tells me it isn't the danger of a near miss with a cyclist in a hurry to get somewhere that's raised my heart rate. It's Ryan, this close, his delicious smell, noticing that despite the fact he doesn't technically work with his hands, they're strong enough to move me out of the line of fire.

He's holding me, his indigo blue eyes studying me for several long seconds, until I finally push back.

When I catch my breath, and we start to walk again, I ask, "Are you Grayson?"

"What? No, of course not. He's a *character* I invented."

"But we all do this to a point, there's something of me in each of my characters. I think there's a lot of you in him. You're Grayson. He doesn't get the girl."

"Some people might decide Grayson worked *too* hard to get Lula. That maybe a love so unbalanced and one-sided could never result in *happily ever after*." He held up air quotes for the last three words, which I did not appreciate.

I mock scowl. "All I want is the end of the story. Please. You can't just leave a reader hanging."

"Luci, I am *not* writing a sequel. Never and that's final. Everyone, including you, is going to have to accept that."

"But—"

"Did you ever think the beauty of the book is in the fact it's not finished? And never will be?"

"No." I shake my head. "That's not it."

He groans. "Why don't you write it then, since you want it so much?"

"Maybe I will." The words come out of me in a huff.

I don't actually want to write this book. Now that the Desdemona window is closed, it might be time to sell my own book. Ryan's generosity should allow me a couple of months in which I can focus on nothing but my writing so I can revise it into perfection and start the querying process all over again.

"The problem is the book was a fluke. There's no way to replicate that kind of success," Ryan says. "Too much luck involved."

"But romance books are still bestsellers," I say. "I admit I'm biased."

"When did you fall in love with romance books?"

"I suppose that's my longest relationship, so, thanks for asking." I step up my stride to meet his. "We've been together close to two decades. I was probably twelve when I snuck the first paperback from my Tia Carmelita's stash. And, you'll be proud to know, it was a historical."

"I'm impressed."

I nod. *Whitney, My Love* by Judith McNaught. It's a classic. I graduated to my monthly Harlequins, Nora Roberts, and the amazing Susan Elizabeth Phillips. Really, anything I could get my hands on because at twelve, I was not supposed to be reading 'those books.'"

"Nothing quite like banning a book for making it soar."

"But I came by love of romance honestly. My mother and father were the best examples of true love. Whenever I give my mother the benefit of the doubt, I try to understand how difficult it must have been to lose the love of her life."

"Tell me about your father."

"Well, he was Hispanic, and everything you might

imagine that sometimes goes along with all that. A little bit of a macho man, kind of old-school. He was left-handed and played on a left-handed acoustic guitar. And he also told me stories, very long ones in which I was a princess saving the world with a toad named Joe."

Ryan chuckled. "Sounds like you inherited something from him even if not his looks."

"He was a born storyteller."

"Do you also think it's overwhelming? Intimidating to know your parents had the perfect relationship?" he says. "That they were the center of each other's world?"

Until he mentioned it, I wasn't aware that could ever be the case.

"Not really. In my books, I try to give them the happy ending they should have had." I pause, then ask, "Were you serious about me writing the sequel?"

"Were you serious about helping me put a little romance into my spy novel?" He quirks a brow.

"I hardly think I need to tell *you* how to do that, but yes. If you want me to, of course I will."

"We'll start Monday. You'll read what I've written so far. And we'll go from there."

"Yay!" I do a little hop skip in the middle of the street to make Ryan give me the smile he rarely bestows. And yes, I get it.

WHEN I GET HOME, my mother and Eddie are in the living room with Abuelita streaming a telenovela. I was raised on the drama of these, and yet I don't understand the continued fascination. I've outgrown them. There's plenty of melodramatics and characters who've been thirty for twenty-five years. Kids, meanwhile, who go from age ten to twenty in a year or two. At the moment, there's an amnesia story going on, which has all three of them on the edge of their seats. What a cozy scene.

"Any mail for me today?" I ask.

"Shhh!" Abuelita says.

"Excuse me," I mutter under by breath, finding the basket where they usually stack my mail.

"I knew it!" my mother exclaims.

"No, no," Abuelita says. "That can't be her husband. He's lying, that's what I think."

"Mami, why would the man lie about that?" Eddie says.

"Mijo, because she's beautiful and he wants her to be *his* wife!" Abuelita says, like d-uh.

"Exactly," my mother says.

Eddie is silent, clearly outnumbered.

I'm looking through my boring mail filled with nothing but bills when Mami joins me by the kitchen. "Anything exciting?"

"Nope."

Mami leans in close. "I want to ask you for a favor. Go with me to a singles event," she says.

"What? No way!"

"Why not? I can see how lonely you are and finding someone new is the best way to get over an ex."

"I am *not* lonely and I don't need anyone. You're talking about yourself. Why don't you sign up for Tinder or one of those later in life silver-haired dating apps?"

She gives me her pouty look. "They're not safe. Besides, I prefer the old-fashioned way. Face to face."

She has a point and I for one will never swipe right. All those apps go about love in the wrong way. Trust me, I'm a romance writer, I know these things. I'm delighted, too, to be wrong about my mother and Eddie. There's nothing there and I should have known. A man getting together with his brother's widow is just too weird. The thought fills me with relief and I suppose if Mami finds someone new, that will further cement the fact Eddie would never be an option, even in a weird alternate reality. I consider the idea because I should encourage her.

"What *kind* of singles event?"

"Abuelita's parish is putting it on, so you know it will be safe. Lots of Catholic singles mingling, looking for love. What could be better?"

I think I'd rather put my honey-covered hand into an ant hill but nevertheless, it sounds like at least not too much funny business will be going on. Still, I'm a bit shocked by the implications. My mother is looking for a nice single man in *my* town. I'm not sure how this will shake out. She's never going to settle for a long-distance relationship.

"I guess you're staying. How much longer?"

"As long as Eddie and Abuelita will have me. This is home, and *you're* here." She pushes a lock of my hair back, but it's a gentle move, with no comments on the length for once. "There's no place I'd rather be."

She's trying, and it's incredibly annoying. I have too much on my plate to indulge her. I have research to do, Ryan's proposal to critique, a sequel to write. An apartment to find.

"Fine. I'll go with you. But I won't be staying long. I absolutely am *not* looking for love! And that's final."

CHAPTER 20

When Monday arrives, Ryan hands me a check the moment after I walk through the door.

After two weeks, it's my first official paycheck but when I open it there are a few too many zeroes. "What's *this*?"

He squints. "I'm no accountant, but it looks like a check."

"But I didn't expect this much."

He's again sitting at the dining table in the middle of his mess. There's a laptop open in front of him but he still takes a moment to look up and nod.

"I added more than we originally agreed, since that was before you decided to help save my reputation." He picks up the coffee I've brought him. "Did you get my order right this time?"

Once. I got his order wrong once and I still blame the barista.

"I'll try not to be offended by your lack of faith." I cross my arms as he takes a sip. "It's been right the last two times. Black, two creams, no sugar."

He nods and goes back to his laptop.

I have much to do, like check my emails for anything

Pepper has scheduled for Elizabeth. I've got interview questions to answer from a major book influencer who has asked to do a podcast about me. I'm firmly in my Elizabeth Brogan era and interested in seeing how it all works from the side of an author who's been successful.

And I should really respond to Holly's email. Late last night, I came up with a plausible explanation.

To: inthequerytrenches@yahoo
From: theghostwriter@hotmail
Re: WTAF
Dear Holly,

I'm so sorry I didn't tell you any of this, but this was one of those "sooper" secret projects you hear about sometimes. You know, all that vague publishing news? The agent and publisher asked me not to talk about it. I didn't tell anyone, or I would have told you! I couldn't let anyone know because I was so nervous about writing a book only from the hero's POV. It's different from anything I've ever done, as you will see when you read it. Please forgive the oversight. I want to share everything I can with you now, so please ask me anything. As you can imagine, I honestly never thought to dream this big.

That a lie. Unlike so many other authors, apparently I dream big. Then I realize I should say something far more important.

By the way, I'm no longer getting married. Sorry I lied. It's been six months now, but that's why I've gone IG silent. Chris decided he wanted to join the Peace Corps instead of getting married. I thought he was being magnanimous but he actually met a woman at the coffee shop we frequented. And he went with her. So, there you have it. I'm a romance writer without a man. Is that an oxymoron? Also, please forgive me.

I revise the email about three times, more than I ever do with Holly, but I finally hit send.

Now, I need to thank Ryan. Properly.

I sit on the chair beside Ryan to get his attention and eventually have to clear my throat for him to look up. "Your generosity. It's more than I could have hoped."

"You mean from a guy who went on a rant about romance books?" He smirks. "You're working for me; I have to pay you. It's the law."

"But you didn't have to pay me *this* much."

"Does this mean your situation will be better now?"

"It's as if a year's worth of savings dropped in my lap."

"Good. I don't think it's fair what your ex did. I'm glad I can be the one to help fix it."

"Get ready, professor, because a hug is incoming," I warn him with a twitch of my finger.

"O-kay," he says slowly, drawing out the word. "But not necessary."

I expect this to be deep in the awkward zone of human hugs but I'm going to do it anyway. I'm already sitting next to him, so all that's required is to move closer and throw my arms around his shoulders. I don't even have to move all that close, turns out. Somehow the distance between us has lessened and the hug is easy. Effortless. That's when it occurs to me Ryan *leaned*. He leaned in for the hug and it's the same lean we discussed the day on the beach, *when a man is interested*. Does he even *realize* he leaned in? It's probably my loneliness that's reading a lot more into this. Maybe, for once, my mother is right.

The hug takes longer than I expected, as his embrace is warm and firm, his arms pausing to linger on my waist. I don't want to stop touching him and at this moment it has nothing to do with his generosity. It has to do with the way he smells of fresh clean soap and rays of sunshine. I have to stop, eventually, and I do, but not before there's a small moment between us when I pull away.

I catch something in his gaze I haven't seen before, which,

in any other man, I'd call desire. Longing. But I'm sure this is more of my active imagination working. I simply have a ridiculous crush on a man who's attractive, knows how to apologize, loves books, and is generous to boot. I need to leave it at that. Perhaps *technically* he's my dream man, but this can't go anywhere so it's best to squash this fantasy.

I abruptly stand and walk to the other side of the table "I better get started answering those interview questions for the podcast. They sent them ahead of time."

Ryan shoves a stack of papers toward me. "That's what I've written so far, the stuff Kate hates."

"She did not hate it, but I'll take a look." I flip through the pages, anxious to read.

"And after that," he says with a bit of a smirk. "You might want to start plotting the sequel to the book. I'm not telling Kate, but if you can write something similar enough to what I wrote, I don't see why you can't be the one with the next contract. Elizabeth Brogan doesn't *have* to be a one-hit wonder if you'd like to continue writing under the name."

I try to imagine taking over as Elizabeth Brogan in perpetuity. It wouldn't be any different from authors who take on a nom d' plume. It would be the opportunity of a lifetime, and I can't refuse to consider it. If I do, it comes down to being too precious. I don't want to copy his voice and that would never work anyway. But if I don't at least try to write the sequel I so desperately want to happen I'll never forgive myself. I'm obviously not going to convince *him* to do it.

"What if we do it together?" I ask.

His brow furrows. "Do what together?"

"Write the book. The sequel."

He groans. "Not me. I thought *you* would be happy about this."

"Hang on, you haven't heard my suggestion. I'll do the

hard work, but I just want your input. I'm awful at plotting a straight contemporary so you can edit, and I'll write."

He seems to consider it then shrugs. "Long as I don't have to write it."

We both get to work and a couple of hours later, I've finished answering the questions for the podcast and trying my best to make my boring life sound fascinating. It's not easy but fortunately I write fiction.

"I have to run an errand," Ryan says as he's gathering his keys and wallet. "If I'm not back in a couple of hours, I'll see you tomorrow."

"When you get back, I'll have my comments on your pages."

"Great," he says and is out the door.

His "great" didn't sound all that enthusiastic if I'm honest. Either way, I don't take it personally. Instead, I dive into Ryan's new story. I'm immediately drawn to the main character, who's working in the shipyards of Richmond during war time. Ryan is particularly skilled at bringing a setting to life, a weakness of mine.

But it isn't until chapter two that he introduces another main character who clearly has possibilities of being *the* love interest. As I read on, it becomes unclear whether or not these two will actually be involved. I furiously write notes in the margins of how Ryan might improve the connection.

"Remember the lean," I write in the column and add a wink emoji. He will know what I mean. He's got to add in movements and gestures that will indicate the first level of interest from the hero. It can be hand holding, hugging, any kind of touching before the kiss that changes things.

My phone pings while I'm editing, a text from Pepper.

Please don't worry about the latest trade review and if you can possibly hide it from Ryan, do. I know the critic, and he doesn't like anything. No big surprise or loss here. Sales are still stellar.

Okay, what? I drop what I'm doing and follow the link she provided to read the review:

The latest splash in the romance world fails in many ways.

I don't know where to begin. Yes, it's a different concept. Tell the story from the lovesick hero's point of view. But honestly, this mess is like reading someone's diary, first person point of view included. There's little plot, and what there is of it is a tough slog. I'm not surprised it hits all the feels for those interested in angsty and emotional journeys but it would help if it were well written, at least. Even the title makes me cringe. Soulmates? There is no such thing, as our poor and utterly ineffective hero soon discovers. The woman he loves is a shrew even if he can't see it. Finally, we have a woman writing a man's point of view but as with almost all romance, it does not at all realistically portray the man. I have to give this my lowest grade. D-

D minus? What? What! Ridiculous! The reporter writes like a pompous ass, which I have no doubt he is. There are some critics that enjoy ripping apart something that's popular with readers. Sometimes there's a great deal of professional jealousy involved, but I've definitely got to hide the review. It's more than ironic since the book *was* written by a man, only by a man who isn't a neanderthal like this lovely critic appears to be. But that's not the point. Bad writing? He's absolutely dead wrong. Even when I hated the book, I loved the prose.

But he does make a point that hadn't occurred to me until now. *Why* did Ryan choose a woman's pen name when the book was written in a male point of view? I hadn't known this when I agreed to be Elizabeth and I never did get a straight answer out of him. He and his publisher could have chosen another male pen name and simply hired an actor. I have questions. So many questions.

I fire off a text to Pepper:

Why did Ryan choose a woman's pen name?

Pepper replies:

I think you should ask him that question. It's complicated.

Complicated? Now she's piqued my curiosity.

Why? Someone he knows?

Pepper ignores the question.

There's also an email from Pepper, sent yesterday:

I'm just putting on the finishing touches for a book signing at the local indie bookstore in Seven Trees. They've been very supportive, even if they usually don't host romance books. But with the success of Soulmates, they couldn't resist. Working on a date but will be in touch via email. I'm already posting teasers on your website.

A *book* signing. They'd warned me this could happen. It's one thing to have performed in front of the monitor with only Ryan for company, knowing any mistakes would be edited out. It will be quite another to be live and in person with actual people. I wonder if they will ask me to speak. I'm one of those people that would rather die than speak in public.

For the next hour, Ryan gone, I put everything else out of my mind and flesh out some ideas for a sequel. It has to be said that I also fight my desire to snoop in his bedroom. But I can't bring myself to breach that line, even if I imagine something significant to Ryan is in the room where he sleeps. Looking around, I see he's added nothing to Professor Henry's décor other than paper and research books, of which there are already plenty.

It all says that Ryan is a short timer here, which I already understood.

When it's time for me to go, Ryan hasn't returned, so I leave him my notes on his proposal and lock up.

. . .

SOFIA HAS MANAGED to talk me into going out tonight and so I drag myself to Sliderbar expecting I'll have to watch her flirt with someone. Flirting is her art and she loves showing off. But if she reads my books, I'll go ahead and watch her flirt. It's only fair to support her art.

When I arrive, she waves me over to a booth.

I sit on the opposite side. "I'm not staying long."

"Why not?" The sound of her voice comes out like a whine.

"Because I'm not interested in flirting with anyone tonight or finding someone new."

She pouts. "When are you going to be interested?"

"Does it matter?"

"Yes, it does, because you're too young to be sidelined with permanent heartache."

"I'm not *sidelined* and it's not permanent. It's only been six months."

"But when are you going to get back on the horse?"

"Maybe I should first figure out why in the world I chose to be with Chris in the first place. He was all wrong for me. A gym bro when I'm an introverted intellectual. He didn't even like to read books. I should have known then we were doomed. Was I that desperate not to be alone? Because that makes me sound too much like my mother!"

"Hmm. Well, he's handsome and has a job unlike some other guys you've dated."

"Like that's enough? I wanted sparks. I wanted—"

"What your parents had."

We're quiet for a moment, both of us, because we both know it's true. I've been so busy chasing after a fantasy, a moment in time, that maybe what I'm missing is something real.

"What about professor McHottie?" She bats her eyelashes.

"Did it ever occur to you that true love might be right in front of you?"

That's a bit of a cliché but I'm going to let that go because I know she's trying to speak my language.

"We'd be a workplace romance," I explain. "But weirdly enough, while that's cute in a romance book, in real life it can result in a lawsuit. I'm sure Ryan wants to avoid one of those."

"Oh my gosh, just tell him you'll never sue and kiss him silly!"

"No. I'm not going to ruin our working relationship."

That's the trouble with real life. Tropes aren't as cute and endearing because you have to live with the ramifications. If only I could live in a romance novel. Life would be perfect. I picture my father dipping my mother in the kitchen while they danced and I giggled. They were perfect. Doesn't anyone else get that? Why can't I have it?

"Your mami is the most beautiful woman in the world," Papi would say. "And she married me!"

"I've been thinking about what you said the other night," Sofia says, pulling me out of my memory. "And I talked to my mother about old times. She wants to get together with your mother. She says they have a lot to talk about."

"I didn't think they even liked each other."

"I'm not sure they do, but Mami said something interesting when I was over for dinner. Apparently your mother met *Eddie* first."

"That's common knowledge. They were both at university together. But then she saw my father and the rest is history. They fell head over heels in love."

"Yes, but you realize she was more than friends with Eddie when they met. She dated him."

"What?" It comes out like a sputter. "You must be wrong about that."

That's not right. It's not the story I've been told.

"What's the big deal? It wasn't serious, and she obviously much preferred your dad. She settled down with him, she loved *him.* You're not wrong about your parents. They had the great love story."

"But…why didn't anyone ever *tell* me this?"

"Ancient history. There's no reason to talk about it unless you're like my mami and love to gossip."

Tia Carmelita does love to gossip.

"Maybe."

But having either imagined or actually seen what I did, I can't deny this new information bothers me.

I don't love anyone messing around with the picture I have in my head of my parents and the love story set in stone in my mind. First love, true love, soulmates. This is the story that plays in my mind when I imagine a forever kind of love.

This is the story I don't ever want to let go.

CHAPTER 21

*I*t's a few days later when I bump into Ryan at Piazza's on Charleston *grocery shopping*. It's a shock to my system because he's out of place in this setting. It's like seeing your doctor at a coffee shop, or your irritating misogynist boss cuddling with his wife at the movie theater. It doesn't quite compute. I join him in the produce aisle where he's loading a carton of grape tomatoes into his basket.

I need to ask him about Elizabeth's name and between his writing hours and my research hours, a good time to bring it up hasn't come up. Particularly since I want to make sure he doesn't read the editorial review, the one that derides a woman from writing a man's point of view. He's going to be sorry he didn't go with a man's name. So far, if he's seen it he hasn't mentioned it.

"Hi," I say now, sidling up next to him.

"What are *you* doing here?" he says, with his infamous eyebrow quirk.

"Skydiving," I deadpan. "You?"

"It's open-mike night and I'm thinking about trying out some new material."

Damn, his is better!

"I like doing this," he says. "What else can we pretend to be doing instead of grocery shopping?"

"Writing?" I snort.

"Writing is hard. You know what's easier? Juggling apples while riding a bicycle over a tightrope. And the bicycle is on fire. *Everything* is on fire."

"It sounds like you mean that. The book isn't going well?"

I'd left him my notes and they were encouraging. His opening is excellent, truly riveting, and I don't quite understand why Kate "hates it." The truth is she probably doesn't hate it at all. Still, I did what I could, adding areas here and there where he could layer in more emotion with his love interest. If there's anything I agree on with Kate, it's that those layers seem stilted when compared to *the book*. But probably *everything* does in comparison. Kate will just need to accept this is a different kind of book and that's okay too.

He doesn't reply, simply studies the label on a carton of cotton candy grapes, as if there's anything interesting to read there. Not exactly riveting material.

"There can't possibly be cotton candy in here, but why are they so sweet?" He throws one in his basket.

I ignore that because I can't help. I don't know why, either, but I add one in my basket too.

"I mean, you can't have every book be *Soulmates*. That would be boring. Didn't you get anything from my notes?"

He nods. "They were good but I'm stuck."

Hoping I don't come off like a stalker, I follow him down the fruit section. I start stocking my cart with cut-up melons, pineapple, and peaches.

"You're going to think this is a weird question, seeing as

it's a little late in the game now. But since I hadn't read the book when you asked me to be Elizabeth, now I wonder why you didn't just take on another male pen name? It was written from the male's perspective."

"Kate and the publisher thought it might make a more intriguing marketing angle."

That sounds like a reasonable answer. You could put everything I know about marketing inside a flea's home, so I can't argue the point. It probably was a stroke of marketing genius. The truth is if *Soulmates* had a man's name attached to it, it wouldn't be called "women's" fiction and it probably wouldn't be called a romance, either. It would be shelved as commercial literary fiction.

Ryan picks up a carton of blueberries. "And Elizabeth Brogan is a family name, so I used it."

That makes sense, but I admit I expected more information. It feels like Pepper could have told me that, but she didn't. However, more pressing at the moment is Ryan's apparent writer's block, which I dare not mention out loud. He's the superstitious sort, probably coming from the love of baseball.

"Okay. Get this. I have an idea for the sequel. And I think, if I say so myself, it's pretty damn brilliant," I say.

"Excuse me," a loud voice behind us says. "Are those organic berries you're standing *right in front of?*"

It's only then we both realize we've been chatting for far too long. Ryan is the first to move out of the woman's way. I don't usually have entire conversations with people at the grocery and am in fact frequently annoyed by people who do. I push my cart to a less bustling section and beckon for Ryan to follow me, which he does.

"The sequel is written entirely from Lula's point of view!" I hold my arms out like, "ta-da!"

Ryan is pensive for a moment, stroking the beard he used to have. He's got stubble again. While I wasn't fond of the full beard, I have to admit this look works for him. And if I'm to go by the attention he's getting from the females in the store, it's working for all of them under forty. Even the white-haired woman not far from us is checking Ryan out.

"I mean, it worked for *50 Shades*."

He still doesn't respond.

"Well, what do you think?" I press when he hasn't spoken for a few seconds.

"I think it could work beautifully as long as I don't have to write it."

But I have my own set of fears that I'll be able to write something to follow up the success of *the book*.

"Do you think Kate will go for it?"

"I think *anything* that means she'll get a sequel is going to be just fine with her."

"Don't mention it until we've fleshed out the plot and have a strong beginning."

"All she expects from me next is my contracted book. The one that isn't going well."

"Is there anything I can do to help you get…unstuck?" I gaze at him from the condiment aisle. "Did my notes help at all?"

"They helped, and you're right. The new book lacks the sentiment of *my old book*."

I notice how he won't even say the title anymore. The distance he's created is getting wider.

"I didn't say that."

"But you meant it."

He looks at me with those unbearably sad eyes, and grief and loss slam into me.

"You helped me a lot the other night when you reminded

me we need to write without a safety net. Maybe that's what's happening to you now. You're being too safe. Too cautious because you've had such massive success. It's got to be intimidating."

I can see he's mulling over the idea in his mind and I count this as a small victory.

WHEN THERE'S a knock on my shed door that evening, I'm surprised to find my mother. Since I got back from the store, I've been writing, alternatively thinking about Ryan, the Elizabeth Brogan family name, and losing track of time.

"Is that what you're wearing?" Mami scans me up and down.

I'm wearing yoga pants and a sweatshirt. It's my writing uniform and I can do without the judgment.

"*Why* do you ask?"

"It's singles night at the parish! Did you forget?" She's wearing her standard sleek pantsuit, black this time, accentuated with red lipstick, purse, and matching heels.

"I changed my mind. I don't want to go." I attempt to shut the door.

She pushes it open. "You *said* you would come with me. I need you for protection."

"Protection?" I shove my hands on my hips. "It's at a church."

"Protection from *myself*. You know I make lousy decisions when it comes to men."

I can't deny this when my mind goes back to oily Seb. If I want her to pick a good man who could at least be *half* the man my father was, maybe I should go along and screen the prospects. Naturally, as a child, I would have loved to be given a choice. And I'm always better at doing this for others than I am for myself. Mami is obviously serious about this. It's not like she can live her life without a *man.* If she's going to stick around—and maybe that wouldn't be the worst thing to ever happen—I have to save her from herself.

"Fine!" I throw my palms up. "I'll be ready in a minute and no comments about what I'm wearing. You're lucky I'm going to wear real pants. *I'm* not the one looking to find a man."

She waves her hand dismissively. "Whatever you say."

I hook a thumb to my chest. "And I get final say on these men or *I won't do it.*"

"Yes, yes."

Once we arrive, park, and walk inside, it's a good thing I'm not looking to find the love of my life here. First, I don't find this romantic in the least. It has the ring of true desperation. Second, everyone here is much older than me. They're using the same room they use for bingo, and the entry fee is a donation for their worldwide charities. Even though I plan to sit in the wings and judge the men to my heart's delight, I pay an entry fee since these days I feel like I actually have money. They've got everyone sitting around a large table, and a timer that goes off every fifteen minutes.

I won't be surprised if the two organizers at the front announce "bingo" at the changing of the guard. They're both standing up there looking expectantly at the couples, like someone here is going to stick and they'll have a wedding soon. They're the kind of couple who are so aggressively happy together they can't stand to see people *choosing* to be alone. Like me. At least they are giving them fifteen whole minutes but I don't see how you can be sure you want to get to know someone better after such a short time.

Still, I want to tell my mother she should simply accept she'll never find anyone like my father again. She had her love story and maybe that's all she'll ever have. Maybe it's greedy to want more. Anyone else and she'll have to settle.

My mother turns on the charm to triple wattage and I swear every man she meets is ready to propose marriage tonight. It would be odd to stand behind her and listen in to the conversation, so for my purposes, everyone is going to be a resounding "no" tonight. It's good practice for her in understanding how *not* to settle.

The timer rings. "Switch tables! Next topic of conversation: Are you a cradle Catholic or a convert? And, go!"

Wow. Such riveting subjects. *So* controversial. I wonder what the odds are this leads to more than two minutes of conversation. They should ask their thoughts about World War II or ask for the title of their favorite book. Something important.

My phone buzzes in my pocket and there's a text from Chris:

Am coming home ahead of schedule. Can you pick me up at the airport tomorrow?

Is he serious? Me, the rejected fiancée, is supposed to give him a ride home. This is some kind of cosmic joke, happening simply because I've stepped inside a church for the first time in years. Instead of striking me dead, God is playing a joke on me because what so many people say is true: He has a sense of humor.

I reply:

You can't be serious. Why don't you ask Nadia?

Chris's response is brief:

Didn't I say we'd talk more when I got back? Please, Luci, otherwise I have to call my parents.

I snort-laugh. He has an army of friends. *And* we broke up. I text back:

Take rideshare like a normal person.

I slip my phone back into my pocket and will ignore any

further buzzing. Chris can buzz off. The one thing I will say about my experience with Ryan is that it's taught me a lot about true love. I don't see why I should ever settle for less than a man who makes me feel like I'll die without him. If I do nothing else while she's here, I want to make my mother feel the same.

It's not until I'm at the back of the room where they keep the coffee machine that I spot him. There's Eddie, sitting at a table talking to an attractive forty-something woman. He doesn't see me when I wave, that's how deep in conversation he is with the woman. I shouldn't be surprised Eddie is here since Abuelita would encourage him to attend if nothing else to support the parish. I never thought he wanted to get married and this is a settling-down place to meet a possible mate. It's not fair of him to get the hopes up of all these desperate single women.

When they have their "bio" break, I sidle up to Eddie.

"What are *you* doing here?" My tone is light, but I'm working him with my accusatory eyes.

I'm not sure he's buying it.

"What? I came after work. Didn't have time to stop by the house."

"Eddie, are you seriously looking to settle down?"

My second try at eyes dripping with accusation. This time I add crossed arms for emphasis.

"Of course! I've been looking all my life." He shakes his head. "Well, at least half of it."

"Huh." I uncross my arms, trying to be a bit more accepting of this previously unknown-to-me information. "I didn't know this. That last lady you were talking to seems nice."

"She is. We're having coffee next week."

"A coffee date is a great way to begin. Low expectations. But you never know."

My mother joins us. "Eddie! You're here."

"What do you mean? You *told* me about it," he says, cocking his head. "You said I should come."

"I didn't think you'd actually listen to me."

I turn to my mother, enjoying my new position of authority over her. "Did you find anyone?"

Without answering me, she turns once more to Eddie. "I asked Luci to screen these men for me since I make such poor choices."

"I wouldn't necessarily say that," Eddie says.

There's a moment that passes between them thick with unsaid words. Which makes sense, of course, because Eddie is of course thinking of his younger brother. And it must be difficult for him to accept anyone taking his place.

"Geneva." A man with a nicely trimmed salt-and-pepper goatee approaches my mother. "Dinner next week?"

Mami flutters her eyelashes at him, smiles, and then looks over to me for approval. Softly, I shake my head and then lower it. Dinner has way too many implications.

"How about coffee? I'll call you," my mother says and then when he's gone, turns to both me and Eddie. "He's very nice. Owns a flower shop in San Jose. Cradle Catholic."

I work hard not to roll my eyes. They actually answered that question. I can think of a million matters far more important.

Do you believe in true love?

How important is it to be honest?

How many books have you read?

What is your favorite period in history?

Do you think romance writers are hacks?

Those would be my questions.

"Is he divorced? Widowed?" I ask.

"Widowed, like me," she says, forgetting all about Seb, which I find entirely hopeful even if a little misleading.

"I'm having coffee next week with my date," Eddie says. "Let's make sure we don't go to the same place at the same time."

"You have a date, Eddie?" my mother asks. "With whom?"

"Sandra Ortiz," Eddie says. "Very nice woman."

My mother snorts. "She's divorced."

"Um, so are you," I whisper. I'd like to forget it too, but it doesn't work that way.

"Anyway, it's just coffee," Eddie says with a shrug. "We will see how it goes."

"Same," my mother says. "I will *also* see how it goes."

"But I remain hopeful," Eddie says with a smile.

"As do I!" my mother says.

This conversation is prickling my spine because my mother's words sound tinged with jealousy. This can't be right. She's probably involved in some odd kind of one-upmanship with Eddie. A competition. That would make sense as she's always been the competitive type.

A woman interrupts. "Aren't you Geneva Santana from *Desperate Hearts?*"

"Yes, I am." My mother turns to her with a beaming smile. "You watched the show?"

"I loved it! Why did they kill you off? You're such a good actress."

My mother flips her hair. "Why, thank you, but you know how it is in Hollywood with aging women. Someone younger took my place."

"That's so unfair! My favorite storyline was when you were kidnapped by the cartel and Enrique found you. He died saving you!"

The woman breaks into tears and now my mother is comforting her, stroking her back.

I'll never understand how real these characters become to their audience. The storylines are so over the top and melodramatic. But Abuelita says these people become like family, because she sees them every day in her own home. They are characters you come to love like members of your family. She cares what happens to them.

I'm not sure what this means, but I know there's something here for me to learn about story.

CHAPTER 22

On the way home, my mother chats incessantly. There were so many nice single men there, but good thing I didn't participate since the men were all much older than me. She's sorry about that, and switches to whether she should suggest the church do outreach for younger people, like she's determined to talk so much I won't be able to get in a word about the weird exchange between her and Eddie.

But followed by the display at the restaurant, I'm not having it. "What is going on with you and Eddie?"

I've now realized it's better to face things head-on rather than be surprised by them later. Some shocks are inevitable, like my father's death. But others are not. Chris leaving me before the wedding shocked me though it shouldn't have. I sensed him pulling away but ignored my instincts. Next time I vow to be prepared, to be aware, to be armed to the teeth.

"What do you *mean* what's going on with me and Eddie?" she asks, eyes focused straight ahead as she drives down University Avenue.

"You know what I mean! Don't play dumb. You two were

trying to one-up each other. And you sounded like you were almost…*jealous*," I hiss.

"Me? Jealous of Eddie's dates? Don't be ridiculous."

I take in a deep breath. It's not *ridiculous* because other than the fact he's my father's brother, Eddie is a very eligible bachelor. He takes good care of himself, has never developed a paunchy middle, and has perfect teeth. I would not blame any woman his age who wanted to have a relationship with him *except* for my mother. I'm allowed to blame her because that would be sacrilegious. There's probably something in the bible about it.

"Sofia's mother said you dated Eddie first," I say, and watch as my mother nearly runs a red light, slamming on the brakes. "Oh my God, be *careful*!"

My heart is in my throat. She knows better than to be a careless driver with me in the car.

"Carmelita has a big mouth."

"But is it true?"

She doesn't answer for far too long. "Yes."

The answer is not what I wanted and the world falls out from under me. I'm spinning like the dial on a washing machine's cycle. Maybe there's some other explanation for this.

"Like, dated *dated*, or just friend dating?" I cover my ears. "No, wait. Don't tell me. I don't want to know, it's too gross. Ay Dios mio, I'm going to be sick."

"Luci, no. Calm down, it's not like that."

"Why did you wind up with my father if you dated Eddie first? You said he thought he was too good for you!"

My mother sighs and pauses for interminable seconds. "Maybe that's what you tell yourself when someone has hurt you."

"What are you *saying*? Eddie dumped you, so you went for the next brother? Honestly, please tell me the truth, because

I'm a writer and I'm making up all kinds of stuff in my head. This is starting to sound like a telenovela, but the worst kind. I'd much rather you be an amnesiac or kidnapped by the cartel."

And I'm only slightly exaggerating.

"I never wanted to talk to you about this. It's ancient history."

"Which seems to be making its way to the present."

"Yes, well. Maybe I want a second chance."

"You want a…you want a *what*?" My throat is closing up at the same moment it sounds like I'm screaming.

"This is my third act. The first one was your father, and you, the happiest times of my life. The second act was Seb and we all know how that went. In this third act, I want to go back to my roots."

"Stop talking about your life like it's a play!"

"Wait until you're my age. The little things don't matter anymore and you don't care what anyone else thinks."

"Did you *ever*?"

Maybe this is unfair but it comes out of me before I can stop myself.

"Of course. Men have ruled my life for far too long. I cared what they thought, what they said, what they wanted, and whether they liked me or not. My life was judged for merit by how well men noticed me. It's how I got myself into this mess."

"What mess?"

"I loved *Eddie*, and he was my first love. But I let him call the shots. He wasn't ready to commit, he wasn't ready for so many things. Then, there was Antonio, so loving and devoted to me."

"You always made your love story sounds so amazing, but my father wasn't even your first love, was he? He wasn't the love of your life!"

"Now you need to be the one to stop thinking about life like a romance novel. Your father knew about me and Eddie. The truth is we both may have hurt Eddie without meaning to. I suppose he thought I'd sit around and wait for him forever."

"Then the next thing you know you're dating his *brother*."

The thought of my father, possibly taking away the woman his brother loved…it's not fitting into my brain. My mind doesn't have the bandwidth or the compartment size for this truth bomb. This puzzle piece is too big to fit the shape. I resist the idea that my father was anything less than a perfect man who was my mother's first and only true love. It's the real reason I resented Seb, but I can't *possibly* hate Eddie for taking my father's place. My mother, as usual, is wreaking havoc in my life. Ruining everything. For the first time, I wish she hadn't come back.

"I realize it's difficult to think of these things but it shouldn't concern you," my mother says. "Your father is still your father, a wonderful man."

"But it's not the great love story you led me to believe all these years!"

She doesn't seem to grasp the significance of this. I would think she realizes what a romantic I am, thanks in part to their love story. I've made a career out of this. And now she's destroyed what's left of my illusions.

"It *was* a great love story," she insists. "Nothing can take away those years I had with him."

"But if not for Eddie's commitment issues, it would be *him* and not my father."

"We will never know but it doesn't matter. Because a person can have many loves in their life."

"Pull over!" I shout. "I need out of this car. Now."

"What? I can't." She glances wildly over her shoulder and all the traffic on University. "Look at all this traffic."

"If you don't pull over, I'll throw up in your car. Is that what you want?"

"It's a rental!" she screeches as she turns onto a side street and pulls over. "What's gotten into you? It's just like when you were a little girl! 'Mami, watch this. Mami watch that.' All the time performing and craving attention. Good thing you were an only child because you never could have shared the spotlight. You needed too much, you had to have things a certain way, or you'd have a fit. Your father always indulged you and that was a mistake. You're a grown-up, Luci. News-flash: Things do not always work out the way you'd like. You need to accept that people in your life make their own choices."

Tears prick my eyes, but I spill out of the car without another word.

"Luci! Wait. I'm sorry!" she says. "I didn't mean all that."

"Of course you did."

Slamming the door, I make my way to the sidewalk. I'll walk home from here. Yes, I *know*, I'm too much. That's what she always said. It might be the reason I made myself smaller, the pieces of me easier for someone to digest. I loved writing but didn't have the courage to put myself out there so I found a job ghostwriting. Falling in love was important, and I fell for someone who thought of himself first in everything.

I've always been behind the scenes, whether in my work or my relationships and grew comfortable there. But there was a time in which I was the center of a man's world. My father's.

It's so long ago I can barely remember.

I walk for thirty minutes, head down, for approximately a mile, texting with Sofia, who is trying to talk me off this metaphorical ledge.

No big deal, she says. These things happen, she says. Eddie is great, she says. It could be worse, she says.

Look, she's far more accepting than she would be if *her* mother had originally dated Eddie, then married her second choice. I'd like to see what she would say then. Sofia doesn't understand, but no one can. I had this image in my mind of my parents, their forever love, cut down in its prime. It was so romantic and tragic. Like so many things, my mother has destroyed that picture for me, too. There's only one person I want to talk to right now and I can't. My poor father. I want to know if he always felt second or if it's true that my mother really loved him as she claims.

My hands are shaking and my stomach is burning. As if all this disillusionment isn't enough, the skies open up in a rare showing of water falling out of the sky in the month of June. This thing we call rain is sprinkling and it's no big deal. No self-respecting Californian ever gets upset about the rain because we always need more. But this Californian never drives in the rain.

As the sprinkle turns into a proper deluge, I don't want to sound ungrateful, but I could do without the timing. The water is in my hair, my eyes, and I'm splashing in puddles I can't avoid. Memories of another rainy night over two decades ago are splintering what's left of my heart.

There's too much sadness in the world and rather than dwell on it, I've chosen to look past it. I've tried to bury myself in imaginary worlds where people are eternally happy. In other words, for half my life I've been lying to myself. One would think by now I should have figured this out and stopped trying so hard. It won't change anything. Ryan was right. Maybe the perfect love story is one without any real answers. That's the best one can expect.

I'm not far from Ryan's neighborhood and before long find myself at his front door. It's hard to explain what draws me to his home as opposed to taking a rideshare to Sofia's or letting her pick me up as she's offered. Suffice it to say it isn't helping that she's not as distraught as I am. I expected a little more support from my ride or die.

It doesn't occur to me Ryan will have much to say on the matter, or that I will even share this with him. I simply want to take my mind off it. I'll think about books when I'm with him, World War II spy novels specifically, because who the hell needs romance. I'm so sick of disappointment. At least with Ryan's books you know you're going to be sad and you can gird your loins and prepare. There's a war, and guess what, nobody gets a happy ending. The end. When I knock, it takes him longer than I would think to open the door. It's not a big house and his car is parked in the front so he must be here. And there's cover over the porch stoop so I'm not getting any wetter. I could stay here all night if he doesn't answer.

I hear him call out, "Hang on!" He opens the door saying, "They said twenty minutes."

I blink. His hair is wet, and he's blocking his body partly behind the cracked door.

"I thought you were the pizza delivery."

"I…I hope I'm not interrupting. Anything."

"No. Sorry, I wasn't expecting company. They *said* twenty minutes."

"Can I come inside? It's raining."

"You *walked* here?" he says, eyes wide.

"Yes, *Ryan*! And I'm starting to feel like there's something you're hiding in there."

He waves me inside, and I realize what he's hiding. He's wearing nothing but a towel on the lower half of his body. It's another shock to my system to firsthand see all that lean muscle, the drops from his wet hair sliding down his neck. His wide shoulders.

My eyes must bug out of my head because he deadpans, "This is what I'm *hiding*. I just hopped out of the shower and don't usually answer the door half naked. With you, in particular, it feels inappropriate."

"B-but you didn't want to miss the pizza delivery?" I'm stammering, keenly aware that Ryan has a man's chest.

I don't know what I *expected*, certainly not a child's chest, or a woman's chest. The thing is, I'm not prepared for all the muscle and…definition. I might be staring. Ryan has a runner's build, not massive, but defined. And abs…um yes, he has those too. There's a light smattering of dark hair across his chest but he's not *furry*, my least favorite type of man chest. While I'm cataloging all this in my mind, I do hope I'm not staring.

He turns down the hall and points. "I'll be right with you."

"Great," I say, standing so I won't ruin his dry couch.

It's a good thing I came here. He's such a great distraction I almost forget why I'm so upset. But then it comes back to me far too easily. *My mother!* She ruins everything. I glance at my buzzing cell. There are now messages from Eddie, too. No doubt by now my mother has filled him in. He wants to "talk to me." I don't currently want to talk to him about this, now or…ever.

First, I have to formulate my thoughts and accept this new reality. The idea of my *uncle* and my mother together…a second chance, she said. This isn't how second chances happen in my romance books. It's supposed to be a good thing for everyone concerned but I guess the books don't ever cover how the daughter feels.

Ryan joins me in the living room wearing an LA Dodgers hoodie and jeans. His floppy wavy hair is combed into place and he's got his retro glasses back on. I should tell him he looks good with or without his glasses. I should tell him he always smells good, like sandalwood cologne. Like sunshine.

I should say so many things and maybe someday I will, when I'm feeling less vulnerable.

He hands me a fresh towel to dry off and after I do, I take a seat on the plush tan leather couch.

"What kind of pizza?" I ask, toweling my hair.

"Pepperoni."

"My favorite. Look, I'm sorry to show up like this." I clear my throat. "It's rude. For all I know, you might have had company."

This is a fishing expedition whether he realizes it or not. I want to know, *who are you, Ryan Brady, now that you're resoundingly single?*

"No worries. I'm glad you're here. This way I don't have to eat alone."

He starts building a fire, with real wood, not the easy-burning log we use at home. It usually takes one match and burns for hours. But Ryan is stacking wood at angles and adding crumpled paper at precise locations like he knows what he's doing. All he needs is a flannel shirt and he'd be the perfect small-town hero in a romance book where the big city woman wants to sell the farm he works but…you know what, I can't do this anymore.

Life is not a romance novel, Luci.

He lights the fire, and it comes to life, flames licking, roaring like a lion. Ryan stands in front of it for several seconds then turns to me.

"Why were you walking in the rain? Did your car break down?"

"No, I…jumped out of my mother's car."

He quirks a brow. "You *what*?"

"I'm not explaining this well," I admit, pulling the towel around my shoulders. "I didn't literally jump. You know, I exaggerate."

He nods. "You are fond of hyperbole, I've noticed."

"We were coming back from the church singles event she wanted to attend."

"Ah." He comes to sit beside me. "You're both looking to meet someone new."

"Not me, it was my mother. I was there to weed out the losers. *She* was there trying to make *someone* jealous."

I'm almost sure of it. Why else would she want Eddie there if not to show him how many other men found her attractive and the dinner dates she could arrange. It's a move straight out of the Geneva Santana playbook of feminine power. She makes her moves with such finesse no one notices. I'm sure Eddie has little clue he's in her scope. She's about to reel him in and he won't even see it coming.

"Trying to make *who* jealous?" Poor Ryan, his forehead is furrowed in confusion. This is what my mother does to reasonable men. "Her ex-husband?"

"My uncle."

And I tell him everything.

CHAPTER 23

"That's… I don't know what to say." Ryan rubs his temples. "This is a later-in-life second chance."

Normally, I'd be thinking the same. But it's more than I can handle at the moment. First, my mother talks about her entire life as if she's in a play, and now Ryan is referring to a romance trope.

"This is real life!" I raise my voice and jerk back in surprise.

I'm not in the habit of yelling but now I've done this twice with Ryan. I remind myself I'm no longer going to make myself smaller. I can be loud if I want to be. And in this setting, the warm fire crackling, the rushing sound of the rain falling outside, it's soothing. I'm starting to feel safe.

"Sorry. You're right. But I studied this and it always surprises me to see how it has a basis in real life even if it's never as clear-cut." He clears his throat. "I thought you liked your uncle. He seems like a nice guy."

"He is, but he's my *father's brother*," I say slowly, like I'm talking to a four-year-old.

"Yeah, that's usually what uncle means." This time, there's

194

no condescension in his tone, and he gives me a little quirk of the lips.

"Don't you think it's strange?"

"Yeah, sure, but it's not like they got together right after he died, right? Your mother married and divorced someone else."

"Ugh, I thought you of all people would know how I feel. You had a great love, and so did my parents. It's all I've ever wanted. The kind of love that comes along once in a lifetime *if* you're lucky."

A flush goes up Ryan's neck. "You're wrong about me. I didn't have this great love, Luci. Don't put me in that category. The book has made you think of me in a different light and that's not fair. It was a *book*, not my reality."

"Look, my entire life I've had this picture of my parents and their perfect marriage. My memories are all good. They adored each other."

"First, there's no perfect marriage, but how has this view of your parents changed? It isn't like they divorced or ever stopped loving each other."

He's right, of course. At least they never grew to hate each other. He never had to wonder whether she'd have been happier with Eddie. It's the upside in all of this.

"I hate thinking someone else was her first love. Especially Eddie. The truth is I'm sad for *him*. All these years, he never found someone. Maybe my mother was his only chance."

I'm being childish, and some part of me knows this, but it's tough to look through another lens when the one you had worked beautifully. My lens had colors, vibrant, bright, and shimmering. It had memories of love, sharp and clear. Now there's a gray film over my lens that comes with a dullness I can never dust off.

"It's silly but my illusions are shattered."

"No, it's not silly. We only have to make sure we see things as they are and not how we want them to be."

But if I haven't seen life the way I should have been all along, it means I've fed my own illusions. The picture I have in my mind, that moment in time when everything was perfect…maybe it wasn't real.

I know Ryan is not wrong, and something in his words, the gentleness in them… I burst into tears.

Ryan is at my side in an instant. "Luci…no. Look, listen, everything is going to be okay."

He's not one of those men that runs the other way when a woman cries. Or worse, gets angry and uncomfortable and begins to question what *he* did to cause the outburst as he desperately tries to stop it. Ryan understands he's not at the root of this problem, or the center of the universe. That's another way he's different from all the men I've met before him.

He's holding me, and it feels so perfect, small strokes of his hand up and down my back while I'm sobbing into his chest. I thought I was done with crying and I'm generally not an overtly emotional person except when I'm writing. I'm humiliated by my actions, but I can't stem the dam. It could be I'm crying about more than my mother and Eddie. Maybe it's my father, and the staggering loss of him, which is still such a deep ache, or maybe it's Chris, and my disillusionment with romance. Either way, it's Ryan who's got me in his arms and is ignoring the knocks and rings of the doorbell. As I've said before, his powers of concentration are enviable.

"I bet it's the pizza," I say, sniffling and pulling away.

"Right."

He heads to the door and I vaguely hear sounds of him speaking to the delivery person, then making his way back into the living room.

I'm curled up on his sofa in the fetal position when Ryan comes back into the room.

"Why don't you stay here tonight?" He hooks his thumb to the hallway. "Take the guest room."

"Thanks, I'm not ready to go home."

Eddie and my mother both now want to talk to me and I don't want to listen. I'm still busy rewriting history.

The smells of fresh-baked dough, melty cheese, and spicy pepperoni are enticing. And distracting. Mami and I skipped dinner, which is something she probably does often.

"I guess that pizza won't eat itself." I sit up, wiping my eyes with the backs of my hands.

"Hungry?" His smile is easy. Slow. "Those tears must have worked up an appetite."

"Well, I will never turn down a carb."

Ryan walks away and comes back with a pair of sweats. "They're probably too big but you don't want to stay in your damp clothes."

"Thank you," I say, and head to the bathroom to change.

When I come out, dressed in the comfy sweats that smell like Ryan, I catch his quick, appraising look before he motions for me to sit down to have some pizza. For the next few minutes, we eat while watching *While You Were Sleeping* on a streaming network. It's a weird combination of hanging out with someone who is part Sofia, arguably my best friend, and part super cute guy I'm attracted to. In a romance novel, Ryan and I would be the classic workplace romance if we ever got that far. Not that I think we ever will, but the more time I spend alone with him, the more I fantasize. Now that I've been in his arms, my imagination has gone into over-drive. His arms are strong, and he smells clean and fresh.

Sofia keeps texting me and I know she won't stop until I respond:

Don't worry, I'm fine. You can tell everyone I walked to Ryan's house and I'm going to stay the night in the guest room. I'm not ready to talk to them yet.

Sofia:

 *Get it, girl!*

I roll my eyes and put my phone away. Enough with the sexy-times innuendos. No more texting tonight. A few minutes into the movie, I nudge Ryan, who is sitting beside me on the sofa. At the appropriate time, such that I couldn't have planned it better were I writing it, we simultaneously say, "The *lean!*"

"I don't know how I ever forgot about this movie. It's like my favorite of all time," I say. "And her name is even Lucy."

He quirks a brow. "Interesting, too, that it's an almost love triangle. Two brothers."

"But one is in a coma, so it doesn't count."

"Why do you think she loves him?" Ryan says.

I know he means the brother in a coma because at this point in the movie, he's the only one Lucy *thinks* she loves.

"I guess it's his good looks that attract her, and a certain je ne sais quoi. A quality about him, the suit, the confidence. She *doesn't* love him, though, because she doesn't even know him."

"She thinks she does. You have to get to know a person to fall in love with them. While she's waiting for him to wake up, she falls for the brother."

"Because c'mon, he's adorable. The whole skating scene?"

"It's called slipping over frozen cement, not skating," he deadpans. "Winters in Chicago."

"Very sexy, falling into each other's arms, holding each other up." I'm probably smiling dreamily as I take another bite of pizza and wash it down with water.

"I think she loved the first brother because it was all smoke and mirrors. A fantasy. In the end, she loved an illusion and those slip through your fingers. It's not real.

Anyway, women like Lucy don't usually fall for men like Jack," he says.

"What are you talking about? You mean the hunky woodsy guy wearing flannel and boots? He's practically a Hallmark movie hero."

"Yeah, as opposed to the rich businessman in a suit."

"Not everyone goes for those types, Ryan." I stretch my arms. "I would love to see you write a take on this movie but set during World War II. Where she's a nurse and falls for an injured soldier in a coma but when his brother shows up to visit him, they spend so much time together, she falls for him instead."

"That would work, but the brother who visits has to be a spy who needs vital information from the one in a coma."

This makes me laugh because Ryan sounds so serious. Before long, he's laughing too. I'm glad he doesn't take himself seriously all the time.

"And of course a lot of bombs dropping and explosions," I chuckle.

"Naturally."

The movie over, I want to go to sleep with this buzzy happy feeling of warmth and coziness floating through my body. Had this been a book first, I wish I'd written it. It's like a hug. And we all need more hugs. From both books and people.

I'm left with the knowledge true love will prevail, even with a few hiccups along the way like comatose brothers and large interfering families who mean well. Love wins even when you don't realize your dream has been right in front of you the entire time. It's comforting to know there's still a hint of the romantic in me. I suppose given everything that's happened, no one will be able to beat it out of me no matter how hard they might try.

I catch Ryan looking at me before he quickly glances away.

"Hope I didn't interrupt any plans you had tonight. I don't imagine there are many thirty-somethings like us who prefer pizza and a classic romcom movie at home."

"No plans and if I did I'd have canceled them."

He must be a homebody like me and this knowledge settles over me like a soft and worn blanket.

We clean up the pizza, throwing away paper plates and napkins. I fold up the throw blanket that covered me throughout most of the movie, thinking about Lucy from Chicago. Thinking about finding love where you don't expect it, by a hospital bed or a subway turnstile. When I return to the kitchen, Ryan is hunched over the sink, arms braced, and I can see the muscles bunching along his fore-arms. His body is one tight coil. I can almost feel the tension, thick and unyielding between us, and I press my face to his back.

"Thank you," I say. "Tonight was exactly what I needed. A friend to listen and hang out with me when I start to spin."

He hangs his head and a sigh of what must be relief comes out of him, but he doesn't turn around.

"Good," he says. "Glad you feel better."

I should move away now but he just smells so amazing and it's been a long while since I held on to a man like this. His arms feel strong and he's so utterly male. It's one of those moments in life when you know you should stop but your body isn't listening. The physical part of you is disconnected from your mind and heart.

When he turns to face me the look in his eyes could best be described as tortured. His blue irises are darker than normal, and they're pinched at the sides. He's Heathcliff on the moor. He's Mr. Darcy. He's every tragic hero rolled into one.

He throws his head back with a groan. "Luci, *please*. I'm not a damned saint."

And even though I wasn't prepared for this reaction from him, I'm ready.

"Maybe I don't want you to be."

We're so close I can see a speck of green in the blues of his right eye. My arms lowered when he turned, and he brings my hand up to his lips. I don't know what I'm doing here. Clearly, not thinking. I would love him to join me in this. He cups the side of my jaw and lowers his head only to stop midway, like he's changed his mind. I can't let that happen. This is what I want and in that flash of a moment, I close the distance. Standing on tiptoes I press my lips to his. I've never been this bold in my life, and the kiss has my entire body thrumming and pulsing. It's quickly reminding me of the fire he built with one match. We are the right kindling and I'm about to burst into flames.

This is bananas. Totally nuts. This is not me. It's not what I do, or how I roll. I'm not looking to jump into a relationship until I figure out a few things for myself. And I never make the first move, but my body isn't listening to my far more lucid brain as he deepens the kiss. The tough bristles of his stubble against my skin are marking me. Changing me. Ryan knows what he's doing. He kisses me with intention and passion. We are taking leaning to a whole new level, bodies pressed together hip to hip, tasting each other. And it's thrilling, romantic, sweet and sexy. It's everything.

But like any great writer, Ryan has words. He pulls back and presses his forehead to mine, his hand still in my hair.

"This is…not a good idea."

My body screeches to a halt and catches up to my far superior brain. I don't like these words but he's right. Still, I'm the one who showed up on my employer's doorstep. And here I am taking liberties with his mouth.

I take a step back, holding up my palms. "No. I'm sorry, you're right."

"I know." He drops his hands to his sides and at least he sounds miserable while he's turning me down.

Even so, a spike of humiliation shoots through me. That's what I get for making the first move. He's used to turning down advances.

"This must happen to you a lot. Sexy young professor, women making the moves on you."

His eyes narrow. "No. It never has. There are clear boundaries I won't ever cross."

"No, of course not. I seem to have crossed them for you." Shame presses down my shoulders, and my cheeks flush with heat.

"You can't possibly think I didn't want that to happen." He looks down at me quizzically. "I almost kissed you myself."

"Almost being the key word here. You didn't. I did." I turn in a circle, frustration bubbling out of me. "I'm so sorry."

"*I'm* not sorry, Luci." His arms are crossed now, perhaps creating the distance to keep me from attacking him again. "There's never been anyone like you before and I don't know how to handle this."

I think of his beautiful ex, with the straight dark hair. "I'm just not your type."

"You're very much my type." He makes air quotes. "But we're not exactly on an even playing field. It would be unfair for me to take advantage of this situation."

It's big of him to take this stance, since I'm the one who initiated the kiss. He's letting me off the hook.

"I understand. You're my boss."

"For now, yes. I'm also six years older than you."

"So what? That's nothing. It wouldn't even rate that as an age-gap romance."

He all but rolls his eyes at me. "And whether or not you realize it, *you're* not available."

I don't correct the available part because I worry he's right. I've been saying this to my mother, Sofia, and anyone who will listen. They don't listen and apparently, my body isn't even listening because it's Ryan and he's the exception.

This is my time. Time to stand up to the people in my life who've always wanted me to adhere to their ideas of who I am or who I should be. Thinner. Forgiving. Easygoing. Happy to settle for what I can get.

Maybe Ryan is on to something. With a marriage behind him, and an understanding of commitment I don't have, he might be right.

"Do you need anything else before bed?" Ryan asks, interrupting my thoughts.

"No, I'll be fine. Thank you," I say and without another word I head to the guest room.

"Luci?" he calls out, and I turn just outside the door. "Sleep well."

"Not a chance, but I'll try," I say before I open and shut the door.

CHAPTER 24

*H*ow do I sleep? Horribly, if you want to know the truth.

First, there's the guest bedroom. If I'd thought I'd find pieces of Ryan in here, I was mistaken. This isn't his home. It's professor Henry's, art collector extraordinaire.

This morning, I wake to a large, framed piece of multimedia art. It's an abstract, with different shapes and Jackson Pollock–inspired swirls of paint. There's a rabbit clearly cut from a greeting card, and a soldier peeking out from another corner behind swirls of paint. It's the kind of art you could study for days and still find more things the artist hid.

And there's a text from Chris:

Thanks a lot! My parents had to pick me up. I had a two-hour lecture on all the mistakes I've made since birth. 😫 *When can I see you? I said we would talk when I got back. I really miss you.*

I don't even know if I should dignify this with a response. He misses the old Luci, the one who will roll over and beg for his scraps. New flash: that Luci doesn't live here anymore. I pull the warm blanket around me tighter. The guest room smells like Ryan. Sandalwood and beachy fresh.

Sunshine. An undetermined and pleasant light musky scent lingers that is all male. A few minutes later, I hear sounds coming from the kitchen, sit up straight, and smack my forehead.

What did I do? I kissed my boss! I kissed *the professor* and he kissed me back. This is the man who hired me as a research assistant even after listening to me word vomit my interview and qualifications. This is the man who's changed my career, breathing new life into it. Sure, I think we decently recovered from the kiss and the moment we shared.

Except I'm not sure I will recover. I've never been kissed like that before. His fingers were threading through my hair, pulling me closer with intent, and it was glorious. The whole thing was hotter than I would have ever imagined. That single kiss was better than most of the *sex* I've had. I thought Ryan was hot, but holy guacamole, he's so much more.

Luci, I'm not a saint.

No, *not* a saint. Pretty sure a saint wouldn't kiss the way he did. Damn it, now I'm picturing all manner of other unsaintly things. I only hope I haven't made things incredibly awkward between us. I'm going to try and behave like we're back to being friends and colleagues, and the kiss never happened. That seems the best approach. I'm pretty good at pretending, which is part of my problem. But screw it, I can't fix everything overnight.

I would ask Sofia what to do but I don't want to hear her sexualize this relationship when I give her ammunition. Because Ryan and I kissed, oh boy we *kissed,* and going farther than that isn't as unlikely anymore. I did hear Ryan when he mentioned even playing fields. Maybe I could quit this job and then technically I'm only working for the publisher. Right? But I'm not sure if it works that way. Besides, now we're writing the sequel together.

I finger-comb my hair, change into my now dry clothes,

and visit the bathroom. I need my toothbrush. I need my face soap. Forced to brush my teeth with my finger, I do my best with his toothpaste, a minty flavor. When I snoop in Ryan's toiletries, I find the soap he uses and vow to order some so I can smell him all the time. He's obviously a low-maintenance guy, given the lack of hair gel, spray, and other metrosexual detritus used by men like my ex. I find an electric shaver and have to wonder why he suddenly seems to have stopped shaving.

I didn't want to go home last night, but this morning I don't know what possessed me. He kissed me—correction, I kissed *him*—and everything changed. Maybe I should have left. I don't know if I'm skilled enough to fake my disinterest despite all my experience faking.

When I find Ryan in the kitchen, he offers me coffee and our hands touch, reminding me of last night.

"Oh, so you *can* make coffee?" I go hand on hip. "You don't need my daily delivery?"

"That was your idea," he says with a smirk.

"Which you definitely leaned into," I say, and now I feel a warm flush creeping up *my* neck. "Um, yeah. I guess I will have a cup. Thanks."

Note to self: Don't use the word lean in his presence.

I take a few sips and sneak looks at Ryan, who is dressed in his usual uniform of jeans and a shirt over a tee. He's not wearing his glasses, which is a different look for him. I resist my impulse to go into his arms again.

"Are you trying to grow a beard again?" I study him because he's still got beard stubble and it looks a bit thicker today.

He runs a hand along his chin and I swear I hear it from where I'm standing two feet away. I felt those bristles last night against my skin.

"My razor broke and I haven't ordered a new one."

"Just so long as you don't go all Grizzly Adams again like in the video."

"Not a good look for me." He shakes his head. "But that's how I usually look after I finish a book. When I'm immersed in a book, I barely eat or sleep, much less bother shaving."

"That doesn't sound healthy."

He shrugs. "It works for me."

I sit my cup on the counter after only a few sips. "I figured I'd go home and change before I come back to work."

He heads to the dining table with his coffee and stops between the two rooms. "If you want to work from home today, that's not a problem."

"Do you want me to work from home?"

He pinches the back of his neck. I've never seen him like this. It's like I make *him* nervous, but in a good way.

"I don't want you to be uncomfortable in any way."

"Because of last night? I don't," I lie. "I'm the opposite of uncomfortable because I didn't do anything wrong."

"I'm not saying you did. Or we did." He waves his arms. "No one in this room should feel uncomfortable because… yeah…I just meant those clothes of yours are probably not comfortable."

It's hard not to chuckle when I realize he might be more nervous than I am. "You're right about that. Plus, my toothbrush. You look all clean and snappy and presentable while I look like…like I had a sleepover without my toothbrush."

At this, he gives me half a smile. "You always look good to me."

Oh. That's nice of him to say. I should accept the compliment, but I can't resist.

"Just so you know, this is the worst I ever look." I hesitate. "Except when I'm sick."

After I say this, I regret the words and want to take them back. I think it's somehow wired into my DNA, which has infected me with the idea I must be presentable and attractive to men at all times. This is something I can thank Geneva for. I've fought this attitude for years, but it's deeply ingrained and not just by my mother but society as a whole. Like the worst thing a woman can be is invisible to men. Newsflash: I don't care anymore. My looks are the least important part of me.

Ryan grabs his keys. "I'll drive you."

As we drive to my neighborhood, I notice Ryan isn't wearing his glasses but a pair of shades he pulled out of the glove compartment.

"Don't you wear prescription glasses?" I say.

"Yeah but just for reading."

This is interesting because I've never seen him not wearing a pair of glasses until today and I've seen him in plenty of situations when he's not reading.

"Are we not going to talk about the kiss?" I say.

"Not unless you want to," Ryan says and I notice his knuckles go white on the steering wheel.

"If we don't talk about it, it's going to be awkward."

"I would hate that."

He sounds the way most guys do when they'd prefer to talk about the splitting of the atom, space exploration, or conspiracy theories. Anything else. Literally.

"We've come a long way from the day you asked me to be Elizabeth."

"I'm with you so far."

Now for the tough part. "I guess you know by now I'm attracted to you."

"Yes."

While I sincerely wish he'd admit he feels the same way, I suppose I don't need him to confess the obvious. I was there when he kissed me back like he wanted to inhale me. I'm not going to do this "does he like me" thing I always do. Who was it that said we're all basically sixteen when we fall in love? I refuse to act like a teenager again crushing on someone. I'm thirty, for crying out loud.

"I never planned for this. You know I hated you after I saw the video."

"Sure."

"Everything is different now but naturally we're not going to do anything about this"—I wave my hand between us—"thing between us."

"Exactly."

I cross my arms and tuck them under my armpits so I'm not temped to smack him. So much for talking things out.

I did all the talking.

"So glad we had this talk."

"Same here."

Woohoo, two whole words. I'm going to punish his lack of vocabulary by pressing to hear more about the real Elizabeth.

"So. Ryan, would you tell me more about Elizabeth Brogan? It's a family name, but who's in the family? A grandmother? Aunt? Is it your mother's maiden name?"

Ryan freezes, his lips pressed together, and he's absolutely white-knuckling that steering wheel.

"I'd rather not say, if you don't mind."

"Sure, but why?"

Maybe I shouldn't press, but we kissed, and I'm Elizabeth now. And maybe I have a small right to know.

"Just trust me. You won't think of me the same way if I tell you."

That's a loaded statement. I can't imagine why I would think of him differently.

"You do know what I'm making up right now is probably worse than it actually is."

"Don't let you imagination get carried away."

"Ha! Fat chance. But you'll tell me someday."

He doesn't respond but gives me a non-committal "uh-huh."

"Just pull over here." I point to the sidewalk in front of the house.

Ryan parks and then says, "I'll walk you."

The idea is old-school, and I kind of like it.

"I don't think that's a good idea, though," I say. "I already spent the night at your place and if you walk me, it might look like—you know—"

"You're right." He reaches for my hand and threads his finger through mine and just stares at our joined hands.

I study them too, with no commentary as to how good they look together, his big hand holding my much smaller one. All I need is a little time and I'm sure the man I want is Ryan. The timing is just off.

"Thanks for understanding my silly family."

Then he abruptly drops my hand as if he's snapped out of a trance. "I'll see you later and we'll talk more about the sequel."

There have been so many times with a favorite book when I've wished I could write a sequel for the author, so I could see how those characters I've become attached to are faring. I even once experimented with fan fiction.

Now I have the chance to write the follow-up to a bestseller and I can write the ending I want, the one readers need. If I do this, I will fully become and own the brand of Elizabeth Brogan and Ryan becomes the ghostwriter for the first book.

He doesn't immediately drive off as I stroll up the walkway to the side gate knowing there are probably eyes on me from inside the main house. I turn to see him watching me, and only when I shut the gate do I hear his car drive off. The house is quiet as is customary on a weekday morning.

Abuelita will be inside folding clothes, or cooking sopa for dinner. Eddie will be at work in San Francisco. My mother's car is still parked, so she will probably be knocking on my door momentarily. True to form, I've been inside for ten whole minutes before she knocks. She's so predictable.

"I don't want to talk right now!" I yell through the door. "I have to get ready for work."

"Mija, it's me."

Eddie.

This is almost worse. I don't know what to say to Eddie. He's one of my favorite people in the world. I adore him and want him to be happy. The thing is, I thought he was until now. Sofia and I used to wonder why he was single, at one time wondering if there was perhaps something he wanted to tell us. Now I know he never chose to be single and has been pining away for my mother for decades. The idea that he's been unhappy all these years, longing for someone he lost, is enough to shatter my heart.

I swing the door open to let him inside. "Why aren't you at work?"

He waves his hand dismissively. "Dr. Marroquin will take my patients."

"You never call in sick."

"I'm never sick." He shrugs.

I walk a few steps and plop down on the love seat. "I guess Mami told you everything."

He nods. "She did, and she was very upset. And since when do you jump out of cars in the rain? That's very dangerous! Cars and rain. I think you know what that does to me."

"It wasn't raining when I got out! I'm sorry but I couldn't talk to her another minute. This is tough for me."

"Your mother thinks you might understand better if I explain."

"What is there to explain? You didn't want her, so she went for your brother. As if there were no other men on campus. I mean, what is that?" I throw my hands up.

"That's not exactly the way it happened." He takes my only chair and straddles it, clasping his hands.

"What do you mean? There's more?"

"It was your father who went after *her*."

"When he knew *you* were dating her?"

He nodded. "Look, you're not wrong about their love story. It was like cupid himself struck your father the moment he met her. I saw it, too, even if he wouldn't admit it. He didn't want to take my girl. He was my little brother, though, and I would have done anything for him. So, I stepped aside. Did I have second thoughts? Yes, sure, a couple of times when I wondered…but no, it worked out the way it should have. He and your mother had many good years together. And of course, they had you, the joy of their lives."

"But what about *you*?" My voice breaks and I'm embarrassed to feel a pinch in my throat.

Everyone deserves true love, that all-encompassing feeling that wraps around your soul.

"What about me?"

"*You* were alone."

"I've almost never been alone. I have my family and there are a lot of us."

"You didn't have someone."

He chuckles and holds up a finger. "I found a lot of someones."

"That's not what I mean and you know it. Someone *special*. The love of your life."

He looks pensive and stares briefly at the ceiling before meeting my eyes.

"Sometimes I think your father was the love of my life."

I've never heard love described in this way, as if it could

be something more than what's between lovers. There's love between friends, between family members, but the love for a significant other should be above all.

"I always thought their love story was unique and special but I never had any idea they hurt someone else by being together. And it's worse because it was you."

"Don't feel sorry for me. I've had a good life. Friends, a big family filled with nieces and nephews. And as for your mother, I firmly believe a person can have more than one true love in a lifetime."

This is similar to what my mother said and it's clear she considers Eddie one of the loves of her life.

Eddie clears his throat. "When Geneva came back this time, she confessed her feelings for me. But she wasn't going to push. She told me to see other people. And I went to that stupid singles event, but I've seen a lot of women over the years. I had to take a hard look and realize I still loved her after all this time. But you should know neither one of us are going to do anything about this until, and unless, you say it's okay."

Relief should spill through me but instead it's shock mixed with a pinch of anger.

"You're going to make *me* responsible for your happiness?"

"Don't think of it that way."

"What other way is there? That's what you're asking me to do."

"Would you rather we do what we want without any regard to your feelings?"

"Well, no, but…is this really what *you* want?"

I suppose it's now up to me to be the parent and gently remind Eddie my mother is not the most reliable woman on the planet.

"What do you mean?"

"Think carefully. I don't have to tell you her track record isn't the best. There's Seb—"

"Seb was not a good man." Eddie shakes his head slowly.

"No kidding! But there's also the fact that she…face it, she doesn't stick around for long. She has to be the center of attention."

"It took a while, but she's changed. I believe her."

"I don't see it yet." I cross my arms and give him the truth because he deserves it. "And you're ready to settle down? With *her*?"

"Like it or not, your mother is still beautiful, and she's funny, and irreverent. She gets me." He shrugs. "I'm over fifty, and I have a few good years left in me. If not now, then when? Marry when I'm eighty? What's the point?"

It hurts me to think of how much time they've lost.

"I…I don't know what to say. What does Abuelita think? You *have* told her, haven't you?"

Eddie nods. "You forget your abuelita had a front row seat to all of this years ago. After your father died, she thought I should marry Geneva and take care of both of you. That didn't sit well with me. It had been too long and Geneva was no longer mine. Hadn't been for years. I couldn't get there, even though of course I adored *you*. I promised to take care of you like you were my own and I have."

"You have."

The thought of Eddie and my mother, all those years ago, when they could have raised me together…this spears into my mind with slicing pain. She wouldn't have dropped me off with Eddie and Abuelita and left. She would have stayed.

The picture of me, Eddie, and my mother as a family brings about fresh pain of what might have been.

CHAPTER 25

By the time I get back to Ryan's later that morning, I don't want to think anymore. I've been given the power to control the future happiness of *two people*. I told Eddie I don't want the responsibility and they should do whatever they want since they're both adults. He insisted I think about it and they will accept whatever my answer is. Can I just say? The pressure is enormous. I appreciate the vote of confidence and clear concern for my well-being. But a person who romanticizes everything isn't going to tell two people who long to be together that they can't because I think it's cringy.

At Ryan's, I have someone who manages to make me feel good about myself. All I want is to fall into this world of make believe we've created where books and words rule the day.

I'm not going to think about last night's kiss or how it made me feel. We're co-workers and co-writers.

"How's the writing going?"

It's the first thing I ask him when I walk in because he's sitting on the sofa, wearing his glasses, scribbling on a notepad. This is a good sign. He looks up at me, one corner of his lip quirked up in a half smile and takes off his glasses.

He holds up his yellow legal pad. "I've got the plot."

"I thought you already had the plot."

"Not for my spy novel. For the sequel to the book."

"You have the entire *plot?*"

I've only been gone a few hours. He might be some kind of plotting savant.

"Of course, there is room for changes and flexibility. But this is an outline you can use that would at least help you get started." He hands me the pad.

I sit beside him. These are hieroglyphics I can now read due to experience. I flip through them quickly.

This is something I can do. It's not all that different from my ghostwriting gig, being given the plot, but this time it's skeletal. This time, I'll be the one to give it flesh and breathe life into it with more of my own ideas. It will be *my* face on this work. This time it's forward facing. Ryan is no longer the ghostwriter of the book. I'm no longer a ghostwriter. Take out the ghost, enter the writer.

"You can make whatever changes you want. It's not set in stone. Remember, this is your book."

He's not wrong to call it my book. I have the passion for this project he lacks.

"I'll get to work on this right away."

"There's one thing." He lightly touches my arm and probably because of last night, a tingle flows through me. "Write this with your own style. Your voice. I don't care if it's different. Make the book, and the story, your own."

"It's Lula's point of view, so maybe it's okay the voices are different," I muse. "They're bound to be."

He splays his hands behind his neck. "I'm so relieved we're going to make everyone happy. There *will* be a sequel and I don't have to write it."

I chuckle at his honesty. "What does Kate think?"

"Kate is nothing less than ecstatic there will be another book, so thank you. Again."

"She's excited even if *I'm* writing? How does she know how I write?" I stand. "Wait. How do *you* know?"

Ryan palms a hand down his face. "Not long ago we both read the latest Desdemona book. The e-book was priced at 99 cents which is honestly too low of a price for such great work."

I wish he'd said something sooner because I could have made a rec. That particular book is replete with open-door love scenes between Desdemona and her longtime lover, Ezekiel. It's what they'd asked for in the book. Their specific instructions were: Don't hold back; we'll tell you if it's too much. Last year was the twenty-five-year anniversary of her long-running vampire series and they wanted scorching hot scenes to celebrate and acknowledge the fact Desdemona, when alive, was a trendsetter.

And so…I didn't hold back. I hold up a palm, clutching the pad to my chest. "I can explain—"

"What's there to explain? The writing is strong. Your voice is irreverent and funny. And that's how I wrote Lula."

I'm now wondering if he skipped over the love scenes in the book or actually read them. He's not giving me any weird looks so I'm hoping for the former.

"I'm guessing the heat level should stay the same as with *the book*?"

I refuse to look at Ryan when I ask this question. There were a few scenes in *Soulmates* between Lula and Grayson that almost set fire to my e-reader.

"Yes, that would work. Might be best."

"Okay." I swallow hard.

"Kate is running the idea by the publisher, but she fully expects the sales from the book to mean they'll send over a deal memo in record time. You'll also need to sign an agency agreement with Kate so that she can officially represent you."

"She's offering me representation?"

My voice is a squeak. Kate is one of the best in the industry, and even I know this. She's closed to queries and has a stable of impressive household names. I never dreamed she'd represent me. Apparently this is one area in which I didn't dream big enough.

"You could seek your own representation if you'd prefer that. We don't need to have the same agency but the publisher does have first right of refusal for any sequels."

I drop the pad and spin around in place. "Of course I want Kate! I want it all! I can't believe I'm finally, after all these years, going to have an agent!"

He chuckles. "Good, because Kate would have probably had a stroke if you went anywhere else."

Anywhere else wouldn't be like having Kate and the same agency who's represented multiple bestselling books and many of my literary heroes. This time I don't warn Ryan a hug is incoming. Instead, I jump into his arms and he catches me.

"I can't thank you enough. You've made all of my dreams come true."

Neither one of us shies away from the embrace, which is tight, and might last a little too long for workplace hours. My face is nestled into his neck, which is so warm, my arms around his strong shoulders. His hands are hovering around my behind. Then I remember to be a professional and am the first to pull away. I want to know that Ryan is working with me because he likes my writing and not because he thinks I'm sexy and wants to sleep with me.

Even so, I see the desire in his shimmering eyes. He's given me everything I ever wanted but there's one thing he can't give me. Back when I dated nothing but selfish losers who put their own needs before my own, I would have loved to meet someone like Ryan.

I stay at Ryan's later than I normally would because working here is easy and inspiring despite the distraction of the hunk in the room. I've been writing in my shed for the past few months, but it's comfortable working beside Ryan as we both write. His face is almost comical. It's one of utter concentration, but every once in a while he gets up, runs a hand through his hair and mutters, "This is hopeless. Maybe it's time for me to quit."

"Are you serious?"

"I had a good run." He sighs and shakes his head.

It's all I can do not to roll my eyes. "Take a break and come back."

He's a rather dramatic writer. I can't imagine what revisions must be like.

It's almost dinner time when I get home and I know I'm going to eat dinner with Eddie and my mother. It's normally not an issue and we've been managing since she arrived. But in light of recent developments, I expect a lot of awkward pauses in conversation. When I walk inside, the succulent smells of arroz con pollo fill Abuelita's kitchen. She's also fried plantains, one of my favorites, which she only makes every few months. I'm beginning to wonder if they're all trying to butter me up. I suppose it makes sense for Abuelita to want to keep us all close and in the family. Eddie would legally be my stepfather, which while strange, fits right into the family dynamic. And she wouldn't worry about Eddie being alone after she's gone.

"Mmm," my mother says. "No one makes rice and chicken like you do, Mami."

"Muy delicioso." Eddie nods.

"You should eat more, Geneva," Abuelita says. "You're too skinny."

"Yes, I will," my mother says, shocking all of us, I'm sure, but mostly me.

For the next few interminable minutes, we all talk about food as if we've never had it before. As if we've just discovered Abuelita can cook. The salt is particularly salty and the rice is so fluffy. It's ridiculous.

"It looks like I'm going to get a contract for a new book," I announce, mostly to change the subject from food.

"Of course you are," Mami says. "You're a *New York Times* bestselling author. It's not time to stop writing now!"

"Yes, but I didn't write *that* book," I say and then conversation stops. Just grinds to halt as Eddie stares at me bug-eyed.

I throw a hand over my mouth. The secret I fought so hard to keep is out. It slipped out. I have just violated my NDA.

"What do you mean you didn't write the book?" Mami says, glancing from Eddie to me, back to Eddie again. "You always write the book. If you didn't, who did?"

Eddie stares straight ahead and Abuelita hasn't even looked up from her plate.

It's too late now, so I just go for it.

"Sorry I didn't tell you, but I wasn't supposed to tell *anyone.* And now you all are sworn to secrecy unless you want me to be sued."

I explain I've violated my non-disclosure agreement and if they love me, they will pretend they didn't hear any of this. All these years they all knew I was a ghostwriter but not for who or which books I wrote. It didn't matter to them as long as I was happy and getting paid to do the work I loved.

Eddie and Abuelita seem to accept my slip just fine, nodding their agreement. But my mother's forehead is crinkly and for the first time I notice she's no longer using Botox. Maybe Eddie *is* right and she has changed.

Mami sets down her fork and crosses her arms. "So, this man has *used* you."

"No, no." Eddie waves his hands dismissively. "This is a good thing."

"I don't see how," my mother says. "He's using her face and body like she's an employed actor or something."

"That's right, I'm acting," I say with a tiny smirk. "It's something you're familiar with."

I half wonder if she's jealous it's a role she can't play. Any moment now I expect her to remind everyone I'm taking after her. It was her influence that led me to this moment in time. Her genes that made me who I am.

But instead, her lower lip is trembling as if she's going to cry.

"Acting is something you never expressed any interest in," Mami says.

"Maybe she's proud of you, Geneva," Eddie says, placing a hand on her shoulder. "And wants to be more like you."

That's a reach but I appreciate Eddie trying to smooth this over.

"That's the last thing *I* want!" Mami says, standing, and dramatically throwing her napkin on the table.

She then turns in the direction of the hallway and stalks off toward the bedrooms.

Eddie and I stare at each other.

"What just happened?" I ask him.

He shrugs. "Don't know."

Abuelita pipes up. "Go talk to your mami, Luci."

"Me?" I put a hand to my chest. First, I'm not done with the fried plantains or my rice. Second, what can I possibly say to her other than I'm sorry I lied, but that's in my job description.

"Do you see any of her other daughters in this room?" Abuelita says.

"Fine!" Now, I get up and storm off.

At the closed bedroom door, I knock. "Let me in, it's me."

"Come in," she says.

When I do, she's hunched over, sitting on the edge of the bed, not prostrate in dramatic diva fashion as I'd expected.

"Okay, listen. See, I don't understand why you're so upset. Want to tell me? I'm the one who should be upset because I shouldn't have said anything at all."

"How can you *not* see why this bothers me?"

"I never wanted to be an actress, you're right. And I'm still not. This was a one-time deal and it's definitely typecasting. It's like having a pen name, which a lot of authors do."

"You don't feel…used?"

"Not at all. It was my choice. My decision. They're paying me well for this. Plus, I've had a lot of doors open and the next book will actually *be* written by me. It's the greatest opportunity I've ever had."

My mother sniffs and I notice she has a rumpled piece of tissue in her trembling hands. "I know how opportunities can pull you in but if you have to change who you are, it will only lead to disappointment."

"I'm not changing who I am. Basically, Elizabeth Brogan is me, and I'm Elizabeth Brogan."

"He's never going to…change his mind who should play Elizabeth?"

It hadn't even occurred to me, because it's too late now, and we have a contract. Still, it's stated to be valid for only one year. I'm not sure what could happen after that but it wouldn't make much sense to hire anyone else.

"We have a contract."

"Contracts can be broken."

"It wouldn't be in his best interest because that would lead to a lot of questions he doesn't want to answer."

Mami puts her hand on mine. "Don't let anyone, especially a man, have too much control over your career."

And just like that, a wave of unwanted sympathy for Mami washes over me.

My mother was raised by a Latina generation of women who had only begun to question a man's role, authority, and control over them, so I'm surprised by this enlightened view. I've never once considered Ryan had any control over my career, but in a small way he does.

"Is that what happened to you? Did Seb take control over your career?"

"And I didn't even see it happening. But it wasn't just him. Him, and all the men who control everything. He even controlled my body. What I ate, and when. I could never be thin enough for any of them."

This is brand new information to me, the idea this obsession with weight and looks didn't originally come from her.

The wave of compassion becomes a tsunami. My poor mother, believing her worth was tied to how men felt about her. And the way they felt about her was based on her looks.

Except for my father.

Except for Eddie.

"I'm sorry he made you feel that way. Your body is beautiful, no matter the size."

She dissolves into tears and I can't take it anymore. I wrap my arms around her and feel her body shake with wracking sobs. Patting her back gently, I remind her I'm here. She's home and no one is going to ever judge her again.

And now that includes me. I won't judge her for leaving me behind. I won't judge her for pursuing her dreams after she lost my father. I won't judge her for marrying my father when she wanted Eddie.

After a while, her sobs become whimpers, then hiccups.

Eddie gently opens the door once, throws my mother a worried look, and I wave him away. I've got this.

"Why did you choose to come home?" She doesn't respond right away, so I prompt. "Was it all about Eddie?"

In the space of that moment, I realize I *want* it to be him. He should be the reason she came back because he *deserves* it. I don't want to hear she came back because she ran out of other acting opportunities.

"No, it was you. I hated myself when I was with Seb, hated that I never stood up for you. And I didn't mean any of those things I said to you yesterday. You're not too much, Luci. I wonder if you'll ever forgive me." She pats her nose with the tissue.

"I know what it's like to say things you don't mean in the heat of the moment," I say. "I hope at least part of you came back for Eddie and that it wasn't just because you had no choice."

She shakes her head. "Eddie always accepted me for who I am. Just like your father did. I wanted to see for myself if there was still something there."

"And there is."

"Yes, but I won't do anything about it. I can learn how to be alone like you have."

"No, you can't," I snort. "But it's nice you want to try."

"I'm not like you and your hip generation. Maybe if I'd started sooner, learning how to rely less on a man…"

"I don't want to be alone *forever*," I explain.

"Oh, thank God. I'd like to be a grandmother someday."

"Eddie is a good man," I say. "He will never leave you, or hurt you, or let you down in any big way. I'm sure of it. He's waited a long time for you, and in my opinion, you two should be together. You've waited for each other long enough."

She brightens through red eyes and it's like someone

turned on her light but it's too much wattage. *"Really?* It's okay with you?"

"You'll need to take care of him. He's about as old-school as you are."

"No doubt."

"But let me be clear." I hook a thumb to my chest, putting some steel into my spine. "If you *ever* hurt him, if you ever leave him, you will have to deal with me. And it won't be pretty."

I don't tell her, but I'll issue Eddie the same threat, though it's hardly necessary.

CHAPTER 26

Since he returned, Chris has been sending me text messages all week, which I've ignored. He wants to see me, he wants to explain, he wants to have closure. And I'm sure he also wants his stuff. I kept very little for him other than the Absolut, and I no longer have that. He's not going to be happy about this, but I wasn't either when I poured half of it down the drain. I'm not sorry.

He doesn't seem to realize we're done. He's the one who ended us by leaving for South America. He chose his coffee-house crush and the Peace Corps over me. I could get past the Peace Corps, but I don't see how we can ever get past Nadia.

When there's a knock on my shed door later that night, I'm shocked to open it and find Chris.

It's been over six months but he still looks the same. Blond, clean-cut, well manicured. A small part of me is happy to see him, like some of the cells in my body forgot what he's done to us. Those memory cells seem to recall only the good times. Thankfully my higher-level brain is in charge.

"*Why* are you here?" I ask.

"You won't return my texts."

I wave him inside. "I didn't see the point. You probably want your stuff, but there isn't much here."

I grab the box of mementos and clothes and dump it at his feet.

He glances around my teeny-weeny living space, especially as compared to the condo we once shared, which actually had a separate dining and living area. And plenty of walls.

"Why are you staying in a shed?"

When he says it, he doesn't sound much different from my mother. But in my mother's case, and defense, *she* wasn't responsible for it.

"There wasn't much I could afford after I didn't have your help with the rent and was left with all those cancellation fees for our wedding."

The color drains out of his face and he covers his eyes, lowering his head.

"Damn, this is just one more example of my many failures. I'm going to pay you back for my half. And I'm so sorry. I feel like I've been in a fever dream for months and I'm only now waking up."

"Wow, Nadia must have sure cast a spell on you with her dark magic." I snort.

It's just like him to blame the woman.

"It wasn't her. It had nothing to do with her in the end. The truth is I was afraid of dying."

"Excuse me?"

"I saw marriage as the end of my youth. It was another stage, the one before I became a parent, and another step closer to death."

This makes me snort-laugh. "Oh my God, you must be the most romantic person *ever*! When you think of me, think of death. That should be a Hallmark card. You're the one who wanted to get married! I would have been fine going along the way things were."

"I've been thinking about all this, while I spent all that time building orphanages. It was good for the soul. Gave me time to think. My parents put all this pressure on me, to accomplish things by their rigid timelines. I was supposed to get married by thirty. It was on their damn calendar like my college graduation! And of course, I love you, so it made sense for us to marry. It just felt at the time that the closer I got to marriage, the closer I got to death."

"Um, gee, thanks?"

No wonder his proposal was so half-hearted. Seriously, at the *gym*? Yeah, I get that's where we met, but clearly he put almost no thought or creativity into it. I neglected it at the time, thrilled someone wanted to *marry* me. The romance of it all held me in a tight grip. I thought Chris was The One. He hit all the markers. He was handsome, intelligent, funny, charming, great body, honest and loyal (I thought) and he said all the right things. Clearly I saw only what I wanted to see. Yes, we were complete opposites, but opposites attract. It was, however, simply difficult to live with him. Eventually, we judged our differences. While I was in the middle of it, I couldn't see how wrong we were together. As a romance writer, I was too in love with the idea of being in love.

"I screwed up big time. Please forgive me and give me another chance." Chris drops to his knees and clasps his hands prayer-like.

I can't believe this guy and his idea of romance. Begging and desperation after he just revealed I remind him of death.

"Get up. This is silly."

Instead of getting up, Chris goes all in. He covers his face with his hands and does something I've never seen him do before, not even the time our cat died.

He *cries.*

It's far more effective than I would have imagined. He looks so pitiful kneeling there, the sobs echoing around the uninsulated shed. An ache forms for this man I loved at one time. It's not his fault his parents had such incredibly strict guidelines for him. And he'd joined the Peace Corps. Even if it was to follow a woman-crush, he'd done that, and put himself through the conditions of living in a third-world country. I'd never seen him as a snob or I wouldn't have fallen for him in the first place.

Tears spring to my eyes and I gently pat his head like I would a young child. "Please don't cry."

"I'm sorry, I know it's not fair but…I just can't believe what I lost because I was too stupid to realize what I had." He glances up at me, his eyes red. "I don't deserve it, I know I don't, but please say you'll give me another chance. I'll do anything."

It seems cruel in his state to outright reject him even if he deserves it. Funny how when the pain you wished on someone actually happens, it doesn't feel good. It's not *satisfying.* Revenge, I'm sorry to say, does *not* taste sweet. Or maybe I'm just a grown-up now.

I've always believed in second chances. It's one of my favorite tropes for a reason. But I can only think about Ryan, his soulful eyes, and the way his lock of hair continually falls over his glasses.

I *want* to be done with Chris. It is true we didn't get closure. He just took off and left me with everything to handle on my own. I'm in this shed because of him. Then again, I met Ryan because of him and all these changes, too. Now I have this opportunity I might have never had otherwise. I see what Ryan meant when he forgave his ex for contacting his agent without his permission. It led him to an amazing book he wouldn't have written otherwise. Then, I might never have met Ryan Brady. Maybe this all happened for a reason, though when it comes to Chris, I know I'm being generous.

Chris leaving showed I don't need a relationship for the sake of one. I proved that I could do hard things. It showed me the person I need most in my life is *myself.* And I've always had her.

"Okay," I say. "Let's talk about it tomorrow."

"Really?"

His voice is laced with the faith of a child and I want to tell him not to get his hopes up because Santa isn't real. He can't bring you everything you want just because you asked for it. It doesn't work that way.

"You're right, we didn't get closure. I'm not willing to take you back like nothing ever happened, but I'm open to seeing what comes next if I can ever manage to forget what you did."

"That's all I want." His voice breaks, he stands and straightens to his full height and brushes off the legs of his khakis. "I'm going to show you why you should pick me again."

"Right. But you also have to give me room, because a lot has happened to me since you've been gone."

"I want to hear all about it." He bends to leaf through the box of the few items he left behind with me. "I can't believe I gave everything else away. That was the sign of a fever dream if there ever was one."

"Actually, I think it was one of the best things to come out of this." I clear my throat. "Now, let me explain something to you about the vodka."

It turns out Chris is both shocked and in awe of what I've accomplished while he was gone. He leaves an hour later, trying for a kiss, which I block. Not going to happen. I don't feel *that* guilty about the vodka. Chris forgave my lapse in judgment in pouring it down the drain in a moment of anger and passion. He agrees this was nothing less than he deserved and for the first time I wonder if this attitude change might actually stick. It doesn't mean I'll take him back but it's nice to know he's learned something.

He's promised he will "show me" he's a better man and he's going to come to the book signing with all his friends to support me. I don't tell him that with a book like *Soulmates*, I hardly need the support of whatever gym bros he can round up. I suppose it's nice to know he's putting in the effort. It will take a lot of forgiveness I'm not sure I have, but if I'd begged someone while crying on bended knees, I would hope they'd at least be a friend to me. That's all I can give him now, or ever. I'm being the mature one here because he deserves far worse and I know it.

I explain to Chris that my career is my focus now. He promises he understands and encourages me to go for my dream, the way he thought he'd gone after his. He was wrong, but my dream might work out better. I try not to remember part of his dream was Nadia. He's conveniently neglecting this fact but I'm not likely to forget it.

The next week is a flurry of activities as Ryan and I both write side by side, and I exchange a flurry of email messages with Pepper as we prepare for the book signing downtown. I decide not to tell Ryan about Chris because it isn't like we're back together. Ryan wants me to resolve this, anyway, if we're ever going to have another one of those hot kisses. For now, we've got a work groove like no other.

Every once in a while, we'll look up at each other from across the room and we both smile. Each time my heart flutters like I'm sixteen years old. There's another feeling, far from pity, that draws me to him like a magnet.

Then there are the moments we both look up at the same time. One of us laughs, usually me, and the other follows suit.

"Why did I decided to be a writer?" Ryan says, mid-laugh.

"You like torture?"

"Must be."

Now, Ryan is in the kitchen getting himself a drink and a few minutes later I decide I also need some water. He's heading back and as he passes by our hands brush against each other, our fingers touching. It's the only contact we're allowing. I don't know how Ryan manages to make the smallest gestures so enticing. I'm pretty sure it will be years before I stop thinking about that one kiss we shared.

During a break I tell Ryan about my mother and Eddie.

Ryan quirks a brow. "And when did you decide to be okay with this?"

It's harder to explain the decision I made to be fine with their relationship. It was unexpected but my mother had a huge part in it. In the end, it wasn't pity, but my eternal respect for true love.

"My mother surprised me. We were having dinner and she got very upset about—" I stop myself, wondering how much of this I should censor for his sake. I violated the NDA but with people I trust will not repeat it.

"What?" he prompts.

"I'm sorry, but I let it slip that I didn't actually write the book. But she's my mother and knows how much trouble I'd get in. She thought maybe you were taking advantage of me in our arrangement. I assured her she's wrong."

I can tell he's concerned when he leans forward and pinches the back of his neck. "We won't tell anyone. That's what I worried about. I didn't ever want you to feel that way."

"Please, no, don't even go there. You haven't taken advantage of me. Apparently we're both in agreement that I should never follow in her footsteps."

I briefly explain to Ryan that my mother has finally come to realize how much of her own self she gave up to please an entire industry, and a man.

Ryan removes his glasses and rubs his eyes. "That's got to be a tough thing for her to admit."

"I'm proud of her. I never realized how deeply she regrets her own choices. She really only ever had my father who accepted her just as she was. And Eddie."

Ryan doesn't say anything but simply studies me with that blue-eyed gaze as if every word coming out of my mouth is something to revere. Something to treasure and value.

"When I think of Eddie, how much I love him, and how long he's waited to be with my mother…I want to cry." My voice breaks. "I would never want to be in the way of him having everything he's ever wanted."

There's utter tenderness in Ryan's eyes and I'm worried if he says a single word, the kindness in his voice will break me. I will *not* cry in front of Ryan. Again.

"I would wait a long time for you," he says, and rather than tears, it's utter shock that runs through me and wakes me up.

This is a splash of cold water rushing over me, the sharp chill of a freezing wind slicing through my skin. They're words I can't ignore. Words I'll never take for granted. Delight pulses through me. He always knows the right thing to say to me, the precise words I need to hear. I want to run to him. I want to plaster my mouth, my whole body to his. I want to *lean* into him and never let him go.

But I don't, because this thing between us can't happen. At least not now.

And for once I'm fresh out of words.

CHAPTER 27

When the day of the book signing arrives, I'm so nervous I arrive three hours ahead of schedule.

As the date neared, Ryan and I talked about this book signing while we worked. He too had no idea what to expect since his own signings have historically not been well attended.

"I can always count on my faculty staff, a few of my students, and two die-hard fans that like anything I write," he said.

"Two?" I gasped. "There have to be more than that!"

"Nope. Just because a reader buys my book doesn't mean they want to leave their home, drive across town, and find parking just so they can get a signed copy."

"And meet you in person!"

He shrugged. "I don't blame them. It's hard to get *me* to attend my signings."

My entire family plans on making an appearance, but they will arrive at the regular time like normal people. Ryan assured me he'd be here for moral support. He can simply wait for me in the bookcases and send me his rays of support via his expressive eyes. Just knowing he's here is enough. That's all I need.

Chris, of course, will show when he shows and it hardly matters. He believes I wrote this book in the six months he was gone, not that he'll ever read it.

He texted me earlier:

Good luck, babe! You're going to kill it. I want a signed copy. 

We're not anywhere near "babe" status again, but I ignore this. A few days ago, he sent me flowers. I can't begin to describe the confusion on the face of the 1-800-Flowers delivery guy when Abuelita pointed him in the direction of the shed. The gesture was nice, but roses are not my favorites, something Chris should know by now. Yellow daffodils are my flowers because they're so bright and hopeful. Kind of like me when I arrive and there's no line of readers waiting to see Elizabeth Brogan.

"Hi," I say to the bookseller, a woman about my age. "How are you?"

"Oh, hello," she says, giving me her full attention. "May I help you find something?"

For one terrifying moment, I think I'm in the wrong place on the wrong day. Worse, I'm not early, I'm late. It's already happened without me.

"I'm here for the book signing?" Damn, I wish I wouldn't have made that into a question.

Her eyes widen and she glances at her watch. "Well, you're a little early. It doesn't start for another three hours."

"I wanted to get here early because I'm so nervous."

She hesitates for a moment, when her entire demeanor switches into "hostess" mode, and she presses her hand to her chest.

"Oh, *you're* the author? Forgive me, for a moment I didn't recognize you."

I smile a little sheepishly. "It's the airbrushing."

Honestly, in my official author photo I look a little like Taylor Swift. I mean, *that's* how good their art department is. Still, today I'm wearing the same dress and signature red lipstick so I'll at least look a little like I do in the photo.

"I was just going to arrange the seating," she says, walking to an open area near the front window.

"Let me help you."

I need to do something to slay these nerves. But my nerves are not at all beaten into submission when I notice the big display in the window. Certainly they're on the alert and ready to have a party with their friends. It's much like the first one Ryan and I saw at my neighborhood bookstore, but on steroids. There's a huge photo of me, one of the ones taken by the photographer before the morning show. It's incredibly intimidating that I don't even look like myself, or my pseudonym alter-ego.

Far more intimidating is the enormous stack of hard-cover books they have available for sale. What if I only sell half of those? What happens to the rest of them? Are they shamefully returned to the publisher? If I sign them all so the bookstore can't return them, will I be sued?

Once we're done setting up, I have nothing to do with myself. She suggests I find a cozy corner in the back and wait for people to start arriving. I settle in the historical fiction section and find one of Ryan's earlier books on the shelf. He will be excited to know it's the only one left in stock. Flipping to the back, I study his author photo. The black-and-white photo is of him outside at a patio table. I notice a photo credit to Millie Brady. She certainly got a good angle of him, and the photo is so similar to the Ryan I know I'm sure he wasn't airbrushed. They probably don't airbrush male authors and a spike of unsettling indignation courses through me. Sure, I'm no Taylor Swift but I think I look *fine* without airbrushing. I've got a few freckles and that teeny-tiny scar from the time I fell off my bicycle but that's no crime.

I text Ryan to commiserate:

*I'm waiting in the histfic area and picked up your book. It's the only one in stock. *You* don't look airbrushed.*

Ryan replies:

I'm probably not, whatever that is. You're already there? You have two hours to go.

Me:

I was nervous so I got here early. When will you be here?

Ryan:

I'll be there before it starts. Promise. Save me a seat near the front.

This means he'll be here beforehand to give me a hug, hold me, encourage and assure me. It would be too odd for any of this to happen without him. Besides, I want him to hear all the praise for *the book* because this is his baby.

There are a few customers in the shop who drop in and out during the three-hour wait and ask about the signing. Some pass by me and give me a patient look, as if I'm taking up too much space. I move when someone reaches for Ryan's first book, *The Brother's Spy.*

"That's a very good one," I say. "You'll like it."

It's the only one I've read other than *the book* and I can no longer tell if my feelings for him are affecting my thoughts about the book.

"He's my favorite author and I'm catching up to all he's ever written." The woman beams, pressing it to her bosom. "It's like he sees me. Pain on every page. So cathartic."

"Yes," I say, biting my lower lip. "You can say that again."

I want to tell her he's also funny, self-deprecating, and the most intelligent man I've ever known. She's going to be thrilled if she stays for the signing because she might actually get to meet him.

"Stay for the signing," I say. "He's a friend and might drop by."

"*Really?*" she gasps.

I nod, though I don't want to jinx myself. Of course he'll be here. He said he would be.

Sofia and all the cousins arrive and she finds me in the back.

"Good luck!" Her tight hug is what I needed. "Is it okay if I film this and share in on social media?"

"I'm sure the publisher wants all the publicity we can get."

"Don't worry, I'll edit," she promises then looks to the front. "I think we're starting. No nerves! Remember, you've got this."

I grab her hands before she goes. "Did you see Ryan out there?"

"I didn't, but the place is jam-packed so I could have missed him."

"We have a full house?"

Sofia smiles. "Actually, there's a line out the door to get in."

It feels like all the breath leaves my body and I'm sure my smile freezes in place because Sofia's eyes narrow. I do not want to disappoint all these people. It would be tragic.

"Are you okay?" she asks.

"I'm f-fine." Though I would very much like Ryan to be with me at the moment. "If you find Ryan, could you send him back here?"

"Will do!" She has to pry my fingers off hers and gives me a thumbs-up.

But before Sofia can fetch Ryan, the bookseller finds me. "It's time!"

I follow her out on my shaky knees and find my spot on the dais next to her chair. She introduces me to the audience as the bestselling author of *Soulmates* and explains I'll do a short reading, then take any questions from the audience.

I'm prepared and pull out my copy with the scene I've chosen. It's a touching scene in which Grayson decides he must let Lula go. It's effective and I hear several sniffles as I read. When I look up, I see my mother and Eddie sitting together, beaming, Abuelita next to my mother. All of my tios and tias are here, with their adult children. No wonder there was a line out the door. My family alone could fill this room. I relax, knowing I'm in a safe space. They love me, no matter what I do or how hard I might fail. Eddie has talked about an impromptu karaoke party to celebrate but so far I've avoided him. It's enough that I've given my blessing for him and my mother. I shouldn't have to suffer through more karaoke so soon.

But as I take questions from the audience, I still can't locate Ryan. I do see someone else I know, however. Someone I didn't expect to be here, though I now wish I'd been far more in touch. She'd sent me one other email I hadn't replied to in which she asked again why I couldn't at least share I had a contract without the particulars.

There's no excuse for being a bad friend and in that moment I realize that's exactly what I've been. Far too caught up in Ryan, this opportunity, then my mother and Eddie. The whole secrecy of the project. But none of that matters. No excuses. I've failed in the friendship department.

Holly is seated in the first row.

She's got a copy of *Soulmates* in her lap, and I swear I can see the whites of her knuckles as she clutches it. Most of the questions are run-of-the-mill and fully expected. Everything from how long I've been writing to how I came up with the idea. Pepper and I have gone over these at length and my answers are easy and ready.

Then it's Holly's turn and she stands.

I give her a smile and wave, something I haven't done with anyone else. It's an "I see you, please forgive me. I'll do better," greeting.

She doesn't return the smile.

"So," she says. "Elizabeth Brogan is a pen name, right?"

"Yes, true." We've never represented anything else. "I also go by Luci Santana."

My abuelita beams from her seat, nodding.

"I thought so." She sets her book down on the chair.

"Everyone, Holly is my long-time critique partner and a friend."

There's a murmur among the crowd as they turn to Holly, giving her their attention.

Holly seems to sag a little but my acknowledgment is not enough for her. "It's just, as you know, I've read your earlier works and this...it just doesn't sound like your voice. The tone is different. The word choice."

"It's a stylistic choice that seemed appropriate for the book."

"Yes, but you're a ghostwriter, so I wonder if you hired one for this book?"

I clear my throat. "You know that if I had I couldn't reveal that to you anyway."

"What do you mean?" the bookseller says, scanning the room nervously.

She's probably never had an author accused of this in her bookstore.

Sofia is filming, but she stops, giving Holly a look through narrowed eyes.

"I guess what I'm trying to ask here," Holly says, meeting

my gaze with nothing short of contempt. "Did you actually *write* this book?"

CHAPTER 28

There's a collective gasp in the room.

Scanning the audience for Ryan I see he's still not here. Neither is Chris, by the way, but I don't need him. Still, he'd at least rally to my defense and so would his gym bros. My poor family is in the audience and those who are paying attention look worried. Eddie's eyes are wide. My mother is chewing on a fingernail with narrowed eyes. Most of my cousins are on their phones so they have no idea there's something more interesting going on right in front of them.

"I'm sorry, but we're not gathered here to accuse an author of plagiarism when she's a *New York Times* bestselling author with a publishing house who *does* their due diligence," the bookseller says, coming to my rescue.

"I'm not accusing her of that," Holly said, chin tipped. "But she's a former ghostwriter so maybe she hired her *own* ghostwriter for this book."

"That's ridiculous," the bookseller says. "She can obviously write a book, why hire someone to do it for her?"

"Is she going to answer the question or *not?*" Holly's eyes narrow.

Holly is angrier than I expected but I'm not surprised. I've ignored her for weeks as my life took a turn I'd never dreamed of. She wanted answers I couldn't give her.

Several seconds lapse in which my life flashes before my eyes. There's a pebble in my windpipe and I can't swallow. My mouth is dry enough to be sandpaper. I was afraid I would freeze up. But of all the things I worried about, not one was a friend flying all the way from Missouri to humiliate me.

But it turns out I don't need Ryan here and I don't need anyone else. I speak for myself and no one needs to do this for me. No one has to stand up and defend me because I can do that myself. I have the words and strength I need. It doesn't matter whether or not I wrote *this* book, I can write books. I've written many for which someone else has always taken the credit. And I've made an arrangement with a man who has come to mean a lot to me. I will honor it for the sake of his reputation and because he's a good man even if he made a mistake.

He doesn't deserve his entire career to go down in flames because of one viral video made when he was suffering. We have access to everything on the Internet now, and it lives forever. Maybe what we all need to learn is how to forgive each other for being human.

"No, I did not hire a ghostwriter for this book."

And that, my friends, is the truth.

"Next question," the bookseller barks.

Holly sits with a grunt.

A man in the back stands. "I'm Brett from the Writing Out Loud podcast. I was actually going to pose a similar question to the author, because this entire book is written from the male's perspective. A single point of view. You're a woman, how can *you* know what a man goes through? What he feels? How can you live his experience? It isn't authentic."

Every woman in the store turns to look at him like he's a flea but none with greater contempt than my mother. I'm happy to say his shoulders slump visibly when it occurs to him that plenty of men have written the female perspective and gotten away with this inauthentically for eons.

It happens so fast no one sees it coming, but my mother heads straight toward the man. I catch Eddie trying to grab her arm but misses. Once she reaches the man she gives him several swats with her purse while everyone, including my cousins, whip out their phones and do their thing. They start *filming.*

And now this too shall live forever.

"How dare you!" Mami yells.

"It's a reasonable question!" the man says, ducking and covering his head.

My mother stops hitting him long enough to yell back, "Do you know how many male writers have told a story from a woman's perspective? ALL of them. Let me tell you, sir, a woman's special place does not look like flower petals! Also, bosoms don't heave and nipples don't talk to each other. How dare you suggest my daughter isn't a wonderful writer? She. Is. A. Wonderful. Writer!"

Mami emphasizes each word with a generous purse slap. She's not really hurting the man but it's quite embarrassing anyway. Everyone with a phone is filming this, which is...everyone. This is going to be all over social media in moments. I'm standing on the dais taking shallow breaths, watching it all unfold, wondering how this will look to Ryan, Kate, Pepper, and the publisher. They're going to be sorry they ever hired *me* for this farce. Hopefully they believe in the old adage, "all publicity is good publicity." Part of me wants to scream and the other wants to run out of here while no one will notice me leaving.

Ryan. Where in the ever-loving hell is *Ryan?*

It isn't until the bookstore clerk uses a bull horn that people stop yelling and my mother stops smacking.

"Inside voices!" The bookseller declares from the chair where she's standing while making the peace sign. "Please form a line if you'd like Elizabeth to sign your book! If you've preordered you're at the front of the line."

Apparently the police don't need to be called and we're all going to behave like civilized people again. The man my mother attacked with her purse rushes out (smart man) and a line begins to form. I'm led to the table and chair where I can sit and sign books. I'm out of breath and having an out-of-body experience but I can do this. I've been hired to straddle this morally gray area and here I am, killing it. I think.

Of course, I'm still wondering *where the hell Ryan is.*

The first person in line is Holly, who says, "Make it out to 'my long-time critique partner who has over the years guided my career with invaluable insight and support.'"

It takes me a while to write it all out, but I do, because it's true. She guessed the truth because she knows me. I *didn't* write the book but I can't admit it, even to her. She could have been nicer and not humiliated me in front of a crowd, but I sign the book and say, "Thank you for your support."

She huffs and walks away.

The long line continues with people I've never met, ending with my family, whom I have met many times. Eddie and Mami have a stack of books for me to sign.

"I'm giving them as Christmas presents," Mami says to those in line behind her, tapping the cover of the book. "This is my daughter's book."

The fact she's proud of me even if she knows the truth fills me with hope. Maybe someday she'll be proud of a book

I've actually written. It would be nice but I don't need her to be proud. I'm proud of myself.

Later, after everyone's gone, I express my deep apologies to the bookseller over the chaos.

"It's a controversial book, I guess, what with the ending, or lack of one." She shrugs. "I just didn't know anyone would be questioning whether or not you wrote it."

"I know, right?" I bite my lower lip, guilt pressing as I lie to a nice lady. "Thank you for handling all this so well."

"I've been around the block a time or two. Can I ask? Why did you leave the ending so open-ended?"

"I actually expected the questions tonight to be more about that. The good news is there's a sequel with a very clear ending."

I already know Lula is going to wind up with Grayson, maybe after a suitable amount of time realizing Derek is a first-class jerk.

Finally, once I'm in my car, I take a moment to text Chris:

Just wanted to let you know, it's not cool that you didn't show up. Tonight was important to me. If you really were my friend you'd understand this.

I don't wait for him to respond but text Ryan instead.

Where are you? I have some important things to tell you and I thought you'd be here.

Maybe he's in the habit of letting people down all the time and this is simply the first time I've personally experienced it. I didn't expect Ryan would blow me off like this. He's always been grateful even if not always entirely supportive when it came to the sequel.

Maybe he has a good excuse, but even if that's true, I'd at least expect a text.

My family asked me to come with them to the local café where they want to treat me to a special dinner so I'll head there next. Before I go, I check social media to see if any of the reels are trending yet. All I have to do is search *book signing* and I find videos of my mother smacking the idiot man with her purse. Some are set to music boomerangs and others have been made into memes with: #whenyouraunt-thoughtthegummieswerecandy. I suspect my cousins.

Someone has commented: *Isn't that Geneva Santana from Desperate Hearts? OMG, I love her!*

The hashtags are all over the place from #anotherway-toreadbooks to #bookattacksman and #thispurseisonfire but thankfully, so far, no mention of the fact the signing was for Elizabeth Brogan. They are too preoccupied with my mother's purse. For a moment, I fool myself into thinking no one will ever make the connection to Elizabeth and the book. No surprise, negative news makes it faster to a reel than anything positive.

My phone pings, displaying Pepper's name, and I pick up. "I can explain."

"You're okay!" Pepper says.

I slink in the driver's seat and cover my face with my hand. "You heard?"

"Yes, and we were just worried you'd been hurt."

"No, not me." I groan, not entirely willing to admit my mother was the one with the attack purse.

There's a small chance no one ever has to know that.

"When Millie let us know, naturally, we were concerned about you, too. Good to know you're fine."

"What does Millie have to do with my book signing?"

There's a long pause. "I'm not sure we're talking about the same thing. Millie called us from the hospital to let us know Ryan was in a car accident on the way to the bookstore."

And that's when my world splits into before and after.

CHAPTER 29

ar accident.

There are no two other words in the English language that, when put together, have such a sickening effect on me. My mind goes back to a rainy night twenty years ago. A policeman at our front door. My mother falling to her knees. Later, Eddie, openly weeping without a hint of shame. And me, wanting *someone* to blame besides the rain and a father who loved driving fast through mountain curves.

There are fissures in a life, moments that define what happened after.

I don't want this to be one of those moments. It can't be. I would not write it this way and I don't even think Ryan would.

"Is he okay?" My voice breaks.

"I don't know, but he's hurt enough that Millie called us. She didn't say much before hanging up, she was too upset."

She would know better than to call his estranged family and an ache forms in my chest that Ryan has no one else in the area who cares. Except me. My heart is racing, beating like it will smash through the wall of my chest. If she was too upset to talk, Ryan might be seriously injured. I've got to get there now.

"What hospital?" I ask.

Pepper tells me Ryan is at El Camino Hospital, which isn't far.

"I've tried calling Ryan, but he's not answering," Pepper says.

He could be unconscious, or in a coma. Of course, he might also not have his phone with him at the hospital. You never want to give an author any room to imagine the worst because we are a creative sort. I am picturing everything from a broken leg to death.

The fact Ryan was with Millie doesn't even register on my radar until I'm halfway to the hospital. The only thing that matters now is that he's alive. He has to be. If he dies, if he's dead, I swear I'm going to…stop writing. Stop dreaming. There would be no point.

Simply imagining this fictional scenario has tears streaming down my face before I even start driving and I'm forced to take a moment to calm down. It will do no one any good if I have an accident of my own on the way to the hospital.

I hang up with Pepper and have enough presence of mind to text Sofia that I can't make dinner due to an emergency but will see everyone later. Then I'm off, pulling onto the street and joining traffic. I make it across town in record time, even with my safe driving skills, which normally keep me well below the speed limit. Parking near the ER entrance, I race across the parking lot and through the double doors to the triage nurse behind the glass window.

"Ryan Brady," I say when I'm able to catch my breath. "I was told he's here."

"And you are…"

I'm…I'm nobody. I wonder if I could get away with saying I'm his wife. After all, I'm like his work wife. There's no way they will let me back there if I say I'm his assistant. They'll laugh me out of the hospital.

"I'm, um, his wife." It's tough not to wince at the lie but I think I've pulled it off.

From behind me, someone clears their throat.

"He doesn't have a wife."

I turn and for a moment, everything feels blurry and out of focus. It's Millie, looking model gorgeous with her jet-black hair and matching pantsuit. I'm encouraged by the fact she doesn't look like she's been crying. Her eyes aren't red or puffy like mine. She knows more than I do, which means Ryan is alive.

But Pepper called me, Ryan did not. Maybe he called Millie. Maybe I'm intruding simply by being here. But I don't care because I'm not leaving until I know he's okay.

"Wife, huh? Hello, Luci," she says. "Or do you want me to call you Elizabeth?"

She inspects me, head to toe, as if expecting to find some defect by the manufacturer. I hate when beautiful women do that to us mere mortals.

"Where is he? How is he?" I manage. "I want to see him and you know they weren't going to let me in."

The interesting thing is she's got a plastic band on her wrist, the kind they give when you're admitted to the hospital or clinic for any reason at all.

"He's going to be fine," she says, and I hear the edge of annoyance in her tone. "*You* didn't have to come. We were in a fender bender."

"Oh. Ohhh." At that moment, every one of my muscles unclenches and I sway in place. A fender bender. I don't like those, either, but I know from my extensive research on accidents before I dared take my driver's test, they're the ones that happen the great majority of the time. Fatal accidents account for only 0.5 percent of the time, which doesn't sound like much, but it's still tens of thousands of people every year.

"Here's the patient now," Millie says and I turn to see him being wheeled out by an attendant.

His arm is in a sling and his hair is ruffled but otherwise he looks fine. There are no missing limbs, no casts, no blood, bruises, scratches, or cuts on his face. I'm going to assume they've done X-rays to look for internal bleeding.

"Were X-rays done to check internal bleeding?" I ask the young woman pushing Ryan's wheelchair.

Millie quirks a brow. "Are you a doctor?"

"No, I'm a writer."

"Yes, all that was done," the attendant says. "He's all clear."

I feel like I can breathe again and take in a great big, beautiful breath of sweet air. Everything that had been flipped off its axis slips right back into place.

Ryan is giving me a big smile when I meet his eyes.

"Wow! Who are you?"

Oh, I recognize *this* Ryan. It's Adorable Ryan once again making an appearance. I'm a bit surprised he doesn't recognize me. But he's also not wearing the glasses he claims he doesn't need for anything other than for reading. Not sure I believe that anymore.

"He's being discharged but he's on a lot of pain medication," the attendant explains.

"Yeah, please thank my doctor." Ryan throws back his head to laugh and winces. "Ow. Not going to do that again."

"Give too much pain medication to a man who barely takes a Tylenol." Millie waves her hand in the air. "And this is what you get."

"Can I take Ryan home? Doesn't he need a ride?" I ask.

"I'll take him," Millie says.

"No." Ryan turns to the attendant and points to me. "This woman will take me home, whoever she is."

"Ryan, it's me, *Luci*."

"Oh, right. I remember now." He squints and nods. "You're the beautiful one who helps me."

"Are you sure, honey?" Millie says, placing a hand on his arm. "I feel like this is all my fault."

"It *is* your fault," Ryan says. "But it's okay! It's really fine. I'm good, good. Just…leave me alone. Please."

"It's fine, I'm headed that way," I lie.

"Alright, let's go." Ryan says and the attendant pushes him toward the sliding glass doors.

Millie brings up the rear, her high heels clacking on the pavement behind me. "I'm sorry. I truly am. I honestly didn't see that car or I would have stopped in time."

"You were in the accident with him?" I ask.

"Fender bender," she corrects, then turns back to him. "I'll find your glasses and get them back to you. If you need me, anytime, day or night, let me know. I'll be there."

Ryan is already over by my car, standing, trying to open the door without success and quite confused it won't open. "What's going on here?"

I run over, clicking the key fob on my way. "It's locked."

"Yeah, that makes sense." He then opens the door and nearly falls into the passenger seat even with the nurse's help.

I go around to the driver's side but not before Millie calls out to me, "Ask him to tell you *how* he came up with the pen name. He doesn't like to talk about it, but you should know."

I've already asked, of course, and received a pat answer. Her comment tells me in no uncertain terms I should dive deeper.

With that she turns and walks back to the hospital, following the attendant with the empty wheelchair.

I join Ryan and start the car.

"No." Ryan leans his head back and groans. "I missed the signing."

It's as if he's just remembered.

"Don't worry about it, you have a good excuse."

"No, I don't. She tricked me. You think I would know by now." He pinches the bridge of his nose.

"Tricked you?"

"The problem is I have too big a heart. It's like"—he looks down at his chest—"three times too big. I'm the opposite of the Grinch."

"You're a little like the Grinch until people get to know you." I bite back a smile.

"I told her I only had a few minutes and had to get to the bookstore but she started *crying* again."

That sounded way too familiar. I'm beginning to wonder if she'd kept him from the signing on purpose. It's not as if he needed to be there except for me.

"It's fine that you missed it," I say. "Everything worked out."

"Yeah, I bet it went well!" He sounds so enthusiastic I don't have the heart to tell him everything now. "Tell me."

"Um, yeah, fine, we sold a ton of books. But we'll talk about that later." I grip the steering wheel tighter. "Why is your arm in a sling but Millie seems fine?"

"Oh, well see the car broadsided *my* side. Isn't that funny?" Ryan closes his eyes like he's dozing. "She has all the luck."

"Yes, she seems pretty lucky to me."

I can barely hear his next words. "If I'd met you first, she wouldn't have stood a chance. And then none of this would have ever happened."

"None of what?"

"No Millie. No *book*," he mumbles. "You're really beautiful, you know, but I can't say that because it would be wrong and inappropriate. I know the rules."

I have to smile at his rigidness. "Why would that be wrong?"

"Inappropriate." He holds his finger to his lips. "Shhhh. Don't tell anyone. It's a secret."

"I think I can speak for myself and I wouldn't mind at all if you say it."

But Ryan's eyes shut and he drifts off on a cloud of pain meds.

Once we get to the house, I realize he's a lot heavier and bigger than he looks. All I do is take off his seatbelt, put my arm around him and I can't budge him. Without his assistance, I will never in a million years get him out of this car. I consider phoning my cousin Diego who is often bragging about how much he can bench press. Last I heard it was two hundred pounds. Ryan can't possibly weigh that much. Can he?

Then he moves and rubs his eyes.

"Hey," he says and groans when he shifts.

The medication might be wearing off. "Is it your arm?"

"It's my ribs. They're bruised." He winces and drags a hand through his hair, mussing it up. "But I'm okay. They'll heal on their own. Four to six weeks, they say. Piece of cake."

I stand by as he heaves one leg out of the car, carefully lifting himself out. Walking ahead of him, I unlock his front door.

Ryan sways a bit, catching himself.

"Whoa. That's funny but too bad I can't laugh because it hurts. Thank for the ride," he says with a wave.

"I'm not just *leaving* you here." I hold the door open for him.

He squints, brow furrowed. "Why not?"

"You're hurt, and anyway I want to talk to you for a while."

"The signing."

I'm not confident with the way he sways and plops down on his couch wincing.

"Unless you want to talk about all that…later," I say.

"You know what? That might be a good thing. Because I don't really know where I am right now." He glances around the room and chuckles. "Oh wait. I *do* remember this place. This is Henry's house."

"Good grief. You need water to flush those pills through your system."

I find him a bottle of water and hand it over. Maybe I should wait to ask my question, but the drugs have become a truth serum for him.

Ryan takes gulps of water, alternately wincing and pinching the bridge of his nose.

"I think I better go to bed. That's a great idea, the best I've had today."

"Let me help."

"No, I can do this." But he's favoring the opposite arm, which makes him walk a bit sideways.

I follow him into the bedroom, the secret portion of the house previously hidden from me. I feel like the heroine in *The Secret Garden*. The ornate mahogany bed in the center of the room looks like a replica of an eighteenth-century one. There is even more of Professor Henry's erotica art on his dresser, on the walls. It looks like Ryan has taken one corner of the room. He's brought no framed photos except of a young girl on the nightstand. She beams into the camera with a familiar smile.

That's Ryan's smile. His niece? Daughter? He's never mentioned her, but maybe it's a delicate subject. Still, if he had a daughter, I know I would have heard that. The beautiful girl has a crooked front tooth, the light in her shimmering blue eyes mischievous. I want to pick up this photo and study it closer.

A groaning sound gets my attention.

Ryan has reached the bed, is attempting to take off his shirt and is doubled over in pain.

I rush to his side. "Let me."

The less he moves his arms the better, so I ease the long-sleeved button-up down one shoulder, insuring him as little movement as possible. I am able to slide it off without having to move his arms.

"Hey, you're really good at this," Ryan says.

He groans, his face a mask of pain. There are purple and blue bruises on his rib cage and now I'm the one wincing.

"Oh, Ryan," I whisper, my fingers hovering over his bruises. "This looks bad."

Ryan lies back and from the expression on his face this move wasn't a good idea.

"Maybe you shouldn't," I say, grabbing the discharge instructions I set down on his dresser and scanning them. "It says here it might be best to sleep in a chair for the first few nights. Less pressure on the rib cage. Isn't that chair in the living room a recliner?"

"But that would mean I have to move again."

"I'll help you." But I can't when he brushes me off.

"I've got it." He's not all that steady but shuffles his way to the chair, sits, and pulls out the recliner portion. "My father has a chair like this."

"Eddie has one, too."

I used to think those chairs were made for old men but then I sat in one. Now I think the idea of making a chair that's a little bit of a bed is pure genius.

"I'm reduced to sleeping in a chair." Ryan shuts his eyes and scowls. "How am I going to finish my book?"

"We'll figure something out." I find a blanket, which I carefully place over him avoiding his injured areas.

He's still not wearing a shirt and this is slightly distracting so covering him helps both of us.

He opens one eye. "Thank you."

"The instructions also say icing is a good idea, so I should go to the store and get some ice packs. The soft ones."

He probably wants to snooze but…well, before he does, I want to know how he came up with the pen name. I want to know specifically who she is. She's my namesake, so to speak, so I have a right to know. In the back of my mind, I hope I don't embarrass myself and that Millie hasn't set me up.

"Ryan? Are you awake?"

"Hmmm," he says, eyes still closed.

"You said Elizabeth Brogan is a family name but you never told me who. A grandmother? Aunt? Cousin?"

"Yeah."

I can see this is going to be another one of those one-word conversations if I don't take the reins.

"So, which one of them is it? Do you have a daughter? Is that Elizabeth?"

He opens one eye. "You think I have a daughter?"

"The photo in your bedroom…she looks like you. Same eyes and smile."

"Oh." He smiles a little, eyes closed. "My sister."

"But I thought you…you only ever mentioned you and your brother." Once the words slide out of me, I can't take them back and I'm afraid of what he'll say next.

"It is," he says, and I can't tell if the pain crossing his features is from bruised ribs or something far deeper. "She died a long time ago. Elizabeth."

CHAPTER 30

"She *died?*"

He nods. "Brogan was her middle name, which is my mother's maiden name. Elizabeth Brogan Brady. I just dropped the Brady."

"I'm so sorry. I shouldn't have brought it up." My voice breaks.

My throat is closing up with thick emotion, and I can't speak.

I shouldn't have listened to Millie. Curiosity got the best of me tonight, but maybe she did set me up. Ryan doesn't need to be reminded of this kind of grief and loss, especially now. Then again, isn't he reminded of her every time he sees *me?* Every time he sees the book cover with her name on it? Maybe this is the real reason he never wanted to write another one again.

But he takes my hand, threads his fingers through mine, giving me a pass. "It's okay. You saw the picture. I have it with me whenever I'm writing. She's become sort of my muse over the years."

It all makes sense now he'd choose a woman's name. It

wasn't a marketing ploy. It wasn't trickery. It was simply… love.

"The pen name means a lot more to me now. Before, it was just another pretty name."

"I read somewhere that most authors try to honor someone they love with a pen name. Sometimes it's a family name, a grandparent, a child. For me, it was my sister."

"Why didn't you tell me?"

He shrugs, his eyes closing again. "I don't want anyone to feel sorry for me. It's hard to talk about it."

"It doesn't mean you shouldn't try."

"She's the real reason I wrote the book. When they offered me all that money…it was a good chance to set up a foundation for Elizabeth. It's a literary one that gives a scholarship every year to underprivileged kids."

This was the literacy foundation I noticed in his paperwork when I snooped. He isn't just a *contributor*. He started the whole thing.

"I kept teaching because my writing barely covered my bills. When Kate explained what kind of money she was talking about, I had to go for it. And then the morning show…well, it meant more exposure and more sales. You understand, don't you?"

Of course I understand. Anyone would take the opportunity, and most for far less benevolent reasons.

"You might not want to talk about it. But how…" I let the sentence trail off, not even sure I want to know.

We've both suffered staggering losses. A sister. A father.

"Drowned. We were at the lake, I was supposed to be watching her, but…well, my new Star Wars Lego set was far more important at the time."

An ache slices through my heart with what feels like a sharp sword. Ryan was a child himself. I can't begin to imagine the pressing guilt he must have felt all those years.

He would have been angry with himself, angry with his parents, then angry at the world.

"That couldn't have been *your* fault. How old were you?"

"Eleven." He sighs. "I was the oldest and should have known better. She wanted to go swimming and I told her she had to wait. Well, like most little kids, she didn't listen."

It's no wonder Ryan isn't close to his family. The odds are that at least some of them blame him even if it's unfair and illogical. Grief can be irrational and I know. I blamed my mother for years because my father was speeding, driving alone in the rain. In my child's mind, I thought she could have stopped him. If she loved him enough, she could have saved him.

And Ryan's parents would have wrestled with their own grief, knowing they shouldn't have put a child in charge of a child. Grief wants logic it can never have. A reason why a world suddenly splinters into pieces and changes every moment from that point forward. Because the heart wants someone to blame for its breaking.

For me, it was my mother. It had to have been *her* fault that my father died, even when it made no sense. Someone besides him had to take responsibility, and she did, for many years. She shouldn't have *let him* drive on that rainy day. Leaving me with my father's family hadn't helped, but now I wonder: Did I reject her before she rejected me? It's impossible to know at this point.

I have no words.

Maybe we only have few words when there's far too much to say.

"Listen. You're the best Elizabeth Brogan I could have ever chosen. When we met that first day," he says, his words beginning to slur with the heaviness of sleep, "I didn't plan on asking *you* to be Elizabeth but then Henry saw you had this gentle quality about you. A joy and a kindness and a solid strength, which reminded me of her."

With that last word, he falls asleep. I can do nothing more for him but I'm rooted to this spot on the couch.

I quietly watch him sleep and breathe and maybe dream.

A FEW HOURS LATER, a shaft of moonlight spills through open blinds and wakes me. It occurs to me that my family has no idea where I am and I probably should let someone know I'm staying here with Ryan. Maybe he doesn't need me, but after the accident, I can't leave him. Life is short. Stuff happens sometimes when you look away and are distracted by something bright and shiny. I won't leave Ryan's side because maybe if I just sit here and keep watch nothing worse can happen. It could be the hospital missed something. Once I watched a show where a kid who'd been in a car accident was sitting up talking, just fine, then later died from internal bleeding. Maybe Ryan has internal bleeding and doesn't know it.

It's after midnight when I text Sofia that Ryan has been in a car accident. She knows what this means to me. For years, I wouldn't get behind the wheel of a car. I was seventeen when I got my license. I drive slower and more cautiously than most people do and I avoid driving in the rain, which is probably the reason I can never leave California.

Sofia:

Mierda! Is he okay? At you at the hospital? WHAT HAPPENED?

I respond:

A car accident. He's got bruised ribs but they gave him too many meds at the hospital. Overmedicated Ryan is hilarious but once the meds wear off I don't expect he's going to be a lot of fun to be around.

Sofia, who is a nurse, after all, responds:

No, he is not. Have him sleep in a chair and try not to cough. Or laugh. Don't make him laugh! He'll be healed up in a few weeks if they're only bruised. If they're cracked it might be longer.

If I can't express my fears to Sofia, there's no one.

What about internal bleeding? Is that a thing that could happen? You should see all the bruises on his rib cage. Poor baby.

Sofia texts back:

I'm sure they checked all that out before they released him. They would have done X-rays and scans.

I'm not sure I believe her. We all know the state of our health care system is a running joke. If Ryan doesn't have good insurance, maybe they cut corners. I'll have to stay here and keep watch.

I find a blanket, curl up on the couch, and try to sleep.

When I wake hours later, I'm blinking, nearly blinded by the sunlight streaming through the windows. Ryan is still dozing. He looks so peaceful, those long dark lashes contrasting against his olive skin. Way too peaceful. It scares me and I check to make sure he's still breathing.

When he is, I decide I'll go get the prescription and ice packs I should have picked up for him last night. Grabbing my purse, I nearly bump into Millie on my way out.

"Oh, sorry." I close the door and lock it. "He's still sleeping."

She holds out his glasses. "You better give these to him. I waited around at the hospital for them after you two left."

I take them, then can't stop myself from being kind. It's in my nature, damn it. "Are you okay? Did you have any injuries?"

She snorts. "No, only to my heart."

I'm never prepared for metaphors or hyperbole from non-writers. I don't know how to respond.

She rolls her eyes, crossing her arms. "I'll be fine. I was

too late, that's all. If you're smart, you won't make the same mistake I did. There's no better man."

"Oh, but we're just—"

She holds up a palm. "Save it. Maybe that's what *you* think, but he loves you whether you want him to or not."

A quake of excitement runs through my body. "You're wrong."

"I wasn't sure he was talking about you, but yesterday he finally told me I should give up on him because there's someone else." She narrows her eyes. "Then you showed up at the hospital and he was completely ga-ga. Who *else* could it be?"

I don't know who else it could be either, but I also didn't know my ex-fiancé was having an emotional affair with his coffeehouse crush. I'm not the best judge.

"But if you break his heart, I'll be back around to pick up the pieces."

With that she starts down the brick path before she stops suddenly.

"You know, he thinks he looks better without his glasses. Make sure you tell him he looks good with them on. It's one of those weird male idiosyncrasies. He only behaves this way when he's in love. I know because it used to be me."

It's a loving thing for an ex-wife to say and I'm impressed by her candor. "Okay."

"I will always love him." She walks to the curb and gets in her vehicle.

Once she's out of earshot, I feel comfortable muttering, "Then you should have *chosen* him."

WHEN I RETURN, I find Ryan sitting at the dining table, his laptop open. He's wearing a shirt now, which is a relief, because knowing what I do now, I don't need to see those abs.

They are logical decision killers.

"You should be resting! What are you *doing*?"

"Swimming."

Oh, so he's back to his smartass self. This I can handle because adorable Ryan is way too attractive.

And he's squinting.

"Here you go." I hand the glasses over with the medicine. "Millie dropped these off earlier."

He slips them back on and winces at the movement. "I have to turn in this revised proposal if I want to get paid."

"Have you ever heard of dictation programs? Maybe that would help. I've heard a lot of authors use them."

"I've never been able to get that to work for me."

"Have you actually tried?" I stand behind him. "You wouldn't have to move your arms as much. Just lay back and dictate. Rest *and* write. All you need is your brain and creativity."

When he struggles with the bottle of pills, I take it from him and open it.

He pops a pill, grimaces, and slams down some water. "I'm fine."

"Please don't be that guy."

"*What* guy?"

"The one who won't accept help when it's offered."

I meet his eyes and wonder if he even remembers our conversation from last night. He'd been so vulnerable then, so open, but now he's shut down.

"This book won't write itself."

"Look, you hired me as your assistant so why don't you let me assist?" I stand behind him, hands on hips, ready to fight.

"That was before I hired you to be Elizabeth Brogan." He

closes his eyes and pinches the bridge of his nose, groaning. "I must have told you about my sister last night, didn't I?"

I nod. "And I'm glad you did."

"I shouldn't have told you that sad story. *Don't* feel sorry for me."

Well, isn't that just like a man. *Don't feel sorry for me because then I'm weak.*

Ryan was right when he said there was a little bit of Grayson in him and a little bit of the other guy.

I pull out the chair next to him, sit, and reach for the laptop, moving it in front of me. "I'm glad you told me. Now, why don't you let me be your hands today. Tell me what you want to write and I'll type it for you. I'm your dictation soft-ware. Just…don't speak too fast."

"That's not how my process works." He grabs the laptop, moving it back, flinching when he does.

"But I want to help you."

"You have, and now you can write the sequel."

"I can do both. You're the one with the closest deadline. I can help you *and* write my book. Believe me, I'm a disciplined writer or I wouldn't have been able to write all those Desdemona books. Let me." With that I shove the laptop back to me and shut it, crossing my arms over it, and giving him a pout. "Please."

He throws his head back. "Damn it!"

Ryan complains, and he argues, but a few minutes later with me giving him puppy-dog eyes the entire time, he begins. Haltingly at first, a few words at a time. But, may I say, they are good words. Every one.

"I'm a slow writer," he says as if to apologize.

"That's okay, I'm a slow typist. We're perfect for each other."

CHAPTER 31

By afternoon, we've made it through an entire chapter. We take breaks for lunch and Ryan is alert, pain no longer distracting him. I even have to slow him down a few times, reminding him I'm not *literally* dictation software.

There's a clear-cut love story now, introduced early, even if I know it won't take over the entire book. I'm sure it's exactly what Kate wants. She doesn't want a carbon copy of *Soulmates,* she just wants the same heart and soul and now she'll get it.

"I love this new direction," I say.

"Just took your advice. You've been a big help. Anyway, you can go. I'll be fine."

I grab my purse, ready to go but then I stop because there's something he should know. Somehow *not* telling him feels equally wrong.

"I didn't have a chance to tell you, but Chris…my ex…he's back."

He quirks a brow. "You didn't think he'd stay in South America forever, did you?"

"No, but, the thing is, he wants me to give him another chance."

"Can't say I'm surprised." If he feels anything at all, I don't see the slightest hint.

I expected a bigger reaction from someone who's *supposed* to be in love with me. There's no hint that this affects him in the least. We might as well be talking about the weather.

I fiddle with my purse strap, like it needs adjusting. It does not.

"What do you think? Should I…give him another chance?"

There's zero hesitation. "You should. He made a mistake."

I wish he'd tell me I shouldn't. I wish he'd tell me that *he* clearly is the one for me. We have everything in common. We're so right together that everyone can see it. Even Millie sees it!

He simply stands and adjusts his glasses. He isn't taking them off in front of me any longer. No male idiosyncrasies here. Sure, Ryan does find me attractive, that much we've established. But true love is another matter entirely. Love is something far deeper when it grows like wildflowers, which thrive even in the worst elements as long as the soil is rich. Ours is merely a powerful physical attraction. No one can build a life on that alone. If that's all a couple has, there's always going to be someone else waiting in the wings. Been there, done that.

I nod. "Okay, I'll do it."

I'm halfway out the door when I hear his voice again. "That's all it takes?"

"What do you mean?"

"Face it, you weren't waiting for *me* to say it's okay. You wanted permission from someone, and I'm here to give it. This decision should come from you no matter what anyone else says. So, yes, if you once loved him or still do…

give him a chance. Second chances are one of my favorite tropes."

My heart aches, but I almost smile at the reference. "You are *such* a romantic."

"No, I'm a realist." He smiles, his eyes tipping down at the corners, giving him his eternally sad look.

"Really?" Anger flushes through me. "Is it because you can't see *yourself* as someone who any woman in their right mind would choose?"

"No. I don't need you to choose me. Damn it, when will you listen? It was just *a book*."

But I see a wounded little boy who felt responsible for his family's happiness for so many years and might still feel that way. There's a grown man who is stuck in the belief he doesn't deserve to be happy because that's the message he was given early on. He's making the choices he's always made even when they're no longer serving him.

For years I also believed I was "too much" and worked my entire life to be easier to love. Easier to swallow, by cutting myself into smaller pieces. I know this is the way Chris sees me. He doesn't see the woman I've become since he's been gone.

Ryan sees *me* and I feel safe with him. Safe enough to leave nothing unsaid.

"You want to know what your problem is?"

"Too many to list." Ryan opens the bottle, pops another pill and slams it down with some water.

I point to him. "You can't see yourself the way others see you. It's easier to fall back into old habits than take a risk. Easier to be a grump than open up your heart and *love* someone."

"I've taken plenty of risks." He scowls. "Most of them didn't take me to a good place."

I would say *the book* was the exception but now I see it was Kate who took the risk. Kate who saw what a gem the book could eventually become, unlike anything Ryan had previously written.

"I agree some people are not worth the risk. But some are."

A moment passes between us, filled with empty words and unexpressed thoughts. On his part, I'm sure.

I take several steps toward him and kiss him on the mouth, hard. I'm careful not to hurt him but I kiss him with everything I have. I kiss him like it's the last time I'm ever getting this chance. Without Ryan, I would have never found the best parts of myself.

Ryan is kissing me back, and it's another one of those kisses where I'm lost. I fall into him, forgetting anyone or anything else. We're forgetting ourselves, forgetting rules, forgetting everything that doesn't fit into this moment.

He's the one who pulls back. "Go."

"But—"

"I told you I'm not a saint." He runs a hand through his hair so hard his glasses shift. "I can't do this with you right now. I know what it feels like to be betrayed."

"So do *I*."

He nods, acknowledging this truth.

It's another one of those little things that connect us. Both of our exes came crawling back to us after breaking our hearts. Ryan is not interested in reconnecting with his, and neither am I. But he knows me well enough to see right through me. He won't give us half a chance until he knows I'm done with Chris.

And I am. I just have to prove it to myself, and to him.

"I'll see you Monday," he says, and then turns to go toward the hallway.

And far too easily, I'm dismissed.

WHEN I ARRIVE at Chef Chu's, Chris is waiting for me. He reaches to give me a kiss but I sidestep it. I feel like I'm betraying Ryan just by being here. He's already told me to give Chris another chance but I kissed *Ryan* this afternoon. It was no different than the first time when my heart nearly burst into flames. I don't know why he keeps pushing me away.

Luci, it's just a book.

But when you're a woman who wants real life to be more like books, sometimes it isn't easy to let go of the fantasy. I want to believe Ryan is that man, the one who will run after the one he loves. In an ideal world, me.

I'm standing next to Chris in the line at the entrance where the walls are filled on both sides with framed photographs of all the famous people who've been here. Heads of states have dined here. Also, Kareem Abdul-Jabar, John F. Kennedy, Jr., Justin Bieber. It's a Wall of Fame.

"That could be you someday," Chris says. "The famous Luci Santana, writer extraordinaire."

But Ryan has the right idea. Obscurity isn't half bad. Besides, I've never been interested in being a celebrity author.

"I don't care about being famous," I say even if Chris doesn't seem to be listening anymore.

He's now chatting with someone in line who he recognizes from the gym. They're talking about how much they can bench press and other nonsensical things that don't matter to anyone who lives in my world.

When we're finally seated, I order my standard chicken salad and Chris orders nearly everything off the menu. He always does. Here's the thing about Chris. He's greedy.

"That's going to be way too much food for you," I tell him.

"Always good for leftovers."

I'm not a fan of leftovers, *or* waste. Chris would often let the food go bad and we wound up pitching it. But he never listens to me. He still wants more, excess, and he can afford it. I'm sure his parents are still proud of him. He's their little man.

"Where are you staying?" I ask.

"The rental on Middlefield. You know, the one my parents usually rent out to university students? It's vacant this summer so I'm staying there until I get back on my feet."

I know the house. It's twice the size of my abuelita's house and Chris has it all to himself.

"God, Luci, I can't tell you how bad I feel that you couldn't stay in the condo." He runs a hand down his face. "It was one of those things I didn't think all the way through."

"Like your coffeehouse crush?"

I haven't pressed him on this issue but it's time. This is the new and improved Luci who doesn't ignore problems. Get straight to the point and attack the plot hole, er, the problem. Working with Ryan taught me that.

"I told you," he says, reaching for my hand. "It didn't work out. We're not good together."

"You mentioned something about a fever dream, but that doesn't make any sense to me." I take my hand back and drum my fingers on the table.

"Babe, it was a mistake. I got all up in my head about the wedding. We already talked about this."

But the thing is, *I* did all the planning. He just had to show up. Even this seemed to be too much for him. If he felt that way about the wedding, I shudder to think what our marriage would have been like.

"You mean when you thought marrying me sounded a lot like dying? So, you decided to join the Peace Corps where, if you died, at least you would die honorably instead of while tied to a ball and chain."

He frowns and shakes his head. "That's not what I said."

"If things were good between us, if we loved each other, I don't think someone else could have come between us. Ever. And you let Nadia come between us."

"It was a fever—"

"Stop with the fever dream!" I slap both hands on the table, shocking Chris. "There's no such thing."

"There *is*. It's when someone turns your head and makes you believe things that aren't real." Chris, as always, doubles down when he thinks he might be wrong.

It's as if he hopes his confidence and self-assurance is going to somehow change *facts*. I've always disliked this about him, and I used to tease him. Now, it's super annoying.

Chris keeps talking. "Listen, Nadia is nothing like you. You're perfect. She was always arguing with me, challenging everything I said or did. The whole Peace Corps thing was her idea. Even that I wasn't doing right according to her. I wasn't a good enough man. I'm sorry it took me a while, but I realize you're the one for me. You're who I need and love. You accept me as I am. For who I am."

And it would have been nice had he returned the favor. There's so much truth to his words and he's absolutely right. I didn't challenge him. I took what he could give me because I didn't think I deserved any better. I hovered in the background, worrying someone was going to notice I didn't belong. The reasons for that don't matter now. It only matters I can't be that woman anymore.

"This is not about me or Nadia. It's about you. You're basically an overgrown frat boy who won't own up to anything. Granted, it's not entirely your fault, because your parents screwed you up. But you're old enough to take personal responsibility. I thought joining the Peace Corps would be good for you until I heard about Nadia. You didn't really want to change the world or make it a better place. What you wanted was someone who would continually remind and reassure you of how wonderful you are."

He spreads his palms. "Well…exactly. Isn't that what love is?"

"I don't think so, Chris. It's a two-way street. You never did that for *me*."

He slumps. "I get it. I wasn't good about telling you but I showed you. You know words are not my thing. That's your thing. We're opposites and we do a good job of complementing each other."

"Yeah? What's my favorite flower?"

"Roses. That's why I sent them." He leans back and smiles with a satisfied look.

"Wrong. I love and have always loved daffodils. Yellow ones."

He's lost his confidence, leaning forward and squinting. "Daffodils? Which ones are those?"

I cover my eyes. "Geez. I used to bring them home from Trader Joe's every season. Put them right on the kitchen table as centerpieces. The next day they'd bloom, their little faces opening up."

He squints. "Daffodils? Nobody likes *daffodils*. Every girl likes roses."

There he goes, doubling down again. *Telling* me what I like. He even says it louder, like that will help. Chris wants to believe all women prefer roses because it makes his life as a man simpler. If all women like the same thing, there's little effort on his part to engage the memory.

"Not every girl. Not me."

"Well, so what, I got one thing wrong." He reaches for my hand, rubs my thumb. "But I know *you*, babe. I know what you like and *where* it matters. Right?"

He's talking about sex again, and I don't want to go there. It has never been as great as *he* believes. Not surprisingly, I faked it most of the time, so he'd feel good about himself. Even now I don't have the heart to tell him the truth because he did try so very hard. It wasn't through lack of effort, let's put it that way.

I'm pretty sure Ryan didn't even try and one kiss sent me spinning out of orbit.

My choice is next.

In the end, it isn't his flaws that make my decision. It's the knowledge that I don't love him anymore. Maybe I did at one time, but mostly, I loved the idea of loving him.

And that's not enough.

CHRIS TAKES IT WELL. There's no more crying. No more begging. Just an overall sadness and resignation and this is something we both share. We couldn't make "us" work, but on the other hand, we're not all that different from the rest of the population. The difference is we are acknowledging it. We are moving on.

I'm proud of us for that.

Either Chris realizes I'm right, or he's already making plans to call Nadia. In any case, it doesn't concern me. I applaud this decision. I've always wanted to be part of a couple, that symbiotic relationship that I've coveted for so long in the books I've treasured. In the memories I had of my parents kissing, and dancing in the kitchen. But now I'm thinking about Eddie and how happy he's been all these years without anyone special.

I think your father was the love of my life, he said.

I haven't realized the beauty in those words until now. There can be many great loves in our lives, and they're not all romantic ones. My mother has been lucky to have two great loves in her life. As for me, I need to be alone for now. So, I didn't find love like in the stories I create and read. Someday. Never say never. I'm not likely to give up, but I might redefine true love. I don't know what it looks like yet, but I have a feeling I'll know when I see it. True love will be selfless, of that I'm sure. Both people will be on even footing and it won't be a one-way street.

Either way, I can't wait to tell Ryan.

ON SUNDAY, Eddie throws another impromptu karaoke party for the family. This time, he tortures us with his "compelling" rendition of Gloria Gaynor's epic "I Will Survive."

"At first I was afraid, I was petrified," he sings directly to my mother.

Abuelita is smiling and I'm sure it's because she's wearing earplugs. My tias are elbowing each other and whispering. Two minutes later, Eddie throws back his head, crooning into the microphone like a superstar. My mother is glowing, a woman clearly in love.

"Go, Eddie!" Diego says, then slams his hands over his ears.

By now, the entire family knows Eddie and my mother are a "thing." No one, apparently, thinks it's as strange as I did, not even Sofia. Then again, some of these folks saw Eddie with my mother before she ever married my father. It wouldn't seem as odd to them. What might have seemed odd at the time was the way Eddie stepped aside.

That's what you do for someone you love. I ask myself whether if I loved the same man Sofia did, I'd be able to step aside. There's no question I would. I'd like to think she'd do the same.

Tonight, she's brought along her latest love interest, a man with so many tattoos I don't know what to read first.

"Brett, this is my cousin, Luci. She's a *New York Times* bestselling author." Sofia winks.

"Wow! Really?" Brett's eyes go wide. "Do you know Meryl Streep?"

"No," I say patiently. "I don't think she writes books?"

"Babe, would you go get me some horchata? Abuelita made a good batch." Sofia points him in the direction of the large pitcher being guarded by Diego's mother. Once, years ago, he'd spiked it with tequila and she has never gotten over it.

"Does Brett own stock in a tattoo shop?" I say once he's off.

"Nah, but he works there."

"That's not dangerous," I say, a bit puzzled. She has a type. *Is it possible Sofia is finally getting serious about dating?*

"No, but he's cute and nice. He was so gentle with me when I went in for my tattoo—"

"You have a *tattoo*? Why don't I know this?"

Sofia shushes me because her mother is nearby. If she hears Sofia has a tattoo, she will probably convene a novena so everyone can pray for Sofia's soul.

"Only one." Sofia holds up a finger. "Had to see what all the fuss was about."

"Which one did you get?"

She moves closer. "The caduceus symbol, you know the two snakes coiled around a winged staff? I'll show you later."

Brett rejoins us not with one but with two glasses of horchata, one of which he offers to me. I have to say, it's very considerate of him. I accept it then excuse myself to go find my abuelita. Since this whole thing with Eddie and Mami became official, I haven't checked in with her. Given that I haven't heard any loud arguments coming from the main house, I have to assume she's okay with all this.

I'm sitting next to her for a whole minute before she realizes I'm even there. Then again, Eddie is still singing. I tap her on the shoulder and smile.

She removes an earplug. "Hola, mija."

I point to Eddie, still serenading my mother, having moved to a love song that is very much out of his vocal range. Diego looks like he might throw up.

I put my arm around her. This woman lost a son, but she's stronger than anyone I've ever known.

"Are you okay with this? Mami and Eddie?"

She nods. "Eddie deserves to be happy. He was always such a good son and an even better brother."

"I had no idea *how* good."

"Family is everything," she says. "People come and go out of our lives but family remains."

"You never stopped thinking of Mami as family." It's a statement of fact, because when Abuelita brings you into the fold, you're in for life.

"She's your mami," she says, patting my knee, as if this explains everything. "And she has a good heart."

I glance over at my mother now and realize I've never seen her this happy. Not when she was married to Seb, nor at any point after my father died. Maybe I've always been too tough on a woman who did the best she could.

"I would have never put those two together," I admit. "But funny how they somehow fit."

"Geneva is good for Eddie. Gracias a Dios he'll have someone now and I won't worry when I die."

"Why? Are you *dying*?"

She laughs. "A little bit every day, mi amor, but that's life. We are all getting older. Best to enjoy every day and stop making happiness so hard. It's everywhere if you look. Look at those two. Your papi is smiling down from heaven with love."

I smile too when I see Eddie kissing my mother's hand as

he finally, thank you Jesus, hands over the microphone to Diego because he's done.

Like Ryan, the second-chance trope has always been a favorite.

And a second chance at love is alive and well at the Santana house.

CHAPTER 32

On Monday morning, I arrive at Ryan's, eager to be his human dictating machine. I want to tell him all about this weekend, how I stood up for myself and my own needs. He needs to know I am done with Chris. It's over. I don't expect Ryan's feelings for me will change in any way but at least he won't feel guilty about kissing me anymore. Should the opportunity arise, that is, and I hope that it will.

The door is open when I arrive and a strange woman I've never seen before is cleaning in the kitchen.

"Hello," she says, looking up as I walk inside.

"I'm looking for Ryan? He's staying here, and I work for him."

"You must be Luci," she says, handing me an envelope. "He said to give this to you when you came in on Monday."

"He's not here?"

"No, he went back early."

He's…gone.

I clutch the envelope. This contains bad news and I should be alone when I read what he has to say to me after clearing out of the house like he's running from the law. But I don't get far before I tear open the envelope and read his note.

Dear Luci,

I've left you a check that should cover the remainder of your salary. Your help has been invaluable but I'm going back to Pasadena to finish this book. It's become too difficult to focus and I don't mean my ribs. Kate will be in touch regarding the sequel. You should have an agency agreement in your inbox soon. I have no doubt you're going to write a much better book than I did. Keep in mind that whether it sells a lot of copies won't have anything to do with the story or your writing. There's a lot of luck involved in this business and you already know this.

Let me make something perfectly clear. Love doesn't mean you chase someone. I know that's what you expect. Chasing after someone like Grayson did in the book, begging them to love you, is nothing but desperation, insecurity, and loneliness. That's not true love. Love can simply be the effort of standing still and having the sense to recognize it when it rotates around you like the sun.

Sometimes real love means letting someone go when you realize they'd be better off without you. Because you see, big declarations of love can be quiet. They can be still. I know that's not how it works in romance books. This is how it works for me.

I'm in love with you, and nothing is ever going to change that.

Write your books and be happy. You deserve it more than anyone I've ever known.

Have a good life.

~R

Have a good life?

Have a good *life*?

What the actual…ugh! I press my back against the wall and dramatically slide to the floor in a heap. And no, I would not *write it this way.*

Ryan loves me, so he's leaving. This is how he's written our ending. I guess that's what you get with a man who isn't a true romance writer. He's a one-hit wonder. I read his stupid note again and again hoping I missed the part where he tells me to join him. Where he tells me he wants to see me again. This all makes about as much sense as his *Soulmates* ending. It's no ending at *all*. Incomplete. A cliffhanger. Author, please elucidate! More feeling here, go deeper. Don't leave the reader hanging, a cardinal sin. I am on the edge of a scream.

"Are you okay?" the woman says, gazing at me with narrowed eyes because I'm now sitting on the floor. "Bad news?"

"The *worst*."

"Oh well, it will get better. After all, tomorrow is another day!" She says in a sing-song tone and goes back to cleaning the oven.

I'm a bit taken aback by her casual attitude but she's right. Tomorrow *is* another day, her insincere platitudes notwithstanding. *So what* if Ryan claims to be in love with me, the point is he left. The point is he put it in writing when he should have said it out loud. The point is he doesn't think *I'm* worth fighting for. Instead of tears, there's a shaking anger that convulses through me. I am *so* done with men. Done!

Maybe I'm just meant to write the romances, not live them. Most people are probably not meant to live out a great love story but simply learn to live with whatever joy comes their way. It turns out some of the "lucky" people have to wait twenty-five years before they can be together.

Well, I will not be waiting. I will be moving on. Like Eddie before my mother, maybe I'll date a whole lot and be the woman that goes to the wedding receptions in my forties and is available to dance with all the single men.

I will be happy with my work and my family. It will be enough.

Since I suddenly have the entire day ahead of me I go back to the coffee shop and pull out my laptop. I will rejoin the mighty droves of aspiring authors and playwrights all around me and rage write. I pull up the beginning of the sequel and add a few hundred words, but they're unhinged words. I'm going to have to revise heavily, maybe even (gasp) delete. There's little I hate worse than throw-away words, but I admit they get the juices flowing.

"What are you doing here?" Lula screams. "I thought you left."

Grayson turns to Lula. "Ignore my stupid letter. I couldn't leave. Because I love you."

"You don't love me. What a load of ~~bullshit~~ ~~baloney~~ bull hockey!" Lula grabs her gun, which is legally registered and for which she has a permit.

"What are you doing?" Grayson asks.

Lula cocks the gun, and shoots Grayson in the heart.

"I'm wounded!" He clutches his chest. "This hurts like hell. It's worse than my bruised ribs."

"Now you know how I feel!"

And…end scene.

This is terrible. Truly awful. I will never write a crime thriller but if I did, while it wouldn't be any good, it would be extremely cathartic. I'd start by killing all the guys who say they love me and then leave. I'd devise evil ways to torture them. Facts are, I can't concentrate. I envy all the writers around me who are lost in the worlds they've created. They remind me of Ryan and his ridiculous powers of concentration.

Since I can't write words that make any sense, I check my email and find the agency agreement from Kate.

To: theghostwriter@hotmail

From: Kate.Emery@EmeryAgency

Re: Agency agreement

Dear Lucia,

Attached please find the agency agreement. Please review and sign. We're all so excited about the sequel to Soulmates. Ryan ran the query by me and I love the idea of a book entirely from Lula's point of view. Please send me the proposal by, shall we say, next month? Do let me know if you need more time. I look forward to working with you.

Best,

Kate

I quickly reply that I'm thrilled and will sign and email the agreement back today.

At least one good thing happened today but it rings hollow for me. All of my long-held dreams are finally happening even if not at all in the way I'd imagined. I have what many in the business would call a "dream agent." This is everything I ever wanted and I should be happier. I should squeal, jump for joy, spill my coffee, call my family, and everyone I've ever met. I should post it on my socials and email everyone in my address book.

But I'm in a mood right now since Ryan wrote a note saying he loved me then skipped town.

My thoughts turn to someone whose feelings I've obviously deeply wounded even if it was never my intention. I email Holly and find out whether she's still in town and might like to meet for coffee. She's probably already going to be on a plane back to Missouri but maybe if she took the time to fly all the way here, she and her family made a vacation out of it.

To: inthequerytrenches@yahoo

From: theghostwriter@hotmail

Re: Please forgive me

I hope you're still in the area. If so, I'd love to chat. Please email or text if you'd like to meet at a coffee shop. I'd love to show you around town if you have time. Most of all, of course, I'm sorry for everything, and I want to talk. What I've done was unfair but I need you to hear my side and I don't feel comfortable explaining this all in an email.

I sign off by leaving her my cell number. I don't expect an immediate reply, but maybe Holly will give me a chance to explain my actions. While I didn't write the first book, I've officially taken on the pen name. From now on, it's me behind Elizabeth Brogan and everything that entails. And because I'm a good friend, no matter what she might think of me now, I want to help Holly in any way I can. Ryan helped me and it's time to pay it forward. Women in publishing need to stick together.

I drive home for an afternoon of working in my shed without interruptions. If I can stop thinking about Ryan for thirty minutes, I might get a few hundred words in. But he's constantly interrupting my flow, as a montage in my mind goes back to the first time we met. Me, giving the wrong professor my entire life's story while behind him, Ryan quietly listened. I segue to the night I saw the video of him, angry and tearing into the genre that made me want to be an author, the genre he'd accidentally fallen into. The day he brought me soup and asked me to do him a gigantic favor.

He changed my life. But in the end, *I* changed my life.

I took a risk, dared to push past my comfort zone. I went on a streaming show seen by millions of people, talked, and I didn't throw up once. I've grown more in the past month than I have in a year, and growing pains ache. Before I know it, I'm crying. They are not just tiny tears but big flowing ones accompanied by wrenching sobs. I know deep down Ryan is hurt and somewhat broken, still carrying the guilt over the real Elizabeth. Still thinking he's not good enough for me and he's so wrong.

"I said I wouldn't do this!"

Fists clenched, I look up at my ceiling, imploring the heavens to take away the part of me that makes me so damn empathetic. It screws with my life and causes me to make bad choices like even for one second considering giving Chris another chance.

There's a knock at my door a few hours later, and I fool myself into thinking it's Ryan. He's come back to tell me he made a mistake. This would be the way I'd write this scene: All this time, he's been sitting at the airport trying to figure out a way to let me know he's sorry about leaving. He wants to take it slow since he realizes I just ended a relationship. But because he loves me he suggests a long-distance relationship since Pasadena isn't *that* far. We can see each other once a month and before long we'll have frequent flyer miles and it won't even be that expensive. We can take the time to get to know each other and go from there. Reasonable. Logical.

And all things he *should* have said!

It's not Ryan because real life isn't like the scenes I write in my head. It's my mother and she's beaming. I'm happy for her, seriously, but I can't take this right now. Being around happy couples isn't going to be on my agenda for a while. They can take their joy and stuff it.

Mami holds up her left hand, the ring on her finger big enough to blind me.

"Eddie asked me to marry him!" She launches herself into my arms.

I pull back to admire the ring the way I know she expects, holding up her finger to the light. It's just the right amount of bling and big enough to suggest Eddie spent a big part of his savings on it.

It takes me a minute but I notice my mother isn't wearing any makeup. What in the actual world is this black magic? She looks better than I would have guessed without it, looking more like a fifty-something mother who simply took care of herself. There are wrinkles, but they are soft. She looks, for the first time, like a real mother. My mother. Damn, I've missed her. I love her.

This love has a way of chasing you, of burrowing inside of you to find shelter, of never letting go. It's the kind of love I feel for my mother. The type of love that is simply... inevitable. I never made the choice to love her. Loving her is uncomfortable. Imperfect. But it is undoubtedly the most real thing in my life.

"When are you getting married?" I walk her further into my shed, and she sits on the seat.

"As soon as possible. I don't need a big wedding, but this is Eddie's first marriage, so..."

"Abuelita wants a church wedding."

She nods. "Exactly."

I want to ask her a question that has been heavy on my mind since the moment I realized how she felt about Eddie.

"I don't understand. Did you just...*always* love him? I mean, you never stopped?"

"Yes," she says, not meeting my eyes. "But I loved your father, too. It is possible to love two men and I stopped thinking of Eddie once I was with your father."

"But after Papi died? Why didn't you just try then?"

She shakes her head. "The grief...it strangled us both. I think for Eddie, especially, he could never get past it. He adored his brother. And I understood. The reason I left you with Abuelita and Eddie is because I loved him too much to stick around, waiting for him to be ready to love me again. You missed your father so much, and Eddie was the next best thing."

"I always thought you left because *I* was "too much." Too needy, too noisy, too...too everything." I bite my lower lip, straining against any more tears.

She reaches for my hands. "No, no, mi amor. You were always this bright light, never too much. Yes, I got frustrated at times like any parent when I was suddenly without my partner. But it wasn't you at all. It was me. I hurt so much that I had to leave but I didn't want to pull you away from the only family you've ever had. Especially not Sofia. You've been like sisters all your life."

I never thought I'd see this through a different point of view but the plot is twisting. It's turning down a lane I don't recognize. Leaving me here instead of taking me away with her *was* selfless. I would have been miserable living away from Sofia, my abuelita, and Eddie.

"I'm sorry that I was angry with you for so long," I say. "You were an easy target, I guess."

"That's what mothers do. We become that target because your arrows of contempt can't ever change the way we love you. I won't deny it can hurt, because it *does*. But I never stopped loving you even when you hated me. After a while, I didn't understand what you needed from me anymore."

"I never *hated* you. I just needed you to be around. It's not like I wanted you every minute of the day but a mother needs to be someone you can go to *when* you do. You're supposed to stand still and let me orbit around you."

"I focused on my own pain and not on yours, or Eddie's. It was easier for me to leave but now I can see, a huge mistake."

"Maybe not," I say, and I know I'm being generous. "Timing is important and if you loved Eddie, you might have had to wait around for him to be ready for your second chance."

"Yes, that's true." She smiles, still holding my hand. "He did a lot of dating, but he tells me there was never anyone else for him but me."

"He's such a sweet talker." I chuckle. "But a terrible singer. Just truly awful and I say that as someone who loves him."

"Please don't tell him that," she says with a wink. "I love

listening to him. Now, what about you and that handsome man you were having dinner with?"

"My boss. My colleague."

"It was more than that, I could tell."

"I didn't know how he felt until it was too late. Now he's gone back to Pasadena."

She cocks her head. "Not perfect, but it's not *that* far."

"That's what I thought." I pull out the note from my pocket. "He told me he loved me…in a note."

I read the note to her because there's no way she would be able to read Ryan's handwriting.

Mami blinks. "Ah, not very romantic, is it?"

"He's not actually a romance writer."

"But then again, I imagine words are his gift." She gestures to the note. "And that one part, *big declarations of love can be quiet. They can be still.* That's kind of beautiful."

"Well, he is a writer." I fold up the note, once again on the verge of tears. "A very good one."

"Ay, querida," Mami says. "I think you might just love him."

For once she's here when I need her to be and I tell her everything.

And for the first time in over a decade, my mother is here to listen, and hold me, and help me heal my broken heart.

CHAPTER 33

Three months later

If you'd told me a year ago that I'd be part of a panel filled with authors I've admired and emulated for decades, I would have asked you whether that was your favorite hallucination.

But here I am, at the Southern California Festival of Books, on a panel with bestselling authors short-listed for major literary awards. Our topic of conversation is raising the stakes in fiction, whether genre fiction or upmarket commercial.

Holly bustles across the room, bringing the microphone to a woman who has raised her hand.

She's here because when we were asked to suggest a moderator I nominated Holly. Since that ugly day at the book signing, we've reconciled as two women who want to lift each other up in this whirlwind business called publishing. Holly didn't take long to reply to my apology-filled email, and responded with some apologies of her own, which I'm not sure I deserved. Hurt and humiliated when she thought I'd snubbed her, she reacted badly. We met at my coffee shop the day before she flew back to Missouri with her husband and children. I couldn't tell her the truth but I gave her the next best thing. The idea, how I originally hated it, but an agent loved it. How I worked to improve it and eventually grew to love it. All mostly true. She read passages of the sequel I'm writing and gave me valuable feedback. Interestingly, she finds the sequel to be far more of the voice she was accustomed to reading.

Funny.

There's someone else whose feedback I'd much prefer but I haven't spoken to him in three months. Three long months in which Mami and I planned a wedding. Three months in which I've written the entire first draft of the tentatively titled, *The Romantic Rejects.* It's just a placeholder title, but Kate thinks it's hilarious. In my fictional world, Grayson and Lula eventually wind up together, even if it's at the last minute, and sail off into the sunset. Literally.

You might wonder if I've asked Kate about Ryan. We share an agent, the only connection we still have. I waited until the news came I'd been officially asked to speak at the conference. Then, I called Kate.

"Will he be there?"

No need for her to ask who "he" was.

"Yes, he's on a panel but not on the same day. Still, there's a good chance you two could meet if you'd like me to arrange it."

"Oh, no. Don't go out of your way."

"Surely you two are still in touch, or is Ryan doing his thing again?" Kate said.

"Doing *his thing* again?"

"The thing where he holes up in his house writing

nonstop, shutting everyone and everything out until he's done. That's how his marriage failed, you know. I don't think he'd mind me telling you, seeing how close you two became."

My heart feels like a raw and aching muscle every time I think of Ryan and I try not to make it often for the sake of self-preservation.

"How much of a love story do you think is enough in a book that wouldn't normally be considered part of the romance genre?"

The audience member's question snaps me out of my daydream.

All panelists take a turn answering the question in regard to raising stakes. My answer is there can never be too much of a love story in any book. I accept that only in the romance genre can one be assured of a happy ending, but love stories come in all shapes and sizes. There are sad endings, and yes, unfinished endings.

"Contemporary, historical, cozy mystery, World War II spy novel," I say, and then lose my train of thought when I see Ryan standing in the back of the room. "Um…yes. Give me all the romance."

Everyone claps and Holly comments, "We are not surprised to hear Elizabeth say this!"

Ryan catches my eye and smiles. I'm pretty sure my face does a weird contortion in which I attempt a smile but look like I'm having a stroke. God, he looks incredible. He's dressed in slate slacks and a navy peacoat that makes him look like a cross between an L.L.Bean model and a modern-day Heathcliff from the moors. His hair is long and unruly, he's wearing what looks like a new pair of glasses, and *the beard* is back. He might be unrecognizable to some but I'm not likely to ever miss him in a crowd. I can hear my heart beating in my *ears* and I hope no one asks me another question because I'm now brain-dead.

I've dated in the past three months as I tried to get over him, don't get me wrong. Well, it was one date. *One*. When I started getting flowers delivered every week with no note I immediately suspected Chris. But one phone call to tell him to quit doing that, and I learned he was already dating someone new. It wasn't him. The flowers continued, mostly daffodils with the occasional daylilies thrown in. I went down the list of possible people, even suspecting Eddie, and they continued to come. Once, the UPS guy was there delivering books at the same time as the flower guy.

"I wish they would just stop coming," I said and the UPS guy burst out laughing.

"There's something you don't hear often."

He asked me out and I still wonder if it was because he assumed I was low-maintenance. It was dinner, very nice, pleasant, though he couldn't even tell me the title of the last book he'd read. He did not have any strong opinions and wasn't much of a history buff. Still, we planned to meet again. That night I went home and cried for hours. I did not want to see him again even though I had no real reason.

It took me weeks to figure out I'm desperately, completely, hopelessly in love with Ryan. Some romance writer, right?

What I feel for him is not admiration, it's not friendship, it's not a workplace relationship. I'm not overtly grateful but just the right amount. He's not a mentor. He's not a teacher.

I just love him because I see him the way I'm not able to see anyone else. I see inside his heart and I know he sees mine.

I've stalked him on social media, which in his case is pretty useless. He shares the occasional book review and photos of some of his research but continues to be impersonal and distant. I suppose it works for him. In other words, he's given me no clue as to whether he even *remembers* me, much less still loves me as he once claimed right before he walked away.

But as I sit here now, waiting for this panel to end, I can see he remembers me. He remembers *us*.

"Thank you, everyone," Holly announces and I realize we're done. "If you have a copy of a book you'd like signed, please form a line behind me."

Now I can't leave because someone might actually want me to sign a book. The line moves at roughly the pace of a snail on antidepressants and when I look up, I catch Ryan leaving the room.

"I'm sorry," I say as I sign a book for a reader. "I have to go, it's an emergency."

This might be rude but I need to get out of here. I have to see Ryan. There are things I need to know. How dare he show up here, smile, and walk away again? As I leave the hall, I take a turn and think I see the sleeve of his peacoat. He's walking fast, like he can't wait to get away from me. Well, not before answering a few questions!

I bump into a small crowd forming in front of an author's booth, making my way around with effusive apologies. Eventually I follow Ryan's back down a long hall and the groups of people around me begin to thin. We're not near any of the action and I know he'll hear me now.

"Ryan!" I call. "Stop!"

He finally stops, turns, and does not look surprised to see me. I, however, am out of breath.

"Hey, you," he says as if we just spoke yesterday.

"Where…where are you going?" Hand to my chest, I try to slow my breathing.

What's happening now in my chest must be the result of my sedentary job mixed with the knowledge that nothing has changed because my heart is hurting just to see him. It's racing and beating like it hasn't in weeks because it just saw something it desperately wants. My heart wants to jump out from behind my rib cage and get Ryan.

"Nowhere. You were busy. Good panel."

I close the distance between us. "Good *panel*? That's all you have to say?"

"No. Actually, it was great. I enjoyed it. No notes. How have you been?"

I take a deep breath. "Pretty shitty, actually. Thanks for asking."

"I'm sorry to hear that."

"Well, you should be! It's *your* fault."

He cocks his head but does not respond. So, I march right up to him, standing inches from his warm body.

"Do you still *love* me, yes or no?"

He looks at me from under hooded eyelids. "Yes."

"What? *Yes?*"

"That's what I said. Nothing has changed for me."

"But—"

A crowd approaches, people on their way to the next panel, which starts in five minutes. Ryan grabs my arm and pulls me aside. We wind up in a small nook. This moment reminds me of the time a bicyclist almost knocked me over and he pulled me out of the way. I'd felt so warm and cherished. I want to cry thinking of all the time we've lost.

"Luci," he says. "I meant what I said. It's not going to change. I never thought I'd feel this way again with a love that's even stronger."

"Then why did you just leave? Was it really to finish *the book*?"

"Yes and no. Look, I fell in love with you first. You were distracting me only because I couldn't see how this could work. It was too painful. I wanted to let you go so you could be happy. It's the most selfless thing I've ever done, so let me have that moment."

I grab him by the lapels of his peacoat. "No! I will not let you *have that moment*. It was wrong. Did it ever occur to you that I love you, too?"

He blinks. "When did that happen?"

"I don't know if it happened when you played the people game with me at the boardwalk, or when you pulled me out of the path of a bicyclist or when you accidentally flirted with me after your car accident. Maybe it was when you told me about your sister, and I understood why you'd want to write something strictly for the money. Maybe it was the first time you kissed me. Or maybe when the thought of dating anyone else made me cry. And I don't want to be the woman that waits twenty years to finally get to be with the man she loves."

"Don't cry," he says, wiping away a tear with his thumb because, yes, now I'm crying a little bit. "I guess things didn't work out with your ex."

"I broke up with him the same weekend you left. You have terrible timing! And why would you encourage me to stay with someone who was obviously not good for me?"

"Because you had to figure it out for yourself. Here's the thing. From the beginning, we were not on equal footing. You were my research assistant, and do you know how many times I've had an assistant? Too many to count and I always behaved appropriately. Workplace romances are great in books, not so much in real life. I broke too many rules with you and I had to end one part of our relationship if we were ever going to have another. And that's the only reason I walked away."

This made a lot of sense and it fit with everything I already know about Ryan. He's without a doubt, one of the most honorable and upstanding men I've ever known.

"But...you could have told me that."

"I sent you flowers every week," he said, studying the floor.

"That was you?"

I want to smack my forehead. Of course it was him. Sofia tried to tell me, even asking me to call the flower shop. I did, and they refused to tell me.

"That was me. I had to keep my distance but I thought maybe I'd at least keep you from forgetting me entirely."

"But they had no note!"

He blinks. "What? No note? For God's sake, I want my money back."

I laugh and slug his shoulder. "I should have figured it out but I was too hurt to believe it. You should have called me. Three months is too long."

"Why do you think I'm here?"

"You have a panel tomorrow."

He shakes his head. "It was canceled."

"So…you came here anyway…for me?"

"What do you think, genius?" He cocks his head and grins, resting his hand on the nape of my neck and tugging me even closer. "I decided I'd punished myself long enough and I was going to take a chance that you'd want to see me again. And when you chased me out of the room, I knew."

"Oh, so that was a test, professor?"

He takes my hand and brings it to his lips to brush a kiss across my knuckles. I lean forward, kissing his shoulder, and then we both lean in the world's most beautiful choreography, and kiss. The kiss is soul-deep, torching every part of me and changing it for the better. I fall into him, forgetting we're in a public place. He has this way of kissing me that feels like an all-body hug.

I finally break for air. "B-but what if I was with someone else?"

"Then it wasn't meant to be, or at least not this decade. I

would have had to accept it as long as you were happy." He presses his forehead to mine. "But I would have been heartbroken."

"You're a much better person than I am." I reach to tug on his beard. "This is interesting but I kind of like it."

"It's how I look when I'm near the end of a book."

"Oh, I finished my first draft."

"I know. Kate has kept me up to date. I managed to ask about you frequently, professional reasons only, of course."

"Of course. What happens now?"

"Anything you want. We're on an even playing field. Nice to meet you, I'm Ryan Brady." He holds out his warm hand and this time, I'm sure he's never going to let go.

"I'm Luci Santana also known as Elizabeth Brogan."

"I've heard a lot about you."

"And one more thing. If we're going to be together, you can't just take off every time you want peace and quiet to finish a book. We have to figure that out."

"Agreed."

I smooth down the lapels of his coat. "Um, I'm staying here, you know. On the 12th floor."

"Yeah?" He kisses me again.

This time when we break apart I take his hand and tug him toward the elevator doors. When we hop on, we're sharing the elevator with two other people, and the woman glances at me.

"Oh, Elizabeth Brogan." She reaches into her cart full of books and pulls out *Soulmates*. "I didn't get your autograph at the signing this morning. The line was too long."

"Who should I make it out to?" I address it to her, then sign and hand it back. "This is Ryan Brady, by the way. He's an award-winning author of historical fiction."

He rolls his eyes at me but gives the woman a smile and nod.

"That's nice," the woman says.

She gets off the elevator first, and Ryan and I ride up the rest of the floors. We laugh some of the way, we kiss the rest of it, we're unable to keep our hands off each other.

But when we get closer to my room, fear rises in me. Fear and nerves. Excitement. Throw in a little angst, too. I'm at the start of a romance book that could practically write itself. The ingenue in a romcom, riding up in the elevator with the man who headlines her dreams. Depending on the spice rating, we were either going to stop the elevator and shag right in that tight space or wait until we opened the door to my suite.

When we're just outside my room my fingers fumble with the card key. I have to try twice. It's Ryan who takes it from me and gets the door to click open.

I suspect he's as nervous as I am. I mean, we've both written these scenes and the expectations are high. Are we as good as our writing would reflect? Those scenes take forever to get right. I don't want my first love scene with Ryan to go by the book. Instead, I want to feel his warm bare skin against mine. I want to kiss him forever. I don't know which one of us is going to take the lead but I vote him.

Ryan doesn't disappoint. We've no sooner shut the door when he's got me against it, kissing me everywhere. He's not shy. He kisses the column of my neck, the pads of my ears, anywhere bare skin is exposed.

"I love you, Luci. So much."

"I love you, too," I say.

He unzips my dress, pulling the sleeves down my arms, and kisses my shoulders. Then he drops to his knees to kiss my now-bare stomach. Heat pulses through me and I pull him up and lead him to bed. At this point, we're removing our own clothes to go faster.

"I've waited so long for this," I breathe, letting my unzipped dress fall to the floor.

"Not longer than me, I bet."

"Yeah? I've wanted this since the moment you came to my shed, apologizing and begging for my help. You are so *sexy* when you're sorry."

"I'm going to remember that," he says, his warm hand pressing against my bare thigh and making me tingle. "But *I've* wanted this since you mistook Henry for me and told us both your life story."

This surprises me so much I blink. "The moment we *met?*"

"Well, I'm a guy. And you're very hot."

"I thought you found me annoying."

"No, that was you. You found *me* annoying."

"Just grumpy."

"Fair."

Now neither one of us is either grumpy or annoying as we roll under the covers to discover each other in a brand-new way. There's zero hesitancy and no holding back. We're passionate and delicious and glorious and everything I've ever fantasized.

But the rest, folks, is fade to black.

Use your imagination.

EPILOGUE

SIX MONTHS LATER

"Are you done?" I ask Ryan.

He rubs his temples. "No, I'll never be finished. It's hopeless. These revisions are killing me. How can I reduce my word count and also add in more emotion? I'm a writer, not a magician!"

He's so cute, just shy of shaking his fist at the heavens.

"You always say that, baby." I stand behind him, rubbing his tight shoulders.

Life is never smooth when Ryan is revising but we've devised a system.

It became necessary to implement one, since for the first few months we lived together in my she-shed. We do love each other, intensely, but every writer needs elbow room. Some days I write at the coffee shop, and other days Ryan does. We have our established work hours and we're strict about those. If Ryan or I are having a tough time letting go of a scene, one of us will shout, "And…end scene!"

The agreement is we stop then, wherever we are in the manuscript.

It works because we both need balance and also it helps that we like each other…a lot.

Our days consist of the work that we love, eating takeout, going for long walks, reading books, watching movies, and hanging out with Sofia and her latest boyfriend. Many nights we wind up at Abuelita's for dinner with Eddie and my mother where we all watch telenovelas. Ryan and I are both fascinated with the melodramatics and lie in bed many nights analyzing how we could layer in more emotion to our stories.

Oh, and the video of my mother's purse smacking the man who insulted me? It went viral. The podcaster got a lot of mileage out of that incident for which he is probably grateful even if he never had the grace to admit it. Interestingly, enough people recognized my mother from her soap opera days that eventually a telenovela producer reached out, wanting to cast her. Shocking everyone, including me, my mother said no, thank you. Her acting days are over.

My mother and Eddie married in a fairly elaborate Catholic ceremony and are living together in a cute single-story craftsman bungalow not far from Abuelita. They don't have to worry about her since Ryan and I are still here. In the backyard.

We had a decision to make: pay a ridiculous price for an executive condo, move out of California, or stay where we are. As writers, we both know the money won't always be flowing. And the truth of it is, we'd much rather give our regular donation to Elizabeth's literacy foundation than buy a big house we can barely afford.

Abuelita was happy to let us break ground in her back-yard. We got a permit, and after combining our funds we bought the kit and materials. In the place of the former she-shed is now an adorable tiny home. It's plenty of room for the two of us, and should we decide at some point to add to our family, we will reconsider.

You might wonder what ever happened to my fantasy time travel romance. Ryan has encouraged me to write the project of my heart, and that first novel of mine is finally ready for prime time. Now that I have a first-rate agent, there is plenty of interest in it, too, because of a new and popular genre they're calling "romantasy." I used to call it romantic fantasy. Go figure.

"Are we still having karaoke night?" Ryan asks.

"I'm afraid so." I kiss him and crawl into his lap to make out for a few minutes.

Karaoke night is not his favorite, but there's no way we can avoid it as it happens right outside our front door. We wouldn't want to, anyway, because it's become a lot more fun since Eddie started sharing the spotlight. It turns out my mother has a lovely singing voice. And one night, pumped with spiked horchata, and high on being short-listed for a major literary award, plus an offer to teach at the local university, we even got Ryan behind the mike. I joined him and together we sang, "I Got You, Babe." A classic.

"Don't quit your day job!" Diego laughed and took the mike back.

Okay, so we're not very good.

We eat a quick dinner now before the family descends and spills out into the backyard for Friday night Santana family karaoke.

Eddie greets us. "Are you two going to sing tonight?"

I hear Ryan groan behind me as he lowers his head to my shoulder and tightens his arms around my waist. My cue to save him.

"Well, Ryan's been editing today, so…"

"Ah, say no more, my friend!" Eddie claps his hands. "It

sounds like it's just me and my Geneva tonight. We've been working on a selection from the musical *Cats*."

Ryan gives me a horrified look and I'll be honest, I'm scared too. Still, this is my family, good or bad. Most of it is good, except for karaoke night.

Ryan has slipped into my family with a kind of easy acceptance and instant connection. And speaking of family, I'm likely the best thing to happen to the Brady one, if I do say so myself. Ryan's mother came to visit us after he permanently moved to Seven Trees. She's a gentle woman with eyes the same dark blue color as Ryan's. It might take time, but I know eventually we will reconcile Ryan with the rest of his family. His honoring of Elizabeth by creating a foundation in her name went a long way, but there's still healing to be done.

I've discovered something on this journey that began on the day my wedding was canceled. There are many *kinds* of love stories. They are all around us every day. From the older couple who has waited a long time to be together, to the couple who jumps right in. With love, anything is possible.

I love Ryan with all my heart, and *he's* my true love.

But my family is the love of my life.

ABOUT THE AUTHOR

Heatherly Bell is the contemporary romance author of over fifty published romances under two different pen names. She loves coffee, craves cupcakes, and occasionally wears real pants.

She lives in Northern California with her family and loves to hear from readers.

Contact her at Heatherly@HeatherlyBell.com